The
Ephesus
Scroll

D1732822

Ben Chenoweth

First published on Smashwords in 2012
(www.smashwords.com/books/view/247876)
Second published by L & R Morgan in 2013
This edition published by Ben Chenoweth 2014
Printed by CreateSpace

ISBN 978-1-5023844-7-8 (Paperback)

Typeset in 11pt Cardo by Ben Chenoweth
Cover design by Ben Chenoweth
Author photograph by Michael Bottomer (Life Through A Lens)

www.ephesusscroll.com
ephesus.scroll@gmail.com

*This book is dedicated to my daughters
Kate & Eleanor.
May it help you make sense of a fascinating book
and remind you of your time in Russia!*

Acknowledgements

The scroll fragment on the front cover is actually from the Septuagint, specifically the book of Joshua, and is dated to approximately 200 AD. The two faces come from Roman funerary paintings; the woman's face is in the British Museum and the man's face is in the Manchester Museum. Both are dated to the second century AD. The painting on the back cover is "The Lomonosov Bridge" (2011) and comes from the Artemis Artists Association (www.artemis-spb.ru); it was used by permission. The cover was designed by the author, with input from a number of very helpful Facebook friends.

The font used for the image of the first line of the scroll is P39LS. This font was created by Allan Loder (individual.utoronto.ca/atloder/GreekUncialFonts.html), and was derived from P^{39}, a papyrus fragment of the New Testament that has been dated to the third century. As such it is merely an approximation as to how the letters in such a scroll as described in this novel would look like.

One book was indispensable for the writing of this one: G. B. Caird's commentary *The Revelation Of Saint John* (A & C Black, 1966). Ben Witherington III's commentary, *Revelation* (Cambridge University Press, 2003) and R. H. Worth, Jr.'s *The Seven Cities Of The Apocalypse & Greco-Asian Culture* (Paulist Press, 1999) were also very helpful. For more information on the 'Great Game' period you simply cannot go past Peter Hopkirk's most excellent history *The Great Game: The Struggle For Empire In Central Asia* (Kodansha International, 1994).

The following people read successive versions of this novel and offered very helpful suggestions and encouragement: Ross & Sarah Nightingale; David Greentree, Jr; Ira Kirichenko; Matthew Clarkson; John Siegel; Michael Greed; Alexander Golubev; Matt Merritt; Allen Travis; and Andrew Carmichael. Any errors that remain are, of course, entirely my own. Also, much thanks to my wife, Kylie, for putting up with my 'writing days' and for many helpful suggestions.

Ephesus – April, AD 1885

Nikolai was posing for a photograph with two low-ranking Turkish officers when the earthquake hit the ancient, ruined city of Ephesus. The photographer had just replaced the lens cap when they all felt the ground rise beneath them. They all lost their balance and staggered sideways, each one reaching out in an attempt to steady himself with whatever he could find. Nikolai managed to stay on his feet by leaning back against the wall of stone blocks in front of which they had been standing. The two Turkish officers ended up sprawled on the ground at his feet. While the ground continued to move in a disconcerting way he reached a hand out to each of them.

"Are you all right?" he asked in perfect French. The men grabbed his outstretched hands and managed to pull themselves upright.

"Yes, thank-you," they replied in rather heavily accented French. Inwardly they were both cursing their stumbles – an earthquake notwithstanding – in front of someone they believed to be a well-to-do Belgian industrialist, who went by the name of André Gibaut. According to what he had told them he was in their country looking for a suitable source of certain raw materials for his factories back home. However, had the two Turks known they were being helped to their feet by a young officer in the Russian army, whose real name was actually Nikolai Alexandrovich Kostenko, they would have arrested him on the spot, taken him back to their barracks in the nearby valley, mistreated him appropriately, and then personally pulled the trigger at his execution once he had been cursorily tried before their commanding officer.

Nikolai was well aware of this possibility. As the earthquake continued, bizarrely his mind started going over the reasons why these solid, Turkish soldiers would treat him in such a way. The simplest reason was that Turkey and Russia were enemies, most recently fighting the Russo-Turkish War only eight years previously. A more complex and multi-faceted reason was that Russia had only the week before successfully taken the tiny oasis-village of Pandjeh in far-off Afghanistan, thereby almost certainly precipitating a major war with Britain, and Britain was looking to Turkey as an ally in its plans to attack Russia through the Caucasus. It was all rather tense, apparently. He had heard reports that the British newspapers were demanding that the Russians be taught a lesson they would never forget. On the other side, during one of those rare moments when he had been able to communicate safely with someone from Russia, he had learned that the papers in St. Petersburg and Moscow were insisting that their government continue pushing southwards through Afghanistan – thereby bringing the ultimate goal, India, ever closer – and warning Britain to keep well out of it.

In this intensely volatile situation Nikolai had been instructed by his superiors to enter Turkey posing as a Belgian and somehow to try and slow up Turkey's alliance with Britain. He knew he was not alone in this task, that other Russians were present elsewhere in the country, but still he had struggled to find a way into the upper echelons of the Turkish army. By frequenting some *very* seedy bars and buying occasionally generous rounds of *barely* drinkable local wines he had managed to befriend these two low-ranking officers. But he had not yet been able to persuade them to introduce him to their commander, a man he had previously targeted as one who could be used to bring about suitable delays. Instead, they had promised to show him the ancient ruins of Ephesus and had brought him out to this grassy hillside with blocks of marble everywhere, statues lying broken in pieces on the ground or buried with only their heads peeking out from the soil, and very occasionally an intact wall. It was definitely the ruin of what must have been a very beautiful city, but it had clearly suffered the indignity of neglect as well as the occasional earthquake like the one currently reducing what still remained standing to little more than disordered piles of rubble.

Ah yes, the earthquake! Nikolai's thoughts returned to the moment with a jolt as he became aware that the large blocks of stone making up the wall he was leaning on were beginning to separate in a way that did not bode well for the continued existence of the wall as a whole. Either it had been built into the side of the hill or the hill had at some time afterwards risen in an attempt to engulf it. Whatever the cause, having turned to face the wall, Nikolai could see small amounts of dirt falling out of the wall, as the cracks between the blocks widened.

"Quick, out of the way!" he called out, pushing the two Turks away. They skittered across the trembling flagstones and out into what they had grandly referred to as the Street of Curetes, one of the central roads of the ruins of Ephesus, but which looked like not much more than a goat track with occasional flagstones peeping through the dirt and grass. But Nikolai, turning to follow them, was suddenly struck by an enormous tremor that left him flat on his back looking up at the wall, helpless, as a large crack opened up between two blocks of stone. Incredibly quickly, the crack widened showering dirt and gravel over his feet. With a desperate scrabble he pulled his feet out of the way as a number of large stone blocks were seemingly levered out of the wall by the earthquake and landed with ear-splitting cracks on the flagstones around him.

And then it was all over. The ground stopped moving, the dust began to settle, and the two Turks had run over to see if he was injured.

"I'm fine," he said, shrugging off their assistance. As Nikolai stood up one of the Turks went back to the photographer to see how he had fared while the other stayed with Nikolai. Out of interest, Nikolai looked back at the wall. He had been partly right: the wall had been built into the side of the hill, so where the blocks had been he could see dirt and rocks. But near the bottom of the wall, behind what would have been the second level of blocks, he noticed an opening, little more than a hole in the side of the hill.

"What's that?" he said, pointing.

The Turk nearest at hand had also noticed the hole and together they went over to it. Nikolai looked in but his head blocked out most of the sunlight.

"Sir, do you see anything?" asked the Turk.

"No, this hole is too small," he replied.

He worked at the edges of the hole to make it a little wider. He felt quite excited about doing this. Since Ephesus was such an ancient city perhaps he might find something valuable. Some coins, perhaps? Gold even? With a larger hole and a little more light he could now see that the hole opened into a hollowed-out space that had been hidden behind the wall. He could also see that taking up most of the space was a stone box about a foot and a half in length and a foot wide and high.

"There's something here."

The Turk caught the edge of excitement in Nikolai's voice. "What is it? Can you reach it?"

"I think so."

With great care he took hold of the box and slowly drew it out of the hole. In the clear light of day it looked very old yet was still intact. Underneath some chips and scratches Nikolai could see some rather beautiful carved decorations. The box also had a lid that was slightly cracked but not broken.

"Oh, sir!" exclaimed the Turk, with a wild look in his eyes. "Put it back: it's an ossuary."

The man had used a word that Nikolai was unfamiliar with. "A what?" he asked, carefully turning the box around with his hands.

"It's an ossuary," the Turk repeated. "It contains the bones of someone great."

"Who?" asked Nikolai in surprise.

"I do not know," said the Turk. "But it is extremely unlucky to meddle with the dead."

It occurred to Nikolai that this Turk may be wanting him to put the box back just so *he* could return – once Nikolai had gone – and take the box for himself. However, Nikolai felt that this treasure of antiquity was his, not only by right of seniority, but mostly for the fact that it was *his* feet that had narrowly escaped being crushed by the blocks of stone that had been guarding this box for who knew how long. And *he* had pulled the box out of the hole in the first place. He was not going to lose possession so easily. Instead, he exclaimed, "Let me see inside!"

"No!" cried the Turk, wringing his hands in a decidedly believable display of either sheer terror or thwarted avarice.

Nikolai took no notice. He placed the box on the floor and tried to remove the lid. It was tightly wedged on but he felt it move slightly, then suddenly it was off. However, much to his disappointment the box did not contain bones, or articles of gold and precious stones, not even a few measly coins. Instead, it seemed full of paper. He reached in and poked the rough paper with his finger to see if there might be anything wrapped up inside.

The Turk seemed to have brightened up considerably. Whether this was from his relief at finding that the box was not after all an ossuary and that his soul was now safe from any ancient curse, or his relief that there was nothing of value inside, Nikolai did not wish to decide. However, Nikolai had taken a fancy to the box itself with its intricate carvings. So he made up his mind to take it as a souvenir of his visit to Ephesus.

"I hope you don't mind if I keep this box," he said, replacing the lid and then tucking the box firmly under one arm.

"Not at all, sir," replied the Turk, magnanimously. "Since it is not an ossuary, you have nothing to fear from the dead."

Indeed, thought Nikolai. *And since it is not valuable, I have nothing to fear from the living either.*

The photographer and his apparatus had apparently survived the earthquake, although he had discovered that the lens cap had come off thereby exposing to the sunlight the plate that he had taken earlier. He loaded another plate and the Turks moved in on either side of Nikolai, his arm still around the box. Once again, they looked serious and the photographer removed and then quickly replaced the lens cap.

As they walked back to the nearby town Nikolai thought that, all in all, it had turned out to be quite an interesting day, certainly one worth writing up in his diary…

∾

Nizhny Novgorod – June, AD 2005

While on holidays in Nizhny Novgorod, Natasha found Nikolai's diary when, after finishing the only book she had brought with her, she went scouring through some bookshelves looking for something else to read. She and her husband Dima – short for Dmitriy – had travelled down from St. Petersburg to spend a couple of weeks with Dima's grandmother, in the city of Dima's birth, an event which had occurred some thirty years previously. Natasha, a few years younger, had met Dima when he had moved to St. Petersburg to study graphic design. They were both good-looking with typical Slavic features: dark hair and fair complexions, with well-defined cheekbones.

The diary itself had looked quite interesting, being bound in leather with filigree patterns of gold on the spine but no title. She had pulled it out to see what the book was, but there had been no title anywhere on the cover either. So she opened it to the first page and was surprised to see that it was all in handwriting. Then, when she looked closer, she realised it was in French. Having studied French at both school and university, and rather intrigued, she returned to her seat in the main room of the apartment and read the first page:

> *Wednesday, 14th January, 1885.*
> *I arrived in the land of the Ottomans with a minimum of attention. The ship docked early and my colleague was not there to meet me. After finalising my affairs with the First Mate and collecting my travelling bag from my cabin I strolled down the gangplank to where my large trunk was waiting for me. I was able to procure the assistance of some lively local lads to help transport my trunk to a suitable place of temporary residence in which I write these few words. I expect my colleague to arrive presently and so I shall know my itinerary shortly.*

Natasha found it slow going. For a start, the handwriting was difficult to read. The writer had used long flowing cursive, and it had faded a little over time. In addition to this, the French was somewhat archaic, and there were quite a few words of which Natasha was a little unsure of their meaning. However, she kept at it and began to form a mental picture of the writer. Apparently, he was a Belgian industrialist who had travelled to Turkey for some reason that was never explicitly stated in the diary. He had moved around for a few months, mostly under the watchful eye of various Turkish officials. Natasha had just finished reading some of the writer's thoughts on the many Turkish factories he had been given tours through when Dima returned from shopping with his grandmother, Nadezhda.

"We're home!" called Dima from the small entryway of the apartment.

Natasha put the diary down and went and helped them with the bags as they removed their street shoes and put on some slippers. Then, as they unpacked and Nadezhda placed items away in their correct locations, she asked Nadezhda about her discovery.

"Grandmother, I found someone's diary on your bookshelves. It's in French. Do you know whose it is?"

Nadezhda paused, the packet of pasta in her hands forgotten for a moment.

"Yes, my child. I know it. It was written by my grandfather."

"Really?" exclaimed Dima. "I didn't know you had French blood in you!"

"Oh, he wasn't French," Nadezhda replied with a chuckle. "Nikolai Alexandrovich was as Russian as they come. He was an officer in the Russian army for many years, you know."

"Yes, I vaguely remember you mentioning him before," said Dima.

"But why was he writing in French?" asked Natasha, with a perplexed frown on her face.

"I seem to recall he was pretending to be Belgian at the time. After all, Turkey was not a very safe place for Russians back then, especially officers in the Russian army."

"Oh, he was spying!" said Natasha excitedly, clapping her hands together. "How thrilling! I'm going to read some more." She left the tiny kitchen and returned to her seat in the other room.

"Read it to me," said Dima, following her. "I don't know French."

"Certainly," she replied.

So with Nadezhda listening from the kitchen, Natasha read the next entry out loud, translating into Russian as she went.

" *'Friday, 24th April, 1885.*

" *'I have befriended two young Turkish officers, Ahmed and Mustafa. They are both great connoisseurs of red wines, despite all Islamic prohibitions to the contrary. We have had many interesting discussions, whilst enjoying the subtle flavours of a worthy local vintage, concerning the politics of army life, especially the shame of being passed over for promotion. I have assured them both of their inestimable qualities and can guarantee great things for them if only they would speak to their commanding officer about doing business with a certain Belgian industrialist of their acquaintance. Perhaps as a result of too many refills of the truly excellent local vintage, I had to explain that I was referring to myself. I am hopeful that this tactic will bear fruit before too long.'* "

Natasha turned the page, and a folded piece of thick paper fell out onto her lap.

"Oh, what's this?" She put the diary down on the nearby table and picked up the paper. She opened it up to reveal a very old photograph of three men standing in front of a stone wall. The two men on either side of the central figure were clearly Turkish soldiers. The man in the middle was tall, elegantly dressed, with quite a long moustache. He was also carrying what looked like a stone box under one arm.

Upon hearing Natasha's exclamation, Nadezhda had come into the room. Looking over Natasha's shoulder, she said, "Yes, that's my grandfather. That's Nikolai."

"He's rather handsome," said Natasha. "I can see where Dima gets his good looks from."

"Oh, yes, he was the handsome one," replied Nadezhda. "He came home from his army days with a bad leg that always gave him grief in the cold. But he had his pick of the girls of the town. I always thought he and *Babushka* made such a beautiful couple."

Dima, a little bemused hearing his grandmother talking about her own grandparents, said, "Keep going, Natasha. I want to hear what happened next."

"OK.

" *Monday, 27th April, 1885.*

" *What an amazing day! I have lived through an earthquake and have made an interesting find as a result. I went on an excursion with Ahmed and Mustafa to see the ruins of Ephesus. It is the done thing, apparently. If one is in the area, they told me, it is essential that one visit the ruins. They even took a photographer along to capture the moment forever.*

" *We had walked up to the top of the hill and then meandered our way down a pathway that Ahmed referred to as the Street of*

Curetes. Personally, there was not a lot to see. However, further down the hill there are some passably intact ruins and some intriguing statuary.

" *'We were posing for the photograph in front of a fairly unprepossessing stone wall opposite what remains of a building Mustafa optimistically referred to as Trajan's Temple when the earthquake struck. My companions all fell over, but I kept my feet until the wall behind me started to collapse. I bravely pushed the others out of the way and barely avoided being flattened by the blocks that fell from the wall. However, once the earthquake ceased I noticed a hole in the wall. Inside this hole I found a stone box, beautifully carved. I have kept it as a reminder of my visit to Ephesus and of my narrow escape from serious injury. From what I have seen it contains some papers – very old – with writing that I cannot read. Perhaps I will show them to someone when I get home.' "*

"Let me see that photograph again," asked Dima, suddenly.

Natasha handed him the photograph and Dima scrutinised it closely.

"Look," he said, pointing, "you can see the hole in the wall, here behind this man. I wonder if that's Ahmed or Mustafa? And that must be the stone box Nikolai's holding."

"Did he bring the box home, *Babushka*?" asked Natasha.

"I don't know," Nadezhda replied with a shrug. "I think there are a few bits and pieces of his at our *dacha*. But I never saw a stone box."

"I'd love to have a look," said Dima.

"So would I," added Natasha.

They both looked at Nadezhda.

"Oh well," she replied. "I guess we can go tomorrow. Victor will be there with his family, but we can all squeeze in. Now, put that book away and come help me make dinner. Then we can go to bed and get an early start."

❧

Patmos – April, AD 93

A man stood on the hill overlooking the small harbour of Patmos, gazing intently out to sea. Occasionally, he would cast a frustrated glance at the empty harbour below.

Three weeks and no ship!

If ever there was a moment that he resented his enforced stay on this tiny island off the coast of Asia[1], this was it. The vision that had been burned across his mind and that he had painstakingly translated into writing was one that the church back home so desperately needed. He knew that things were getting worse. The last report he had received had been a couple of months ago and it had told him of the martyrdom of Antipas, his beloved brother in Christos. Tears rose in his eyes as he recalled that fateful message.

And now, he had a message of his own and no ship to bear it away to Ephesus.

Wearily, he turned around to find something suitable to sit upon. Off to his left he spotted a rounded boulder. Moving over to it, he sat down and turned his attention back to the empty sea, scratching aimlessly at his thick black beard.

---

1 That is, Asia Minor, modern-day Turkey.

But the sea was no longer empty. There, on the horizon, a sail could be seen.

His weariness forgotten, the man jumped to his feet and set off down the goat path back to the town and the small empty harbour that was soon to be empty no longer.

Oh, thank-you, Lord, for bringing this ship, he prayed as he jogged down the path. *I know that Your timing is perfect, even if I have felt this delay so keenly. Please, go with this message and quickly bring back Loukas, the one on whose shoulders so much will be borne. I pray that you will be strengthening him for the task even now. You know he will need it…*

᠊ᢀ᠊

A *dacha* near Nizhny Novgorod – June, AD 2005

"Hey, Dima, look at this!"

The train had just pulled out of the main station in Nizhny Novgorod. Dima, Natasha and Nadezhda were on their way to the family's *dacha*, a couple of stations away from the edge of the city. Natasha had been reading Nikolai's diary but now she leant over to Dima, holding the book out for him to examine.

"Look," she said. "Nikolai has reverted to Russian now."

Sure enough, the entry that Natasha was pointing to was in Russian so that even Dima would have been able to read it.

"I wonder why?" he said.

"He explains it in the text," Natasha replied. "Listen.

" *'Thursday, 25th June, 1885.*

" *'I finally managed to get across the Turkish border into Russian-controlled territory, and have made it as far as Baku.*

20

Oh, it feels good to be able to speak (and write!) in Russian again, and not have to pretend to be that boorish Belgian industrialist. If I never have to speak French again, it will be too soon!

" '*My mission was reasonably successful. I may not have single-handedly prevented Turkey from joining Britain in a war against Mother Russia. But I feel that as a result of a few small incidents such a thing may be less likely in the foreseeable future. Be that as it may, as soon as I made contact with a superior officer, I was re-assigned to Bokhara and must immediately set sail across the Caspian Sea. I have been issued passage on the Prince Bariatinski – an aging paddle-steamer that has seen better days – and from there take the Transcaspian Railway as far as its continuing construction allows. All of this will be something to see, I have been told. Apparently, the only way to make a civilised crossing of the many deserts of Central Asia is by train. One certainly avoids a lot of messing about with camels and having to carry your own body weight in water.*' "

Dima laughed. "I think I would have liked Nikolai."

"Yes," replied Nadezhda with a smile, "I think you would have."

"I wonder what he meant by 'a few small incidents'?" pondered Natasha.

"Best not to dig too deeply, my dear," replied Nadezhda, the smile fading quickly. "It was a different world back then. People in military service often had to perform certain activities which we might be horrified by."

"Like desecrating a significant archaeological site without even blinking?" exclaimed Dima.

"That wasn't quite what I had in mind," said Nadezhda, "but it's a good example of the times. In some ways, it's surprising there is anything at all left to see of these ancient ruined cities."

"Which stop is it again, *Babushka?*" asked Dima, looking out the window of the train at a station, trying to catch a glimpse of a sign as they accelerated away.

"Ours is the next one. We should probably get ready to get off since the train will not stay motionless for very long."

Indeed, when the train pulled into their station shortly afterwards there was barely time for the three of them to open the doors and step down onto the platform with their bags before the train blew its whistle and took off.

Uncle Victor was waiting for them. There was no telephone at the *dacha* – in fact, while they did have electricity, there was no running water and they cooked on a wood stove – but he had happened to ring from the bar in town the night before requesting that his mother, Nadezhda, bring a few items from her kitchen when she next made the trip out. She had told him of their plans to come the next day and so here he was to meet them. Uncle Victor was a big bear of a man, with huge arms stuffed full of hard muscle from years working in a timber yard. He gave Natasha and Dima each a spine-cracking hug that would have made a chiropractor cringe in horror, before grabbing their bags, one in each hand, and leading the way off the platform. Dima followed, carrying Nadezhda's bag, with the others close behind.

They had to walk to their *dacha*. It was located approximately three kilometres from the station, so one did not want to make the journey too many times a day. There were a few shops – and the bar, of course – near the station, so they made a few necessary purchases and then began their walk. The dirt track took off straight as an arrow through a forested area that was riddled with *dachas*. On either side of the track, smaller, windier tracks took off through the forest leading to the rickety shacks and carefully cultivated vegetable gardens neatly surrounded by wooden fences, which made up each family's *dacha*. Everywhere, Dima saw old friends of his family who had been working these plots of land for decades. Many stopped what they were doing to wave at Dima and Natasha who they had not seen for quite a few years. Dima knew that he would have to stop in when he next walked past and say a proper greeting to many of them.

Eventually, the main track dwindled down to the size of the side tracks and then it suddenly turned to the left. And there, on the right of the path stood their *dacha*. It was quite large with an upstairs consisting of a few bedrooms simply crammed with beds and chairs that fold out into beds. Downstairs, there were another couple of bedrooms, a living area, and a kitchen. There was an outhouse located at a suitably discrete distance from the main house and a wash room not too far away. There were also a number of ramshackle sheds in which Dima and Natasha were hoping to locate any remaining items of Nikolai's.

It was quite late, despite the fact that it was still quite light outside. For these were the White Nights, that time of the year when the sun barely dips below the horizon resulting in nearly 24 hours of daylight for a few weeks. Uncle Victor's wife Aunt Olga had cooked up a batch of *borscht*, so they all sat down to big bowlfuls of the soup – garnished with a little sour cream and dill – accompanied by chunks of bread. After the walk from the station it was quite satisfying, despite the incessant noise generated by Uncle Victor and Aunt Olga's three young children as they fought over the remaining chunks of bread.

Dima and Natasha had been allocated a room upstairs so after the meal they excused themselves and went up to get their bed ready.

"I guess we can't look for anything now, can we?" asked Dima, wistfully.

"No," replied Natasha. "It will be better to start in the morning. We wouldn't want to disturb anyone by making any noise."

"True. Nikolai's stuff, if it is still here, must be well and truly buried under more recent deposits."

"Do you want to hear some more from the diary?"

"Sure."

They changed into their night clothes, then climbed into bed. Natasha opened the diary to the next entry.

" *'Tuesday, 30th June, 1885.*

" *'The Prince Bariatinski actually managed to get to Krasnovodsk, despite the best efforts of the captain and crew to sink her in the middle of the Caspian Sea. Granted the weather was foul, but that isn't really an excuse for nearly capsizing a paddle-steamer, something I would have thought should be rather difficult to achieve in any circumstance. I am rather grateful that my trunk escaped any significant damage, especially since it contains my charming stone box. Anyway, we are here now and I am waiting to embark upon the Central Asian express!'* "

"Excellent!" exclaimed Dima. "He still has the box!"

"Had," replied Natasha. "At the time of writing, he still had the box. Whether he managed to get it back to Russia is another story. You do realise where he was heading, don't you?"

"Well, of course. The Transcaspian Railway provided a backbone for all of Russia's activities in the Central Asian region, most especially the carrying of troops from one point to another with amazing speed, putting down native rebellions here, extending their territory southwards there. In some ways I'm surprised we never did attempt an invasion on the British in India."

"Yes, I don't need the lecture, but I'm glad you know he was taking the stone box into what was essentially a war-zone."

"Is that the end of the entry?" asked Dima.

"Yes," replied Natasha. "That's all for that day."

"Perhaps," said Dima with a yawn, "that should be all for our day, too. Good-night."

"Good-night, Dima."

As Natasha placed the diary down on the floor Dima reached over to turn off the reading light. Switching it off made little discernible difference to the ambient light in the room even with some curtains drawn across the windows. With a groan, Dima pulled the light blanket over his head in an attempt to block out the light.

It must have worked, for when he woke up and glanced at his watch Dima discovered that it was just past 7 o'clock the next morning. Natasha must have already got up so he got out of bed, quickly got dressed and headed downstairs for breakfast.

He found Natasha stirring some *kasha* on the wood stove. The porridge looked to be ready so he gave Natasha a good morning kiss then helped by getting out some bowls.

"Wanting an early start, were you?" asked Dima.

"Early?" laughed Natasha. "You're the last one to get up! Aunt Olga has taken the children into town for groceries. Uncle Victor's out in the garden working."

Somewhat chastened, Dima ate his *kasha* quickly.

"Actually, I did want to get up early," said Natasha. "I wanted to start looking for the box. I've gone over most of the house, already."

"Find anything?" asked Dima, chasing the remaining dollop of *kasha* around his bowl with his spoon.

"Nothing so far," she said. "But I'm expecting that if it's here at all it will be in one of the sheds. Your grandmother said there was quite a lot of old junk in those sheds."

"I was thinking about that last diary entry. I think we should probably look for Nikolai's trunk."

"Why? Because the box was in it when he was crossing the Caspian Sea? That doesn't mean he left it there for good."

"No, but it's a distinct possibility. Anyway," said Dima, getting up suddenly and giving his bowl a quick rinse using some water from the bucket next to the stove, "let's get out there and have a look!"

Natasha followed him out of the kitchen and along the short passageway to the back door. Outside, it was already quite warm and very sunny. They greeted Uncle Victor who was digging in the garden, preparing to plant some radishes judging from the seed packets off to one side. The biggest shed was near the outhouse. Dima opened the door and stepped inside.

It was rather gloomy. There was dust everywhere, covering most of the tools lying on a long bench that took up one of the walls. You could quite easily deduce Uncle Victor's most recent hobby simply by looking at which tools were mostly dust-free. Currently, it appeared that he was going through a wood-carving phase; all the chisels were clean.

Along the back wall various generations of Dima's family had placed boxes of stuff they no longer had room for in their city apartments. As Dima and Natasha started looking in boxes they unearthed many strange and interesting objects. Dima found a box that contained some of his childhood toys. Forgetting about the search for Nikolai's stone box for a few moments he idly flicked through the toys, remembering events from his past, many happy, a few that were sad.

Dima's reverie was broken when Natasha exclaimed, "Hey, look at this!"

Thinking she had found the box, Dima dropped his childhood memories and rushed over to where Natasha was kneeling, peering into a large cardboard box.

"What is it?" he asked, somewhat breathlessly.

He looked into the box and was at first disappointed to see what looked like a few very old x-rays made of thick plastic. However, on closer inspection he could see what looked like concentric circles – or was it one long spiral? – etched into the surface of the x-rays.

"Do you know what these are?" asked Natasha, eagerly.

"Not really," replied Dima.

"I think these could be illegally-distributed pop music records. During the sixties, the latest music was recorded off short-wave radio and then somehow transferred onto this thick x-ray plastic. Then you play them on a record player. If the KGB found you with one of these they would arrest you, since western pop music was considered highly subversive. This could be an old Beatles LP or something."

"Goodness me! I wonder who the radical was in my family? It couldn't have been my father. I don't think he ever spoke about liking the Beatles. Perhaps Uncle Victor would know."

Dima took the x-ray out to Uncle Victor while Natasha continued searching through the boxes. He came back shortly afterwards with a surprised expression on his face.

"Apparently they were my father's after all. And, yes, they are the Beatles. Uncle Victor doesn't think they would still play but he remembers sitting with my father while he played them to his friends. These must be worth a small fortune!"

He put them carefully to one side and continued searching.

Lunchtime came and went without them finding anything else of note, let alone the stone box of Nikolai's diary. After lunch they moved to the other shed and quickly discovered that the roof of this shed had been much less waterproof than the other one. There were a number of wooden boxes full of papers that had been wet, then frozen, then thawed, then dried every year for some decades. Dima pulled out paper bricks more suitable for use as building material than for reading.

They were about to break for an afternoon coffee when Dima pushed aside the lid of a wooden crate to reveal a large box made of dark wood. It looked old and worn as if it had seen much of the world. If this was not Nikolai's trunk then it was some other member of the family's trunk from about the same period and certainly worth a look inside.

"This *must* be it," said Dima.

Natasha had been taking a short breather, sitting on a pile of books. She quickly got up and came over to Dima.

"It certainly looks promising."

Together, they pulled the trunk out into the middle of the cleared area of floor. The trunk was locked with an ancient and heavily rusted padlock. Dima ran to the other shed and returned with one of Uncle Victor's chisels and a hammer. With a nervous look at Natasha, Dima took the chisel, positioned it over the arch of the padlock, and then gave it a heavy blow with the hammer. The padlock practically disintegrated before them.

"Careful!" exclaimed Natasha.

"It's all right," said Dima, placing the hammer and chisel on the ground. "Help me with the lid."

The lid must have seized many years previously. Even with Natasha's help it would not budge. Eventually, Dima took the hammer and chisel again and carefully used them to pry apart the lid from the rest of the trunk. When the lid came open with a nasty creak the contents of the trunk were finally on display.

Dima was pleased to see that everything in the trunk looked to be in surprisingly good condition. There were articles of clothing that were not the least bit affected by insects; there were books that could be opened; there were papers that were dry and readable; there were a couple of knives that still looked sharp enough to cut through sizable logs with little physical exertion. And there at the bottom of the trunk, underneath an old army coat, was a stone box looking exactly like the one in the photograph of Nikolai taken at Ephesus.

"There it is," whispered Natasha in awe.

"We found it," said Dima, solemnly.

"Let's take it inside."

"OK."

Dima picked the stone box up, carefully lifting it out of the trunk. Then he went outside and made his way over to the house followed closely by Natasha. They quickly went up to their room, shut the door, and Dima placed the stone box carefully on their bed. He looked up at Natasha and gave her a nervous grin.

"Here goes."

Slowly, he removed the lid of the box. Immediately they could see that the box was not empty; there was something made of paper, or possibly something wrapped in paper, taking up almost the entire box. He put the lid down carefully on the bed beside him. Then he gently prodded the paper. It was quite coarse in construction, a light orange in colour. It showed no immediate signs of disintegrating. Nevertheless, Dima did not want to pick it up yet.

"What is it?" Natasha asked.

"I'm not sure," he replied.

He bent a little closer. Actually, upon closer inspection it looked to be a roll of paper with the leading edge visible on top. He gently lifted up the edge by the right corner and saw that there were letters on the underside. Greek letters.

"Natasha, can you turn on the reading light?"

She got up switched on the lamp, positioning it so that the light fell onto the inside of the box. Dima looked again at the first line of letters that were visible. They were all hand-written capital letters and there were no spaces:

ΑΠΟΚΑΛΥΨΙϹΙΗϹΟΥΧΡΙϹΤΟΥ

"Can you read it?" Natasha asked.

"Well, I'm not sure where the word breaks are, if there are any, that is."

"Try reading it aloud."

"OK."

Dima paused.

"I'm guessing the first letter is an 'A'," he said, uncertainly. "Then the next three are just like Cyrillic, so the message starts, 'A-PO-KA'…"

He paused again.

"I'm not sure about the next one," he continued, eventually. "It *could* be an 'L'. I mean, it's *fairly* similar to a Cyrillic 'L'. Then comes a 'U', just like the Cyrillic."

Again, Dima paused. The next symbol had him stumped. It was nothing like a letter from either the Cyrillic or the English alphabets.

"What's wrong?" asked Natasha.

"I'm stuck," Dima replied. "I don't know this next one."

"Well, what have you got so far?"

" 'APOKALU'," he stated, and suddenly he had it. "I know! The next one is a PSI. I remember it coming up in a Physics formula back in high school. So that makes it 'APOKALUPS'."

Natasha's eyes widened.

"Apocalypse?" she asked, wonderingly.

"Maybe," replied Dima.

"What's next?"

"Well, the next letters are 'ISI' assuming that they are all like the Cyrillic. Then the next one could be an 'N' if it's like the Cyrillic, or 'H' if it's like the English, but I don't know which is right."

"Try them out," suggested Natasha.

"OK," replied Dima. " 'APOKALUPS ISIN'? Maybe. 'APOKALUPS ISIH'? Not very easy to say. So let's stick with 'N'. Then comes 'S', 'O', 'U', 'CH'…" (Dima pronounced this sound as it appears in the German name 'Bach' or in the Scottish word 'loch') "…'R', 'I', 'S', 'T', 'O' and 'U' – all just like the Cyrillic."

"Can you see any more?" asked Natasha.

"No, not without opening the roll up further."

"So what does is say?"

" 'APOKALUPS ISIN SOUCHRISTOU'."

"The last part sounds like 'Christ'," said Natasha.

" 'APOKALUPS ISINSOU CHRISTOU'," repeated Dima.

They sat there quietly for a few moments. "Are you sure about that 'N'?" asked Natasha, finally.

"Not really," replied Dima.

"Because," continued Natasha, "if you said 'I-*AY*-SOU', then you would have something that sounds very much like 'Jesus Christ'."[1]

"And then the whole thing would be 'APOKALUPSIS I-AYSOU CHRISTOU…' " said Dima, excitedly.

"And *that* sounds a lot like 'apocalypse Jesus Christ'," said Natasha.

"It does," said Dima, with a slight shake of his head as if he did not quite believe it. "I didn't know Jesus Christ wrote an apocalypse."

"What about the book of Revelation?"

"Well, that's possible," replied Dima, uncertainly. "But if you're right, that would make this what looks to be a very old copy of Revelation."

"*Oy!*" exclaimed Natasha, using a Russian exclamation similar to the English 'Oh!' but usually said with much more feeling.

"Yes," agreed Dima, "*oy!*"

❦

Off the coast of Asia – April, AD 93

A young man stood near the prow of a small cargo ship as it forged its way through the choppy waves of the Aegean Sea. The wind tousled his dark hair, forcing it over his eyes, apparently trying to prevent him from staring at the coastline of a small island in the distance.

1 The Russian name for Jesus is much closer in sound to the Greek than it is in English.

"Is that it?" he asked one of the deckhands who happened to be passing at that moment fiddling with a rope.

"Aye, that's Patmos."

Loukas smiled to himself. He had been travelling now for just short of a week and he was pleased to be nearing the end of the voyage. In fact, he was excited, but not because he was sick of the constant rolling of the sea that made it difficult to walk around and keep down the meagre provisions that comprised a sailor's diet. He was excited because he would very soon be in the presence of Ioanneis once again.

Ioanneis! Just the name was enough to send shivers of anticipation down Loukas' spine. The man had been one of the many Christian refugees fleeing from the horrific Jewish War that had left Jerusalem in ruins. He had quickly become a leader in the church of Ephesus. After all, he had been converted by one of the very Apostles themselves! He always used to say that the gospel written down by Markos was his favourite: it reminded him of the forthright and colourful way that Petros spoke. That's right, he actually knew Petros! At least, before Petros went to the church in Rome, soon after to be beheaded by the emperor… Neron. Loukas could barely bring himself even to think that beastly name.

Ten years ago Ioanneis had baptised Loukas into the Way. But then just last year Ioanneis had fallen foul of the local authorities. Apparently, some of the residents of Ephesus had objected to comments he had made about eating food that had been first offered to the goddess Artemis. Ioanneis had been teaching in the church that Christians should not eat such meat for it had been associated with demons. Some of the followers of Artemis had heard about this and had become enraged. They had laid in wait for him one dark night as he had come out of the Agora, followed him as he headed to his house, and then jumped him. That probably would have been the end of it had not a Roman patrol been within earshot. They had heard his cries for help and come running. However, applying the principle of mob rule they immediately arrested *Ioanneis*. After all, following the logic of the situation, if a mob wanted him dead then he must have done something wrong.[1]

Ioanneis then appeared before the public tribunal and had promptly been found guilty of treason against the State. This new charge had been necessary since treason against Artemis was not in itself something the authorities could punish. Of course, everyone knew he was not guilty of treason against the State, even the members of the tribunal themselves, and this was reflected in his sentence. People found guilty of treason were usually beheaded if they were a Roman citizen; if they were not a Roman citizen they were crucified. Since Ioanneis was a Roman citizen from a well-respected and, more importantly, wealthy family instead of losing his head he lost his freedom: he was sent into exile to the penal colony on the island of Patmos.

This had happened over a year ago. Since that time word had come from Ioanneis occasionally. Essentially, when a ship that had recently travelled from Patmos came into the harbour of Ephesus someone from the church would ask the sailors about him. Usually, one would have a verbal message

1 The Apostle Paul had been arrested by the Romans exactly the same way in Jerusalem many decades earlier. See Acts 21:30-36.

or occasionally even a written letter. Similarly, the churches of Asia had sent letters back, informing him of recent events such as who the authorities had imprisoned and how the church was coping with this and other forms of persecution. In this manner he had continued to have a leadership role in the church even from a distance.

Then, a week ago, the church had received a brief and rather enigmatic letter:

> *From Ioanneis a servant of God on Patmos for the sake of the word of God,*
> *To the church in Ephesus.*
> *Grace to you and peace from our God and Father and from the Lord Iēsus[1].*
> *I have something important to say to you and to all the churches of Asia. Send Loukas son of Theseus and I will prepare him for what is to come. Be encouraged! The Lord knows you and your deeds.*
> *The brothers here with me send their greetings.*

Everyone had been quite excited to hear what he had to say, although they had wondered why he had not just said it right then and there in the letter. And the line 'The Lord knows you and your deeds' had given some of the more mature members of the congregation pause for thought for it could be taken either positively or negatively.

So the church had prayed for Loukas and within a few days he was on a ship bound for Patmos. They had hugged

[1] This is pronounced "YAY-soos", with 'oo' as in 'book'. (See Appendix 1 for a pronunciation guide for this and other names.)

the coast until they had reached Miletus where they had stayed for a couple of days, and then they had headed westward – island-hopping so as not to get lost – until Patmos came into view. Now, he watched the island get bigger and bigger as they sailed closer, but it was not until they rounded the peninsular and the small harbour of Patmos lay before them that he uttered a brief prayer of thanks for his safe arrival.

There was no one waiting for him when the deck hands leapt over the side to tie the boat to the small, wooden dock. This was not surprising since Ioanneis would have had no way of knowing when he was arriving. However, he had no idea where to go. He picked up the small cloth bag that contained his few travelling possessions and clambered onto the dock himself.

The island of Patmos was a penal colony. But it was not one enormous prison. Certainly, there was a prison camp on the island where criminals were sent *deportio ad insulam*, that is deported by the Emperor himself and confined to a prison where they would serve out a life sentence of hard labour. But there were also people here *relegatio in insulam*, that is, those who had been relegated by the provincial governor to the island but who then had considerable freedom of movement within the island context. They could earn a living and even own property. As a result a small town had sprung up to service the Roman garrison and those who had been forced to make Patmos their home for the rest of their lives. Despite its relative isolation, there had been a few entrepreneurial types willing to move to Patmos in order to make a living providing goods and services to the often wealthy men and women who had fallen foul of the Roman government for whatever reason.

From the messages and letters the church in Ephesus had received from Ioanneis, he had apparently adapted quickly to his new setting. He had immediately started speaking to his fellow 'relegatees' about Iēsus and had quickly made a few converts. Their regular meeting together had formed the seed of a growing church. Before long they were visiting the more serious criminals in the prison and had even made some converts amongst the Roman soldiers doing their tour of duty maintaining order in the small colony.

Loukas made his way from the dock into the township. It was late in the day and there were only few people about. The light was draining quickly from the sky and darkening clouds to the north promised stormy weather in the near future. In need of directions, Loukas caught the attention of a man sitting near a grain store mending some clothing in the fading light.

"Excuse me, sir, I'm looking for Ioanneis of Ephesus."

"Ah, yes, I know the man. A *relegatio*, yes?"

"That's right. Do you know where I might find him?"

"Certainly. Follow this road up the hill until you come to the statue of our lord and god Emperor Domitianus. Turn left and when you come to the gymnasium the house you are seeking will be on the right."

"Thank-you."

Loukas took his leave and followed the man's directions. As he passed the statue of Domitianus he shuddered slightly, refusing to make the required sign of obeisance, but no one was present to see this tiny act of treason. He quickly located the gymnasium and was pleased to see light emanating from the house next to it. He knocked at the door.

It was opened by a large, broad-shouldered man with a full, black beard. His friendly eyes were surrounded by laugh-lines that crinkled when he smiled. He was smiling now.

"Loukas, son of Theseus, come in, come in!" he boomed.

"Ioanneis. It's good to see you again."

Ioanneis grabbed him around the shoulders with one arm, and, taking Loukas' bag with his other hand, ushered him into the house. Inside, there were five or six men and women sitting on the floor. There were a few lamps burning and a large scroll lay open on the floor.

"Loukas, you come near the end of our meeting. We have been reading from the prophet Isaiah." He indicated a place for Loukas to sit, then sat himself. "Daria, please continue."

A woman wearing a brightly coloured shawl over her head was sitting closest to the scroll. Hesitantly, she began to read.

" 'Behold, I will create new heavens and a new earth. The former things will not be remembered, nor will they come to mind. But be glad and rejoice forever in what I will create, for I will create Jerusalem to be a delight and its people a joy. I will rejoice over Jerusalem and take delight in my people; the sound of weeping and of crying will be heard in it no more.'[1]"

She stopped, and after a brief silence Ioanneis spoke softly.

---

1 Isaiah 65:17-19.

"This is how the story ends, my friends. Through all the pain and suffering that you have already experienced and all that is yet to come remember this: it will be forgotten entirely when we are living in the joy of God's New Jerusalem."

The others nodded their heads in agreement as if this was not the first time they had heard Ioanneis say something like this. For Loukas, it was good to sit once again at the feet of someone he had looked up to for so long.

But it was over all too soon. When Ioanneis had finished speaking the others stood up and quickly left leaving Loukas and Ioanneis alone. There was a silence as Ioanneis looked at Loukas carefully, sizing him up for the task ahead.

"How is your family?" he asked, eventually.

"They are well," Loukas replied.

"And how is Iounia?"

Loukas blushed, suddenly.

"My fiancée? How did you know about her? We were only betrothed a couple of months ago."

"Oh, I have my sources," laughed Ioanneis good-naturedly.

"Of course!" exclaimed Loukas. "You receive letters."

"That's right, and you haven't answered my question."

"Well, she was fine when I left," he replied, although she had cried a little, as had he. Just thinking about her now had him blinking more rapidly. Ioanneis must have noticed for he changed the subject.

"Are you hungry?" asked Ioanneis. "Was the voyage difficult?"

"Yes I am, and no it wasn't," replied Loukas. "From Miletus we made good time, and I wasn't sick… much."

Ioanneis laughed. "Well then, let me get you something to eat. I'm afraid what I have will not compare to the usual fare back home in Ephesus. We get by with less here."

"That's fine. I'll be back there before long…" Loukas trailed off.

"… And I'll still be here," finished Ioanneis, smiling. "That's fine. I don't mind suffering for the sake of Iēsus who suffered much worse on my behalf. And who knows? I may not be here forever. The new proconsul may grant a pardon to those of us imprisoned by the previous one…"

He prepared a small meal of bread, cheese and dried fruits. When the food was ready Loukas and Ioanneis lay down on couches and ate.

"Speaking of departures: when will the ship you came on leave?" asked Ioanneis, through a mouthful of bread.

"They intend to leave in two days. They have some goods to unload tomorrow. Then, they'll head back to Miletus."

"Then we'll speak to them tomorrow. You *must* return with them. It is necessary for you to begin what I have called you here to do as soon as possible."

Loukas swallowed hurriedly in order to speak. "And what is that? All this time travelling I have been wondering what it was you wanted me for."

"Simply this," replied Ioanneis. He moved to the other side of the room, bent down, and lifted a large, bulky scroll from its resting place on a scroll-holder.

Between Nizhny Novgorod and St. Petersburg – June, AD 2005

Dima and Natasha whiled away the train trip from Nizhny Novgorod to Moscow alternately talking about the stone box with its mysterious contents and reading Nikolai's on-going exploits from the diary. He had had a very interesting time, apparently, crossing Russian-controlled Central Asia on the Transcaspian railway. At Geok-Tepe he had seen the ruined Turcoman fortress, its mud walls pock-marked with shell holes yet dominated by a huge breach. Only four years before, General Mikhail Skobelev's engineers had tunnelled under the wall and with two tonnes of explosives had blasted their way through, closely followed by the Russian infantry, thereby bringing about the complete desolation of the defenders. Nikolai had heard all about the victory, but it was quite another thing to see the ruins with his own eyes.

Merv, by comparison, had been occupied by the Russian army without a shot being fired only a year before Nikolai arrived there, through some secretive and rather unscrupulous diplomacy. There, in the city that had formerly been known throughout Central Asia as the Queen of the World, Nikolai had witnessed the once proud Turcoman people living under the oppressive yoke of the Russians.

From Merv the railway was only being used to ferry building materials up the line towards Bokhara, since the Russians were still in the process of laying tracks and constructing an enormous wooden bridge across the River Oxus. Nikolai managed to catch a lift on one of these goods trains and had devoted a number of pages in his diary to describing the river, once he had arrived there, and the bridge that was slowly taking shape before his eyes.

At that point, however, Nikolai had run out of pages and the diary ended.

"It's a good thing we found his trunk and the stone box," Natasha had commented, "or else we would never have known if he managed to get it back to Russia."

With no further distractions Dima was left to muse about the stone box and the scroll contained within. How old was this scroll? How had it ended up in Ephesus? As a fairly typical Russian growing up under atheistic communism Dima had learned nothing about the Bible. However, he and Natasha had recently got involved with a small church that met one Metro stop away from their apartment building. The congregation had been mostly comprised of younger people and they played contemporary-sounding worship music that he and Natasha had enjoyed. And they had started hearing about the Bible. Someone usually preached every week and they had both found it fascinating to discover that the Bible was still very relevant to life in the twenty-first century. He had bought a copy – something that would have been impossible only a decade and a half before – and had been reading it ever since. He had loved the Gospels but had struggled through Paul's letters. However, it had been the book of Revelation that had puzzled him the most. It was disconcertingly easy to read but utterly impenetrable as far as what it meant. He did not remember hearing any sermons on the book so he really was in the dark about how one was supposed to approach it. The stone box resting at the bottom of his backpack safely stowed between his feet was therefore an exciting challenge. He wanted to understand Revelation and what better way than by being involved in the study of an ancient manuscript of the book.

If that was what it really was. He was basing the identification of the scroll on three words and the fact that they reminded him of the start of Revelation. He could well be wrong.

Once they arrived in Moscow all thoughts of the stone box and its scroll were forgotten in the mayhem of getting themselves and their luggage from Kursky Station, the station they had arrived at, to Leningradsky Station, the station from which trains departed Moscow to go to St. Petersburg. This meant catching the Moscow Metro, and Dima, not having lived in Moscow at all, needed to concentrate a little. However, they only had to go one station anti-clockwise around the Brown Circle Line, from Kurskaya to Komsomolskaya Metro Station, which was the one closest to Leningradsky Station. He was eternally grateful that they did not have to change lines at any stage!

It was only when they were sitting in the McDonalds adjacent to Leningradsky Station, eating a well-deserved hamburger and fries, that he allowed himself to relax and think about what they had found on his family's *dacha*.

"What do you know about the book of Revelation?" Dima asked Natasha, as she was dipping a fry into some unidentifiable sauce.

"Not a lot," she replied, hesitantly. "There's a lot of death and disasters, some grotesque monsters, and a happy ending – at least, for Christians."

"Yes, that seems to be a good description. But I just remember pages and pages of graphic details. I mean, for a book with no pictures it is very *visual*."

"Well, you are a graphic designer. It makes sense that that is how you would approach it."

"True," said Dima, with a frown. "But do those details have any meaning?"

"I don't know."

"I really want to find out."

They were silent for a few minutes. Finally, Natasha spoke.

"You know, Dima, I think God really wanted us to find the scroll."

"Really, why?"

"I don't know." Natasha stopped to consider the question. "Maybe the time has come for the book to be fulfilled," she continued hesitantly. "It's all about the end times, isn't it?"

"Yes, I guess so."

"Well then, start looking for death and disasters, grotesque monsters and a happy ending."

They laughed. Dima happened to glance at his watch and realised their train would be departing soon. So they finished their meal quickly, collected their bags that had been safely stored under the table, and headed off to the station.

Once on the platform, they presented their tickets and passports to the guard waiting outside their carriage and he nodded, ripped off his portion of the ticket, and returned their passports. Once on the train, they made their way along the corridor of the carriage until they reached their *coupé*, the small room consisting of four beds and a small fold-away table beneath the window. It was still quite light outside, but it was already late evening – their train was an overnight sleeper – so they drew the curtains and waited to see who would occupy the remaining two beds. A woman stewardess came by with their blankets and pillows, so they paid her the small extra fee, and prepared their beds. They had been fortunate to get the two lower beds, so they sat facing one another, each reading a magazine they had purchased in the station.

Suddenly, there was a knock on the door of their coupe. Looking through the window, Dima could see two policemen standing there. He opened the door and one of the policemen stepped into the *coupé*.

"Baggage check," the man said, brusquely.

Dima, suddenly very conscious of the stone box in his backpack stowed carefully up next to his pillow, began to feel a little anxious.

"Is that really necessary?" he asked.

The policeman, not appearing to be the least perturbed by Dima's question, replied, "Yes, yes, just routine. You just need to open all your bags, we'll have a quick look, and we'll be on our way."

Natasha had by this time put down her magazine. Dima could see her looking at his backpack with a worried expression on her face. The policeman must have noticed it, too, for he also looked over at the backpack.

Dima thought quickly. Standing up, he pulled out some money from a front pocket of his jeans, and placed it into the palm of his hand. Then, he reached out as if to shake the policeman's hand.

"Look," he said, pleasantly. "Of course you can look in our bags."

The policeman saw the hand outstretched and shook it warmly. The money changed owners.

"Oh," he replied, "that won't be necessary. I'm sure your bags are fine."

With that, he turned and quickly left the coupe. Dima, still standing, shut the door behind him. They were silent for a few minutes.

"Well done," said Natasha eventually.

"Thanks," he replied, a little shakily.

A few minutes later, the other two occupants of their *coupé* arrived: two businessmen who obviously made the journey between Moscow and St. Petersburg frequently, since they greeted Dima and Natasha, set up their beds, and by the time the train pulled out of the station they were already asleep.

It had been a fairly long day so Dima and Natasha also settled down for the night. After saying good-night to one another Dima lay back on his bed and looked at the bottom of the bunk above him. He had his backpack up near his head so that no one would be able to grab it while he was sleeping, but it still took him a while to relax enough to fall asleep. Natasha, lulled by the rocking of the train as it plunged through the gloomy Russian countryside, went to sleep quite quickly.

Dima woke first, as the train slowed in its approach to Moskovsky Station in St. Petersburg. He gently roused Natasha and they quickly packed up their things and tried to straighten their hair. The businessmen, too, had awoken and were preparing to disembark.

Moving ever more slowly, the train gradually eased into the platform and came to a gentle stop. Collecting their bags, including the now precious backpack, Dima and Natasha followed the businessmen out of the *coupé* and into the carriage corridor where the other passengers were now lining up waiting to leave the carriage. Eventually, they made it onto the platform and then they followed the steady stream of people walking in the direction of the station's exit gates.

"Do you want to take the Metro home?" asked Natasha, wearily.

Dima considered it for only a second.

"No, not really," he replied. "Let's get a taxi."

Outside in the square, they found a taxi driver, negotiated a suitable price, then walked over to his taxi. After putting their bags in the boot – Dima kept the backpack with him – they got in and the taxi driver started off. At one point, the taxi driver took an unexpected detour, but explained it was because they were setting up for a Paul McCartney concert to be held in Palace Square next to the Hermitage that evening. Dima looked at Natasha, thinking of the musical x-rays they had unearthed back at the *dacha*, but at the same time they both shook their heads. They had something far more interesting to think about now. They had managed to get the scroll safely to St. Petersburg. The question was what to do with it now.

Patmos – April, AD 93

The next morning Ioanneis woke Loukas early as the roosters were crowing in the dawn. After a quick breakfast of bread and honey they headed off to the dock to speak to the captain of the ship Loukas had arrived in. There had been a storm overnight but it had blown itself out leaving the pathways muddy and leaf-strewn. They did not speak as they walked passed the statue of Domitianus and then down the hill to the harbour. They found the captain overseeing the unloading of the cargo under the watchful eye of a Roman patrol and confirmed with him that Loukas would depart with them the next day. Then they turned around and headed back to Ioanneis' house.

"So, what's the scroll?" asked Loukas finally.

After showing Loukas the scroll last night Ioanneis had immediately replaced it on the stand saying that there was not enough time to discuss it then and there. They had then prepared Loukas' bedding and retired for the evening.

"Ah yes, the scroll," replied Ioanneis. He was silent for quite some time. Then, after drawing near to the statue of Domitianus at the top of the hill, Ioanneis stopped to look at it.

"When you look at this statue what do you see?" Ioanneis asked, suddenly.

Loukas thought for a moment then had a quick look around to see if anyone was close enough to overhear their conversation. There was no one nearby. The town was very small and most of the activity was clustered around the dock at the bottom of the hill where there were a few shops lining a tiny Agora. In the area around Ioanneis and Loukas there were a few private houses and some civic buildings such as the gymnasium to the left and baths to the right. But it was far from a bustling metropolis.

"I see a mere mortal deluded into thinking he is somehow divine," replied Loukas quietly but with some heat.

Ioanneis smiled. "You are right to be cautious in saying such things. If anyone had overheard you would probably be very fortunate indeed to end up here on Patmos with me for good. However, you have spoken truly. Domitianus' delusions of divinity are bad enough but he has been abusing his position of power by forcing others into believing those delusions too. I don't think I need to remind you of our friends who have been persecuted for not going to the Temple of the Emperors. But it's only going to get worse…"

They continued on in silence until they came to Ioanneis' house and went inside. Once again Ioanneis went over to the scroll and picked it up.

"Loukas, this is for the churches of Asia. I want you to take this scroll and read it in Ephesus. Stay there only long enough for it to be copied, then go to Smyrna, Pergamum, Thyatira, Sardis, Philadelphia and Laodicea. In every place stay only long enough to read the scroll and for a copy to be made. When you have been to the seven churches return to Ephesus and encourage the church through what is to come."

"Why?" asked Loukas. "What is coming?"

Solemnly, he handed the scroll to Loukas. "Tribulation," he replied, sadly. "But then vindication will follow as surely as the dawn follows night."

Loukas looked at the scroll with a puzzled look on his face. "So what's in the scroll."

Ioanneis seemed unwilling to answer the question directly. "I know that many of the young people back in Ephesus used to call me 'the Seer' behind my back," he said. Loukas smiled guiltily, for he had certainly done so. "However, it's true: God has given me the gift of prophecy which I have used in the churches over many years. Well, a few months ago I had a vision. This scroll is my attempt at putting the indescribable into words. What I heard I have reproduced faithfully; what I saw I have tried as best I could to give my impressions of the experience."

Loukas was suddenly eager to read the scroll. He unrolled the beginning and read aloud, " 'The revelation of Iēsus Christos, which God gave him to show his servants what must soon take place…' "

Ioanneis interrupted kindly. "That's enough for now. You can read it on the way home."

"So, this is an apocalypse?"

"Well, it's not like those that have been circulating recently. After all, I've signed it. I haven't hid behind some important figure out of the Scriptures, trying to borrow their authority for what I've written. No, my authority comes directly from Iēsus Christos the Lamb of God!"

Ioanneis had got a little worked up thinking about pseudonymity and took a few moments to calm down before continuing. "No, this is a prophecy not an apocalypse. But it is somewhat like them in that there's a lot of mysterious language and only some of it is explained. You'll soon work out why. But you should have no difficulty working it all out. Just keep your Scriptures handy!"

Loukas rolled up the scroll. Ioanneis passed him a cloth cover and he placed this over the scroll before putting it in his bag.

"Do you know whom you were named after?" asked Ioanneis.

"Yes," replied Loukas. "He who wrote one of the Gospels."

"Well, you will be *my* evangelist sharing the good news to the churches of Asia. But I'm afraid this good news will be bitter in the stomach…"

❧

St. Petersburg – June, AD 2005

When Dima woke up the next morning he was disconcerted to find Natasha, already awake, staring at him.

"Finally!" she exclaimed. "I've been awake for ages just waiting for you."

Dima sat up and groaned as he rubbed his eyes. "What time is it?" he said, looking at the sunlight streaming in around the sides of the curtains.

"Seven," Natasha replied. "Don't look at the light; it's been like that for hours."

Dima groaned again. He had lived in St. Petersburg for over ten years now but he had never been thrilled about the White Nights.

"So," he asked finally once he was in control of his thought processes, "what got you up so early?"

"You have to ask?" she responded.

They both looked over to the desk in the corner of their tiny bedroom where the stone box stood.

"No, not really," Dima replied. "But what do we do with it now?"

"I've been thinking about that," said Natasha eagerly. "We should show it to Zhenya." Yevgeny, or Zhenya for short, was the pastor of their small church. "He may know someone who could help," she continued. "Someone at the Christian University, perhaps."

"That's a good idea. And it is Sunday, after all."

They had a leisurely breakfast, for their church met in the afternoon. When Natasha went out to do the shopping, Dima got out their Bible – he had neglected to take it with them to Nizhny Novgorod – and started reading the book of Revelation. He enjoyed the first chapter with its description of Jesus. The letters to the Seven Churches in chapters two and three was reasonably clear, apart from some baffling references to the Nicolaitans, Balaam and Jezebel. But things went downhill from there. The more he read the more puzzled his expression became. *What on earth is this book trying to say?* he thought. *I hope Zhenya knows what's going on here.*

When Natasha returned he had got as far as the '666' at the end of chapter 13, so he stopped reading and helped her unpack the groceries.

"It's a mess!" he said angrily, carelessly waving a carton of eggs.

"Oh, are they broken?" asked Natasha, thinking that she had neglected to check the eggs in the shop.

"No, I'm talking about Revelation," replied Dima, sliding the eggs into their place in the refrigerator. "I've been trying to read it all morning, but it's just a complete mess."

"Well, wait until we talk to Zhenya. He's studied the Bible at University; he'll know something."

"I hope so."

After the groceries were packed away Dima made some tea for Natasha and some coffee for himself. Then they sat at the small table in their tiny kitchen and ate some chocolates.

"Do we take it to church?" asked Natasha after a while.

"I've been thinking about that," replied Dima. "I'm guessing the less we move it the better. Why don't we invite Zhenya and Marina around after church?" Marina was Yevgeny's wife, responsible for running the children's programme that ran at the same time as the church service. Natasha would help her out occasionally.

"Sure."

Once they had finished their drinks they got ready to leave. Dima locked their front door carefully and then they walked down the three flights of stairs to the ground floor of their apartment building. As he opened the security door at the front of the building he saw a bus coming down the street towards them.

"Quick," he said to Natasha, "here it comes."

The bus had already pulled in to the stop as they hurried across the road, but a *babushka* was slowly getting off, so they had time enough to jump in the back doors before they closed and the bus pulled away from the curb. There were plenty of seats at that time of day, as well as it being a Sunday, so they were able to sit together.

Dima was preoccupied with Revelation, especially that last chapter he had just read. He had heard of the expression 'the mark of the beast', but he had not realised there were in fact *two* beasts, one that came out of the sea and one that came out of the earth. Then there was the dragon in the previous chapter; but at least whoever wrote the book had provided a key for that one: the dragon was Satan, the one who had appeared as a serpent in the Garden of Eden and deceived Adam and Eve into eating from the tree of the knowledge of good and evil. It looked as though the dragon had called up the beast from the sea, so what did that make it? Instinctively, he knew that identifying the beast would help work out what the book as a whole meant.

Suddenly, Dima realised Natasha had been speaking to him. He looked up and saw that they had reached their stop. They got out in front of Vasileostrovskaya Metro station, conveniently located opposite a McDonalds restaurant. They crossed the road and lined up at the outside order window – the pedestrian equivalent of 'drive-through' – and bought lunch. Then, it was not a long walk to the building where their church met, eating their lunch as they went.

There were a few people already there, and some of their friends came up and welcomed them back from their holiday. Yevgeny was there but was busy talking with the worship team up the front. Dima had thought it would be better to wait until after the service anyway.

They enjoyed the service, and as usual Yevgeny's message was worth listening to. But both Dima and Natasha had their minds on the stone box sitting in the corner of their bedroom with its mysterious scroll. So as soon as the service was over, they went straight up to the front.

"Welcome home!" exclaimed Yevgeny when he saw them approaching. He was a tall man, mid-thirties, with strong, piercing eyes.

"Thanks," replied Dima. "We had a good time."

"Actually we wanted to speak to you about something that happened on the trip," said Natasha eagerly. "We found something that belonged to Dima's great-great-grandfather; something *he* found in Ephesus."

"What did he find?" asked Yevgeny. "A coin?"

"No," replied Dima. "Look, we would like you and Marina to come over to our place for dinner and we'll show you what we found. I'd rather not spoil it by just simply telling you about it."

Yevgeny looked intrigued. "Let me check with Marina."

Marina, his wife, was not far away. She was a little younger than Yevgeny with pale skin and long dark hair. After briefly conversing with her Yevgeny was back.

"OK," he replied. "If you can wait half an hour or so, we'll come over with you, if that's alright."

Forty minutes later the four of them made their way to the nearest bus stop. While they waited for a bus, Dima and Natasha spoke about their holiday, without mentioning Ephesus again. The bus, once it arrived, was more crowded than earlier; they were able to find seats for Marina and Natasha but they were not together, so further conversation was impossible.

Then, once they got off the bus right outside Dima and Natasha's apartment building, Dima asked Yevgeny cryptically, "So, do you know much about the book of Revelation?"

"Well, I studied it a little at university, but why do you ask?"

"Just wondering," replied Dima as he opened the security door using a three number code.

They were silent as they climbed the three flights of stairs. Dima unlocked their front door and then they were inside the apartment. Everyone took off their shoes, located appropriate slippers from the rack near the door, and followed Dima through the living room into the bedroom.

"My great-great-grandfather wrote a diary," Dima began solemnly. "Natasha found it on a book shelf when she was looking for something to read. Apparently, when he was visiting Ephesus with some Turks there was a small earthquake. Part of a wall collapsed close to where he was standing revealing a hole behind it. And in the hole he found this." With an air of ceremony, Dima indicated the stone box.

"Is there anything in it?" asked Yevgeny as he stepped forward to take a closer look.

"Yes," replied Natasha. "A couple of things, as far as we can make out. Maybe more."

Dima lifted the lid off.

"It looks like a scroll," said Yevgeny.

"It is," said Dima. "We've only looked at the very start of it but I think it's a copy of the book of Revelation."

With great care Yevgeny examined the scroll, his lips moving as he slowly read the Greek words to himself.

"You could well be right," he said after a while. "It certainly starts like Revelation." He reluctantly let the scroll go and stepped back from the box, speaking quickly. "But this is huge! This scroll looks extremely old. You do realise that Revelation was written to Ephesus and some of the churches nearby? This could be one of their earliest copies. It could even be the original. No, that would be impossible. I don't think there are *any* manuscripts of the New Testament that go back that far. No, this must be an early copy, but I wonder how early? You have to take this to the Christian University. Let them roll it out properly; translate it." Turning to Dima he asked, "How did your great–great-grandfather get it out of Turkey?"

Dima was laughing at Yevgeny's lengthy outburst. "Well, we haven't finished reading his diary. He was quite a character, apparently, and thought that only cowards took the most direct way home."

"When can we take it to the University?"

"Well, I'm back at work this week, but I might be able to negotiate an early afternoon, maybe Thursday or Friday."

"That will do nicely. I'll work out the day and we'll meet here. We can take it over together."

"I'm coming, too," said Natasha. "Marina?"

"Yes," Marina replied, "I'll come and keep you company."

"Well, then," exclaimed Yevgeny excitedly, "that's settled!"

Patmos – April, AD 93

The ship sailed shortly after daybreak. There was a favourable wind that would have them in Miletus by nightfall so the captain wanted to get away as soon as possible. But first the Roman guards had to satisfy themselves that only those permitted to leave Patmos were on board.

Once they were under way the weather was delightful but Loukas saw none of it. He found himself a sheltered corner with enough light to read and immersed himself in the vision that Ioanneis had recorded. He began reading with great pleasure and was immediately entranced by the vision of one like a son of man – Loukas recognised the reference to the prophet Daniel – but described as if he were the Ancient of Days.[1] He knew that Ioanneis was referring to Iēsus but making it very clear that he is also God. He could feel the awe that Ioanneis had felt in seeing the one who holds the power over death and the grave and he was himself awestruck. He could not wait to read this out to the churches back in Asia.

However, as he continued reading the scroll his expression became more solemn. At one point he stopped reading with a puzzled expression on his face and then he searched about until he found a rusty nail in a corner. He spent a few minutes scratching some letters and numbers on the deck and then doing some addition sums. Then, when a name emerged from the collection of letters he nodded his head in satisfaction and continued reading. Many times he felt tears start up in his eyes, but it was not until he read the last words,

1 See Daniel 7:9, 13-14.

words that clearly recalled the passage of Isaiah that Daria had read for the little group on Patmos, that he allowed himself to release the pent-up emotion and then he cried for a long time.

"Oh Lord, give me strength," he prayed once he had ceased crying. "I cannot do this on my own. And I know not if I can be faithful even unto death…"

Loukas placed the scroll back in its covering, stowed it safely in his bag, and then hid it under his sleeping mat. Once he was sure it was safe he went out on deck to stretch his legs. He joined a man standing near the prow of the ship looking out at the sunlight sparkling on the Aegean Sea. After they had been standing there a while the other man spoke.

"It's beautiful, is it not?"

"Yes," replied Loukas noncommittally, who had not really been looking at the scenery. He had been thinking about what he had just read.

"My name's Sergius Maximus. And you?"

"Lucius," Loukas replied, using the Latinised form of his name since this man was clearly Roman. Turning to face the man, Loukas was somewhat disconcerted by the strength of the other man's gaze: his eyes were a piercing light blue and seemed capable of penetrating to the back of one's skull.

"Pleased to meet you. So what brings you to Patmos?"

The man was presumably just making small talk but Loukas did not really feel like answering questions.

"I met with an old friend."

"A resident, eh?" asked Sergius with a sly smile. When Loukas did not immediately answer he continued. "Don't worry! There are plenty of decent people holed up on islands like these all over the Empire. I'm sure your friend is one of those."

After an uncomfortable pause Loukas asked, "And you? Why were you on Patmos?"

"I had been posted there for a while working as a clerk in the garrison. But I'm moving on. I've been assigned to Pergamum after a few days in Ephesus."

"Really," exclaimed Loukas, trying to muster some enthusiasm. "I'm from Ephesus."

"Well, it seems we'll be travelling together for a few days, perhaps."

"What will you do in Pergamum?"

"Same sort of thing." He turned and leant his back on the rail. "The new proconsul has requested a legal clerk to assist him in his communications with Rome. So I'll mostly be reading and writing official letters. Not terribly interesting most of the time. But I am looking forward to browsing the library there. I hear it is second only to the great library of Alexandria, and that's only because someone gave most of their scrolls to Queen Cleopatra not that long ago. But enough about me! What about you? What do you do?"

"My father is a trader. I have been in training to assist him in the work."

"An honourable profession. What does he trade?"

"Pottery, linen, some food stuffs, things like that."

"So you're good with numbers?"

Loukas started and looked at the other man guiltily, thinking of those numbers he had just scratched into the deck. *Has he seen those numbers?* he thought with horror.

Did he see the name? But he had been using Hebrew letters, he recalled with relief, so the chances of this Roman official knowing how to read those was extremely slight. In any event, Sergius Maximus had turned back to the Aegean again, seemingly oblivious to Loukas' inner distress.

"Yes," answered Loukas eventually, "you could say so."

The Roman official appeared to have exhausted his repertoire of small-talk. He lapsed into silence for a while, and Loukas was certainly in no mood for initiating further conversation.

"Well," said Sergius Maximus suddenly, "I guess we may be seeing more of each other in the near future."

"Indeed," replied Loukas as the other man turned from the railing to go inside.

Once he was alone Loukas relaxed a little. But he was still deeply concerned about what Ioanneis had written in the scroll. He was not at all sure he was ready to die the death of a martyr, but according to Ioanneis this was a distinct possibility of Loukas' immediate future.

∾

St. Petersburg – July, AD 2005

As it turned out, it was a couple of weeks later that Dima found himself travelling with the scroll again. It had taken Yevgeny longer than he had at first anticipated to organise an appropriate time with his contact at the Christian University. But eventually, Yevgeny had rung Dima informing him that the following day would be the one.

So when Yevgeny and Marina had rung the security bell of their apartment building, Dima and Natasha had picked up their backpack with the scroll in its stone box nestling in the depths, and had exited their apartment to join the others waiting on the street. After exchanging greetings they walked over to the curb and waited for a *marshrutka* – privately-owned mini-vans that travel along predetermined bus routes, more frequent than state-owned buses and consequently slightly more expensive – to take them to the nearest Metro station.

"We will be seeing my friend Dr. Williams," Yevgeny said, as he flagged down a half-empty *marshrutka*. "He's an American who has been lecturing at the University for many years. His Russian is excellent, and he has a good rapport with the students. He was my New Testament lecturer during my theological training some five years ago."

They all climbed aboard, passed their money forward to the driver, then sorted out the change that was passed back. Since there were a couple of other passengers, they did not speak. But once the *marshrutka* reached the Metro station they all climbed out and resumed the conversation.

"Did you tell him about the scroll?" asked Natasha.

"No," replied Yevgeny. "I thought it would be better to surprise him just as you surprised me."

They pushed their way through the heavy, swinging doors of the Metro station, went through the turnstiles using either an electronic card or a token, and were swept onto the escalators by the crowds of people using the Metro to return home after work. The escalators for the Primorskaya Metro take two and a half minutes to move you from the surface down to the level of the trains. This is typical of the Metro stations in St. Petersburg. Since the city was built on a swamp, the tunnels of the St. Petersburg Metro had to be located in the solid rock far below. As Dima and the others descended, they listened to the brief snatches of surprisingly clear conversation of the people going up on the opposite escalator, their voices reflecting off the curved surface of the roof. Dima always enjoyed trying to see who was actually speaking, but it was often difficult to see whose lips were moving in the dim light of the escalator shaft.

At the bottom, there was a wide corridor that curved to the left, followed by quite a lot of steps, a sharp turn to the right, then more steps that led down to the platform area. Since there had been many people going up the escalators, Dima assumed that a train had just arrived. Primorskaya was at the end of the Third Line, so this same train would then move up the tunnel a short distance, stop, and then drive back to the station arriving on the opposite platform. Dima was therefore not expecting they would have to wait too long. Sure enough, as they moved down the platform area, trying to get away from the denser crowd of people who waited nearer the bottom of the stairs, a train came roaring in along the platform to their right, before eventually coming to a halt. The doors opened, and people got on, quickly filling up the few seats that lined the walls of the train. Dima and Natasha managed to get seats together; Yevgeny and Marina also sat together opposite them. Within a minute, there was the usual warning about standing clear of the doors, before they shut hard with a bang. The train quickly accelerated into the tunnel.

Any conversation was impractical unless you were able to speak loudly into a person's ear. They had quite a few stops to travel before changing to another line, so Dima sat there, with his backpack on his lap, thinking about the unrolling of the scroll that was soon to take place. He really hoped the scroll was as old as it looked, but more than that he hoped that it truly was a copy of Revelation. He had been reading the book in *Joyful News*, a new translation of the New Testament recently completed by the Bible Society of Russia. However, despite the more modern language, he still did not feel he understood what was going on. There seemed to be a lot of 'sevens' in the book: seven lamp stands, seven seals, seven trumpets, seven thunders, seven bowls. There were beasts and women and the destruction of a city. There were disasters of increasingly greater proportions. Then there was a period of 1000 years. He had gone online and found a *lot* of different sites dedicated to particular interpretations of those 1000 years. Unfortunately (or was it fortunately?) most of them had been in English so he had not bothered to read them; those that were in Russian seemed to present alternatives without necessarily helping to reach any decision as to which was correct. Dima was hoping that Yevgeny's old New Testament lecturer might be able to shed light on some of these enigmatic puzzles. Somehow, though, Dima was getting more and more pessimistic. After all, the book was nearly 2000 years old. Could anyone today say with any certainty how the original author had intended his work to be understood?

They changed from the Third Line to the First Line at Mayakovskaya, taking the subterranean pedestrian tunnel that

linked Mayakovskaya to Ploshad Vosstaniya. This latter
station was one of the oldest stations in St. Petersburg,
decorated with beautiful red marble pillars and Soviet
ironwork, in this case, arrangements of spears. Then, after
boarding another train, five stops later they reached
Narvskaya, the station closest to the Christian University.
Upon exiting the station, with the huge World War II
memorial archway in front of them, they turned to the right
and headed anti-clockwise around the large circular roadway.
Once they were on Narvsky Prospect it was only a short
walk to the University, nestled in an area surrounded by
larger buildings.

Once inside the University, Yevgeny confidently led the
way to Dr. Williams' tiny office at the back of the building
on the second floor. He knocked on the door.

"Come in," called someone from inside the room.

Yevgeny opened the door and entered, followed by the
others, Dima bringing up the rear with his backpack in his
hands. The office was fairly small, with bookshelves taking
up most of the available wall-space. Dima glanced at some of
the titles and was pleased to see that many of the books were
in Russian. There were also plenty of books in English,
many with titles involving long words that were, at least to
him, of uncertain meaning.

He turned from the bookshelves to look at Dr. Williams.
The man was sitting behind a small desk that was quite
orderly. He looked to be about fifty years old, wore glasses,
and had a tinge of grey in the hair surrounding his ears. He
had a neat moustache and beard, and a pleasant smile that was

in evidence now as he stood up from his chair and came around the desk to greet his visitors.

"Zhenya! And Marina, always a pleasure," he said, shaking both their hands simultaneously, Yevgeny's with his right, Marina's with his left. "You're both looking well."

"Thank-you," replied Yevgeny. "So do you."

"And your friends. Welcome to my little study."

Yevgeny introduced Dima and Natasha and their hands were promptly shaken simultaneously as well.

"Now, I'd ask you to all sit, but there would not be room for all the chairs we would need, so I'm afraid you'll have to decide between yourselves." He indicated the empty chair in front of his desk. He, himself, sat back in his own chair. Dima noted that Dr. Williams' Russian was indeed excellent, as Yevgeny had said, although he could still detect an American accent.

Without consulting each other, everyone turned to Dima with his backpack. Dima slowly lowered the backpack onto the chair. Dr. Williams was looking at Yevgeny expectantly, but Yevgeny signalled Dima to speak. Nervously, Dima cleared his throat.

"Dr. Williams…" he began.

"Please," interrupted Dr. Williams, "call me Ed."

"Oh. Well, my wife and I have just returned from a holiday in Nizhny Novgorod."

"Nice place, I believe," said Dr. Williams.

"Thank-you, it's my home-town," replied Dima. "Anyway, we came across something my great-great-grandfather apparently found in Ephesus."

"Ah, Ephesus," sighed Dr. Williams. "That's one of my favourites. So much to see, especially if you can get special permission to see the excavations in the hill. They have it all covered over now. You know they are still finding stuff in those diggings."

Dima glanced at Natasha before continuing. "Yes, that doesn't surprise me. Now, according to his diary, while he was there, there was a small earthquake."

"Oh, he wasn't injured at all?" asked Dr. Williams.

"No, he was fine. But the earthquake shifted some blocks and behind the blocks, he found…" He paused, uncertainly.

"What?" asked Dr. Williams, somewhat impatiently. He was not exactly sure what these young Russians were doing in his office. He guessed they would want him to date a coin or something similar. He was happy to do that, if that was what they wanted, but really, he had essays to mark, an article to write, and some books to read in preparation for an upcoming lecture.

Dima replied by opening the backpack, and taking a deep breath to quell the reluctance, he pulled out the stone box.

"This," he said quietly, laying it carefully on Dr. Williams' desk.

Dr. Williams was immediately entranced. All essays, articles and books were forgotten as he looked at the stone box.

"It looks like it's quite old," he said at first. He stood up, and reached out to run his finger across the lid. "Have you opened it?" he asked Dima, without taking his eyes off the box.

"Yes, Dr. Williams."

"Call me Ed," replied Dr. Williams absently. He reached up with his other hand and made as if to open the lid. "May I?" he asked.

"Certainly."

Reverently, Dr. Williams lifted off the lid as Dima, Natasha, Yevgeny and Marina looked on. The scroll was revealed in all its ancient glory.

"It's a scroll," said Dr. Williams immediately. He placed the lid down on the desk.

"Yes," said Dima. "We think it's a copy of the book of Revelation. I looked at the first few words, and…"

"You've touched it?" said Dr. Williams sharply.

"Only a little," replied Dima. "I didn't know what it was at first."

"Oh, I'm sorry for my little outburst. But if this is really old, and at first glance it looks like it is, then it could collapse into a pile of dust if we even breathe too heavily near it." Dr. Williams immediately replaced the lid. "We'll need to prepare somewhere to do this properly," he murmured to himself as he sat back in his chair. "I'll need some long benches and some imaging equipment…"

Then he stopped, and turned to the others in the room.

"I'm sorry, but this is astounding. Occasionally manuscripts of the New Testament turn up in old European monasteries or piles of scrap paper in Egyptian rubbish dumps, but not very often in St. Petersburg. Yes, I know your great-great-grandfather found it in Ephesus. That makes it all the more amazing."

"So you know how to unroll it?" asked Yevgeny.

"Yes, indeed," replied Dr. Williams. "I was fortunate enough to have been given a tour of the manuscript preservation and reconstruction of the Dead Sea Scrolls, years ago now, when I visited Israel. I found it interesting at the time, and I've kept reading about the process since."

"And you can do it here?" asked Dima.

"Well, not really," replied Dr. Williams, the disappointment audible for all to hear. "We are a little short of space. But I know someone who works in the Hermitage – quite high up, actually. He's a specialist in document preservation, so he will probably have everything already set up. But you will need to leave the scroll here with me, until we work out where we can take it. It would be dangerous to move the scroll any more than we have to."

"Will we be able to watch, then?" asked Natasha, the question that was on everyone's minds.

Dr. Williams shrugged. "I don't see why not. Yes, of course you can. The scroll was in your possession, after all." Then he paused. "Though I don't think it's really *yours*," he said slowly. "I'm thinking the Turkish government may have some ideas on the matter."

"It was a long time ago," said Dima. "Plenty of stuff has been looted from the ruins around the Mediterranean."

"True," replied Dr. Williams, with a shrug. He stood up quickly. "Right, then, let me make a few calls and we can work out where we can examine the scroll."

"Well, I guess we'll be going then," said Yevgeny. "Thank-you Dr. Williams."

"Not at all, not at all. Thank *you*!" Dr. Williams replied, turning to face Dima and Natasha. "This scroll could be of immense scholastic worth. It is my honour to be involved in its unrolling. And, please, call me Ed."

With one last look at the stone box sitting on Dr. Williams' desk, Dima and the others turned around and exited the tiny office.

Once they were outside in the sunshine, Dima, Natasha, Yevgeny and Marina just stood there staring at each other, clearly at a loss to know what to do next. Eventually, Marina broke the silence.

"Zhenya, we should pray," she exclaimed. "Pray that the unrolling of the scroll proceeds according to God's will. Perhaps God has some special purpose in the scroll coming to light at this time."

"Marina, that's a good idea."

Standing around the desk, they all bowed their heads as Yevgeny prayed.

"Lord, you are sovereign. We thank you that you led Dima and Natasha to find this scroll. We pray that nothing will prevent your will being done as it is unrolled. May we see your hand at work as Dr. Williams and others prepare this text for your church both here and around the world. May the scroll remain intact; may the writing be clear; may you give Dr. Williams steady hands as he works on the scroll. We pray these things in Jesus' name. Amen."

"Amen," replied Dima, Natasha and Marina.

∽

Ephesus – May, AD 93

As the ship wound its way up the narrow canal from the River Cayster Loukas was at the prow wondering if anyone was going to be waiting for him. But once they came into the harbour of Ephesus he could quickly see there was no one in the midst of all the bustling activity who was there for him. It was not to be expected, after all, since no one would have known when he was to return. However, he had been half-hoping to see Iounia standing near the marble pillars lining the Arcadian Way.

They had been betrothed at an early age. Their respective families had long been close and the two of them had grown up as friends, so it had been an easy decision on the part of their fathers to bring about their union. Both families were quite wealthy and well respected in the community, despite the fact that they had both aligned themselves with the group calling themselves Christians. Both Loukas' and Iounia's fathers were elders in the church.

Since the ship was now tied up to the dock he turned to pick up his travel bag with its precious cargo and found himself looking once again into the piercing eyes of Sergius Maximus.

"Farewell, Lucius," Sergius said with a smile. "Perhaps I will see you again over the next few days. At the theatre, or the Agora?"

"Indeed, Sergius Maximus, that will be an honour."

"Well, until then." Turning to the dock, he added dryly: "I see that my welcoming committee is eager to make my acquaintance."

Loukas looked over the ship's railing to see a group of official-looking men waiting in a group, peering uncertainly at the ship, wondering if the Proconsul's new legal clerk was on board. Then suddenly, behind them, Loukas caught a glimpse of a familiar face. It was Iounia; she was there after all!

Sergius Maximus made his way down the gangplank. Loukas followed eagerly and made his way through the throng of labourers unloading cargo to where Iounia was standing.

"Iounia!"

"Loukas! It is good to see you again, and so soon!"

"Yes, I am surprised to see you myself. Have you been waiting here ever since I left?" He recalled watching her standing on the dock as the ship slowly made its way down the channel to the River Cayster, watching until she could no longer be seen and yet unable to look away.

"No, silly!" she laughed. "I was running an errand for my father that brought me down here to the harbour. When I saw a sail in the distance, I thought I would wait and see if you were on board. But you can't have been with Ioanneis long."

"No." Suddenly Loukas was feeling more solemn again. The news he had brought from Ioanneis was one that he was not looking forward to sharing with the church, let alone his fiancée.

When Loukas said no more Iounia asked, "What did Ioanneis want of you? That he asked for you by name has been perplexing me."

Loukas had a quick look about him. They had started up the Arcadian Way, past the imposing buildings of the *palaestra* and gymnasium, and were nearing the Great Theatre of Ephesus. There were people milling about on their way to and from the Agora but no one was paying them any special attention. Given the burden he was carrying Loukas felt that they should be.

"Ioanneis gave me a letter to be read in the church. And not just here in Ephesus. He wants me to read it elsewhere in Asia."

"Oh, how exciting! There hasn't been a letter from him for ages. Have you read it?"

"Yes, I had time on the ship. But I'm afraid it's far more serious than exciting."

"Can I have a look?"

"Not here. I think we need to call the church together as soon as possible. When the scroll has been read I will need to leave for Smyrna immediately."

Iounia had caught the note of seriousness in Loukas' tone. They walked quickly and without speaking along the street that overlooked the ever-noisy Agora, heading towards Curetes Street where Loukas' family home was located. It was a rather spacious house for the times, indicative of Loukas' father's business acumen. Given its size it was also where the church of Ephesus met each Sunday. Within a few minutes he was home, being hugged by his mother and surrounded by loyal servants offering food and water to refresh him after his journey.

"Mother, is Father home?" he asked, between mouthfuls. They were reclining on couches in the central atrium of the private quarters of the house.

"No, dear," she replied. "He's out at the warehouse. Another shipment of dates has arrived in an inedible state and he is trying to sort out a replacement."

"And recompense, too, presumably! I need to speak with him immediately. I'm sorry to leave so soon, but I'm afraid it's too important to wait."

After concluding the short meal he got up and went back out to Curetes Street followed by Iounia.

"First, though," he said to her, "I'll also need to speak to your father."

Together, they walked up the Street until they came to her family's home. While not quite as large as Loukas' family's it was still a beautiful building, with some stunning statues overlooking a shapely archway that led into a small courtyard. Iounia's father, Stephanos by name and a lawyer by profession, was sitting in one of the rooms opening onto the courtyard. It was his study and library. He was seated on a low stool reading a scroll. There were a couple of tablets nearby that one could place on one's knees and lean on to write. The walls were completely obscured by shelves stacked high with scrolls and various writing implements. It could have been the workshop of a professional scribe, for Iounia's father was a conscientious man, often taking notes himself whilst interviewing clients and potential witnesses. He was known to be a formidable speaker when he was presenting his case in the law courts and his trials often drew crowds. And when he spoke in church he could argue very persuasively about the merits of Christianity and the belief in only one God whose Son had died to pay for the sins of all mankind. His parents, Christians through the evangelistic work of Paulos himself, had named him after the first martyr of the church, and he clearly took after his namesake in his ability to more than hold his own in a debate.[1]

"Loukas, my son-to-be, come in, come in!" exclaimed Stephanos as he stood up and carefully replaced the scroll he had been reading on a shelf. "You are back from Patmos, and with news from Ioanneis, I presume."

"Indeed, sir," replied Loukas as he entered Stephanos' study while somewhere behind him Iounia disappeared into another room of the house. "News in the form of a letter. Ioanneis has written to seven of the churches of Asia. We need to call the church together and read it as soon as possible."

"Can it not wait until Sunday?" asked Stephanos with a puzzled expression. Sunday was only a few days away.

"I guess we can," said Loukas unwillingly, "although I am eager to take it out to the other churches."

"Until then, perhaps a copy can be made? I take it from your haste that you have read the letter and that what it contains is serious." As a successful lawyer, Stephanos was a good reader of persons.

"Yes, sir."

"Then, allow me to have a copy made. We can use my own personal scribe, Tertios."

---

1 See Acts 6:8-10.

"Very well," replied Loukas, "but can I ask that he do the work in my house? I am unwilling to let the scroll out of my sight or, at the very least, my home."

"Certainly! There is just the one scroll, then?"

Loukas nodded.

"Then I guarantee the work will be done in time for the Sunday gathering. I will send him off as soon as he returns from the courts."

"Thank you, Stephanos. Now, I must bid you farewell. I need to speak with my father, too."

"Of course. He will be glad to see you returned safe and sound."

As he stepped back into the courtyard, Iounia emerged from another doorway.

"Loukas, I need to remain here and help Mother."

"That's fine."

"But we would love you to come for the midday meal tomorrow."

"That will be a pleasure indeed," Loukas replied with a smile.

"Until then." Iounia smiled also and turned back inside with a swirl of expensive cloth and a tantalising whiff of delicious perfume.

Loukas found it hard to drag himself away from Iounia's house, but somehow he found himself back on Curetes Street, walking in the direction of his father's warehouse.

His father's name was Theseus, after the Greek hero of legend who slew the Minotaur in the Labyrinth of Minos. He had been named by typical, pagan parents, but when he had become a Christian through the ministry of Tychicus[1], they had reacted in the traditional way: cutting off all ties with their son. Loukas had never met his grandparents since they had drowned in a shipwreck before he had been born. But his father had shared many of the happy memories he had of his parents, and so Loukas felt he knew them to some extent. Theseus' father had been a merchant, so it was only natural for Theseus to follow in his footsteps. But it was much harder to build up a trading business from scratch compared to inheriting an existing, successful business. However, Theseus was a shrewd businessman and a canny merchant, often sensing the trends of the market well before they became apparent to others. Consequently, he had quite quickly made his fortune.

The warehouse was located near the Harbour where Loukas had come ashore not a few hours before. He entered through the side door, and made his way through the rows of stacked bundles of goods. Knowing where dates were usually stored, Loukas quickly located his father, with his arm buried up to his elbow in the side of a huge hessian bag of dates. Loukas' younger brother, Markos – also named after one of the gospel writers – was standing nearby holding some papyrus sheets.

"Loukas! I'm glad you're back. Just look at *this*!"

Theseus had a big, booming voice, not unlike Ioanneis, with a tendency to over-emphasise his words. He withdrew his arm, and held a putrid handful of rotting dates under

[1] Tychicus had been sent to Ephesus by Paul during his imprisonment in Rome (2 Tim. 4:12).

Loukas' nose. Loukas shrank back as his father continued angrily.

"Oh, they're not like this at the *top* of the bag, oh no! The ones up *there* are as succulent as the best Asian peaches. But *these* ones from down here, they're not fit to be fed to pigs!" Turning to Markos, he said, "Make a note against bag 5, too." Markos made an annotation on a papyrus sheet then raised his eyebrows at Loukas in silent greeting.

"Well, Father," said Loukas with a smile, "you always say it pays to check."

"Indeed, and don't you forget it. I will *personally* see to it that the man who brought *these* bags to me – and yes, the other bags are *identical* to this one – will sit down to a large plateful of the *best* dates I can find! And I think *these* will do nicely."

So saying, he placed the handful of rotting dates on a large wooden platter that was lying on the floor next to him. Loukas was only too glad to have them out of the immediate vicinity of his face.

"Now what other *monstrosities* can I find in here?" said Theseus, almost to himself. He reached back into the bag and began groping around for the squishiest dates he could find.

"I can see you're a little preoccupied, Father, but I just wanted to say that Ioanneis sent for me to give me a letter for the churches in Asia."

"Oh yes?" replied Theseus, distantly.

"Yes, and I'll be reading it to the church on Sunday. It's rather important." At this point Loukas lost his nerve and he did not continue as he had planned by saying, "And I'm afraid there's something in it you won't like." *I guess he'll just have to wait until Sunday*, he thought to himself.

"That's good. I'll look forward to it," Theseus replied absently, pulling another handful of 'choice' specimens from the depths of the hessian bag. "In the meantime, are you here to help, or are you tired from the journey?"

"The latter, Father. I need to have a rest, but I'll be ready for anything tomorrow."

"Very good, son."

Just as Loukas was walking away, one of Theseus' employees came up to Theseus.

"Sir, you have a visitor. It's Julius the date merchant."

"Ah, *excellent*!" Loukas heard his father reply. Theseus wiped his hands on a rag, then picked up the platter. "I hope he's *hungry*…"

∽

St. Petersburg – July, AD 2005

A few days after handing the scroll over to Dr. Williams, Dima and Natasha returned to the Christian University. They found Dr. Williams just as he was leaving his office.

"Ah, the scroll discoverers!" exclaimed, Dr. Williams, shaking their hands warmly. "Thanks for coming. I'm just on my way over to the Unrolling Room. We've already started – I hope you don't mind – and even at this early stage of the process I can definitely say that you have found a remarkably well-preserved, very early copy of the book of Revelation."

The disappointment of not being present as the scroll was first unrolled quickly turned into excitement as the scroll's identity was confirmed.

"Where are you doing the work?" asked Dima, curiously.

"You may know that the Hermitage owns many buildings scattered all over St. Petersburg. Some are used for storage, others are used for art restoration. Well, it turns out that the Hermitage owns a warehouse not far from here. When I spoke to Dr. Sergey – that's the friend I was telling you about – he made immediate arrangements for us to use this building. And he kindly agreed to let me supervise the process."

They headed back towards the Metro station, but turned off a side street to the right. As they walked, Dr. Williams continued talking.

"The papyrus is in remarkable condition. I was afraid it may have become too brittle and that it would collapse into dust, or at the very least tiny fragments that would then have to be painstakingly reassembled like a jigsaw with no picture to follow. But we are finding that as we unroll the scroll it is breaking up into quite sizable sections, presumably along the original joins where sheets of papyrus were glued together to form the scroll as a whole. Furthermore, the characters themselves are still quite clear and readable. It's almost as though this scroll has not been read too many times, has not had its letters faded by repeated exposure to the Sun's rays, but has sat in its box for nearly two millennia. Sorry for the little lecture, but what this means is that the text is proving very easy to recover. Well, this is the place."

They stopped outside a fairly nondescript door in a typically run-down-looking red-brick building. Dr. Williams took out a key and unlocked the door. Dima noticed that the lock looked new. Presumably, Dr. Williams was taking no chances with security.

The door opened into a dingy corridor. There was a beefy security guard sitting in a tiny cubicle watching TV on an even tinier TV set. He looked up as they entered, nodded to Dr. Williams, and continued watching what looked to be a riveting game show.

"This way," said Dr. Williams, ushering them down the corridor and up a flight of stairs. On the second level there was another dingy corridor with a few doors scattered here and there. Near the end of the corridor there was another door, but this one looked new and very, very solid. It was also locked. This time, Dr. Williams took out a transponder key, and placed it in the receptacle. When the electromagnets holding the door tightly shut switched off, he pushed open the heavy door.

"Please, enter," said Dr. Williams.

Despite his eagerness to see what was happening, Dima allowed Natasha to enter first although he followed close behind. Dr. Williams entered and Dima heard the door close firmly behind them.

The room appeared to have been a laboratory of some kind, with long benches and the occasional sink. There were windows along the wall opposite where they had come in through which endless summer sunlight would have been pouring had it not been for the thick, black cardboard that had been placed over them. The room opened out to their right, and in this direction they saw a number of tables placed in a row surrounded by a few, dim lights on stands. At the nearest end a woman was placing large sheets of glass on top of what must have been pieces of the scroll that were already lying on some sort of backing. As they watched, she taped around the edges, carefully lifting the resulting sandwich off the table and placing it in a box nearby.

"We're working backwards through the process, but I'm sure you'll understand," said Dr. Williams. "Tanya, here, is getting the scroll ready for long-term storage – and public display if it ever comes to that. As you can see, we haven't done a lot yet." He indicated the box into which Tanya had just placed the scroll piece. There were only three pieces there.

One man was manoeuvring a bulky piece of equipment positioned directly above the second table. As they watched, there was a sudden increase in light emanating from the machine. It lasted longer than the flash of a camera, but it was clearly imaging the pieces of scroll lying on the table below, somewhat like a photocopier. Behind the imaging equipment Dima could see a computer with another man sitting at the monitor.

"Here," continued Dr Williams, "Boris and Sasha are making a scan of each section of the scroll. What you can't see is that that computer is connected to the University's network, and in another room I have a couple of my Advanced New Testament Greek course students translating the text from the scans, making detailed notes about how the text differs from other known manuscripts of Revelation as they go. We're also making preliminary judgments about the age of the manuscript based on palaeographical considerations."

"Excuse me," asked Dima. "What does that mean?"

"Oh, I'm sorry," replied Dr. Williams. "Palaeography is the study of writing. Basically, we can get a good approximation of the date of a manuscript by comparing the characters with manuscripts of known date. The way the Greek letters were written changed over the years, you see. And as I said earlier, we can already tell this particular manuscript is very old."

At the next table a woman wearing gloves was carefully arranging pieces of the scroll with tweezers. The unrolled portion of the scroll was sitting under a glass box on the third table.

"Lyuda and I have been working here. We've been carefully extracting the next section of scroll, trying not to allow it to fall apart too greatly, then arranging the pieces on these sheets of glass. I was expecting this to be the hardest part of the process, but as I said, it has been surprisingly easy."

The short tour seemed to be over.

Dima noticed on a table right up against the far wall of the room the stone box in which the scroll had been found. Dr. Williams saw him glance in that direction.

"Yes, there's the box," he said. "We'll spend some time analysing it later. It may help to shed some light on the date of the scroll itself."

Dima and Natasha looked back at the remaining part of the scroll sitting in its glass box.

"So," Natasha said, "it really is the book of Revelation."

"Yes, indeed. And judging from the size of the scroll, it appears to be a complete text. To think it may have been found in Ephesus. This scroll could provide us with an unprecedented window onto the original text of the book, depending on its age, of course. It may not be too far removed from the original letter the church in Ephesus received from John while he was exiled on the Isle of Patmos."

Dima frowned slightly.

"What do you mean 'original text'?" he asked. "Don't we have that in our Bibles?"

"Ah, you haven't studied at the Christian University, have you?" replied Dr. Williams. "And I'm guessing that textual criticism doesn't feature very often in sermons, either. No, but that isn't unusual."

Dr. Williams looked longingly towards the scroll pieces currently being arranged by Lyuda before turning back to Dima and Natasha.

"Look, if you want, I can explain a little of it to you, but we'd better get out of here. I don't want to disturb the work, here, you see."

"Of course," said Dima.

Dr. Williams spoke briefly to Lyuda, and then he walked back to the door with Dima and Natasha, unlocked it by pressing a button next to the door, then they exited the Unrolling Room. It turned out that one of the other doorways in the dingy upper corridor opened into a workers' lounge, complete with a small kitchen. As Dr. Williams prepared some refreshments he began his explanation.

"It's really quite simple in theory, rather complicated in practice. The text that we have in our Bibles is derived from the thousands and thousands of manuscripts of the New Testament that have been discovered all over the Mediterranean. Some manuscripts are just a book; some are just the Gospels; some are the whole thing. There are even some early manuscript fragments that are really not much more than a verse. Now, the important thing about all these manuscripts is that they are not all the same. Yes, that's right, if you take any two manuscripts of a particular book there will be differences between them."

Dima and Natasha must have looked a little shocked at this, for Dr. Williams continued, "This is not a problem. Far from it, by comparing all these manuscripts we can actually get rather a good idea about the original text. As they copy manuscripts, scribes occasionally make little corrections but more often they tend to make little errors. I mean, it's not like they had computers and could just print out a second copy whenever they wanted to! No, they would have had to painstakingly copy out the text character by character, sitting on the ground, having to dip their little pen into an inkwell after nearly every third character. Now, you've seen the scroll. You noticed there were no word breaks? Yes? Good. And there's no punctuation, either. So it's hardly surprising that these little errors occur. Anyway, as I said, by comparing all these manuscripts we can deduce the original text, by knowing the sort of changes that are likely. You'll be pleased to know that most of the differences are absolutely insignificant – slight grammatical changes, inserting the word 'Christ' after 'Jesus' – that sort of thing."

Dr. Williams paused for breath. Dima saw his chance to ask a question.

"What would happen if you happened to have the original manuscript? Could you tell?"

"No, not really," replied Dr. Williams. "It would just be one of the many manuscripts, with its own unique differences to all the others. However, it would hopefully be closer than all the others to the scholarly reconstruction of the original text." When Dima and Natasha looked like they had not understood this, he continued. "For example, as part of this restoration work, we will be comparing the text of your scroll to the current text supplied by the United Bible Society – fourth edition, which explains why it's called the UBS 4. Anyway, if we assume for the sake of the argument that your scroll is the original text, then we would hope that it would be the same as the UBS 4, thereby proving the reliability of the textual critical methodology used to derive the UBS 4 text."

The water was ready, so Dr. Williams finished preparing the teas and coffees.

"Actually there's a good example in Revelation," he said, handing Dima a cup of tea. "There's an interesting textual variant in Revelation 13:18. Most manuscripts say that the number of the Beast is 666. But a few manuscripts, some quite old and usually reliable, say 616. Which one is the original number? Basically, you have to weigh up the internal evidence – which one fits the context of the book – against the external evidence – which manuscripts are more reliable – to deduce the original text. At this point, scholars believe it was originally 666."

"What does my… I mean, our scroll say?" asked Dima.

"We don't know yet," replied Dr. Williams. "We're barely halfway through chapter one."

There was a lengthy pause as Dima and Natasha sipped their tea and struggled to get their minds around these new concepts. Dr. Williams appeared to be slightly distracted by something. Eventually, Dima broke the silence.

"I'm guessing you would like to get back to the scroll. We should leave you to it. But can we come back again sometime?"

"That would be fine. Any time! I will make sure that the guard knows to let you in."

Dr. Williams ushered them out the door and back into the dingy corridor.

"Allow me to thank you again," he said as they were just about to walk down the corridor. "We are doing as careful a job as we can with this scroll."

"We can tell," replied Dima. "We'll see you again, soon."

"Until then."

❧

Ephesus – May, AD 93

Every eye was on Loukas. With mixed feelings, Loukas was standing at the front of the room of his family's house where the church of Ephesus met. He was holding the scroll open to the first column of close-written capitals. He took a deep breath, and then began reading:

" 'The revelation of Iēsus Christos, which God gave him to show his servants what must soon take place…' "

When Loukas had returned to his home after speaking with his father, Tertios the scribe had been waiting for him. Loukas had shown him the scroll, and showed him a place to sit on the floor in Loukas' own room. Tertios had wasted no time and had begun the arduous task of copying the scroll, letter by letter. Occasionally, he had looked up and said things like, "Ioanneis, himself, wrote this down. I recognise his distinctive Sigmas."; or, "Oh, that's not how 'angel' is spelt! Gamma Gamma not Nu Gamma!"; or, "He's good with his margins. I like a scroll with neat margins."; or, "Ooh! What are you doing? Is this supposed to be Greek or Aramaic?" Loukas had fairly rapidly fallen asleep, and was wakened only by the scribe leaving at the end of the day when there was simply not enough light to see by.

Tertios had returned the next day and the next. However, as Stephanos had promised, the copying had been completed by Sunday; and now, here Loukas was, reading Ioanneis' scroll to the church.

" 'From Ioanneis, to the seven churches in the province of Asia: grace and peace to you from him who is, and who was, and who is to come, and from the seven spirits before the throne, and from Iēsus Christos, who is the faithful witness, the firstborn from the dead, and the ruler of the kings of the earth.'[1]"

Already he could sense some puzzlement from those gathered there. The reference to God seemed clear enough, but who were the seven spirits? Loukas knew from later references that these were the angels of the seven churches,

1 Rev. 1:4–5a.

sent to keep watch over them.[1] But he did not stop reading to explain; they would work it out soon enough.

As he read through Ioanneis' vision of Iēsus, he could sense everyone listening with rapt attention. They were as awe-struck as he had been when he had first read those words back on the ship. When he reached the end of that section he paused, mainly to give the people a chance to fully appreciate the glory of the One they followed, but also partly to prepare himself to read out the next part: the words addressed to the Ephesian church personally. He caught Iounia's eyes, sitting with the women off to one side. She smiled encouragement so he continued with more boldness.

" 'To the angel of the church in Ephesus write: These are the words of him who holds the seven stars in his right hand and who walks among the seven golden lamp stands: I know your deeds, your hard work and your perseverance. I know that you cannot tolerate wicked men, that you have tested those who claim to be apostles but are not, and have found them false. You have persevered and have endured hardships for my name, and have not grown weary.'[2]"

So far, so good, thought Loukas. People were nodding and smiling at one another. *Ioanneis was right, as always*, he could see them thinking. *How kind of him to recognise us!* Loukas continued, and the smiles were quickly replaced by frowns.

" 'Yet I hold this against you: you have forsaken your first love. Remember the height from which you have fallen! Repent and do the things you did at first. If you do not repent, I will come to you and remove your lamp stand from

1 See Rev. 3:1; 5:6.
2 Rev. 2:1-3.

its place. But you have this in your favour: you hate the practices of the Nicolaitans, which I also hate.'[1]"

There was a stunned silence. He could see people sitting there with affronted looks, clearly thinking, *How could Ioanneis make such a claim? How could he possibly know the strength of our love for God?* But then realisation dawned: this was not Ioanneis speaking, this was Iēsus. After all Ioanneis could not come to them and remove the lamp stand, the symbol of their church, very clearly implying judgment.

With this knowledge came reflection: the church had certainly begun strongly. The apostle Paulos himself had founded the church some four decades previously. There had been amazing and miraculous signs and wonders: even handkerchiefs Paulos had used had been taken to sick people and they had been healed.[2] Evil spirits had been exorcised, one even from Loukas' mother's mother. There had been many conversions and these new converts had burned their scrolls of magic and sorcery to the value of fifty thousand drachmas, an unbelievably large sum of money.

Sure, there had been a backlash. Demetrios the silversmith had seen to it that Paulos was banished, never to enter the city again because of the threat of certain death by lynch mob. There had been some persecution in the years following: some businesses had been shunned, some individuals had been wrongfully accused – much as Ioanneis had been – and had been sent to prison. But things had mostly settled down. And the Ephesian church had lost much of that initial enthusiasm. Loukas looked around the

1 Rev. 2:4-6.
2 See Acts 19:12.

room. Certainly, it was a large room as far as houses were concerned. But *this* was the church of Ephesus: one roomful of men and women, and a few children playing in the next room. There had not been on-going growth equal to the way the church had begun.

As the silence continued, reflection turned to repentance. There were tears in the eyes of some; many sat with heads bowed. Suddenly the silence was broken by Stephanos as he prayed on behalf of the church. Despite his own tears, Loukas smiled to himself. It seemed their lamp stand was safe.

When Stephanos finished praying, Loukas continued reading from the scroll.

" 'He who has an ear, let him hear what the Spirit says to the churches. To him who overcomes, I will give the right to eat from the tree of life, which is in the paradise of God.'[1]"

He then read through the personal messages for the other six churches. Ioanneis had not instructed otherwise. If all the churches were aware of the issues raised then perhaps there could be some measure of accountability.

Having previously read the scroll many times Loukas was aware that after the personal letters a new section of the scroll began, emphasised by the repetition of the phrase 'in the Spirit'[2], so he paused briefly before continuing:

" 'After this I looked, and there before me was a door standing open in heaven. And the voice I had first heard speaking to me like a trumpet said, "Come up here and I will

1 Rev. 2:7.
2 See also Rev. 1:10; 17:3; 21:10.

show you what must take place after this." At once I was in the Spirit, and there before me was a throne…'[1]"

As Loukas continued reading, the people were rapidly caught up in the awe-inspiring description of God in heaven surrounded by the twenty-four elders and the four living creatures all of whom are there to worship God continually. In his mind, Loukas was comparing this scene with that of the Roman Emperor in *his* throne room, surrounded by his council, with hymnic acclamations pouring from the mouths of those around him. Domitianus had decreed that people refer to him as 'Lord and God'; but in *this* vision of God on his throne Ioanneis was reminding the church that there is only one true Lord and God. He is the one with the power; he is the one who will bring justice to the world; he is therefore the true Ruler of the world, not some mere human upstart with delusions of divinity who is only able to get away with it because he has the might of Rome behind him.

Then as Loukas read out the description of the scroll in God's hands, the one written on both the front side and the back side, and sealed with seven seals, he could see the curiosity on the faces of the people listening. What could possibly be contained in the scroll? And why was there no one in heaven or on earth who was able to open the scroll?

Loukas read out: " 'Then one of the Elders said to me, 'Do not weep! See, the Lion of the tribe of Judah, the Root of David, has triumphed. He is able to open the scroll and its seven seals.'[2]" Loukas personally loved this moment. It was one of several where what Ioanneis had *heard* and what he

1 Rev. 4:1–2.
2 Rev. 5:5.

then *sees* differed significantly. The titles 'Lion of Judah' and 'Root of David' were, of course, good Scriptural references to the Jewish Messiah. And, as the Elder in the vision had said, this Messiah had triumphed. But then what Ioanneis *sees* is a Lamb looking as though it had been slain. The images from the Jewish Scriptures had been transformed by the startling fact that Iēsus, God's Messiah, had been executed by the Romans. But it was precisely Iēsus' death, and his subsequent resurrection from the dead, that made him worthy to open the scroll. *This* was the Messiah's triumph, and certainly worthy of hymnic acclamations infinitely more so than the mortal Domitianus.

When Loukas reached the end of the hymns of praise to God and the Lamb he paused a trifle melodramatically before continuing: " 'I watched as the Lamb opened the first of the seven seals…'[1]"

❧

St. Petersburg – August, AD 2005

"I hear the scanning is proceeding well," said Yevgeny.

"Yes, they're up to chapter 6 now," replied Dima.

Dima and Yevgeny were sitting on one of the grassy banks lining the canal near Primorskaya Metro, close to Dima and Natasha's apartment building. Around them, men and women were making the most of the brief St. Petersburg summer by sun-bathing on towels, reading novels, and

---

1 Rev. 6:1.

drinking beer, quite oblivious to the exegetical discussion that was about to begin nearby.

"Ah, the seals," exclaimed Yevgeny.

"That's right. Look, can you help me out? I'm really struggling to understand this book. I mean, it's all over the place!"

"What do you mean?"

"Well, for a start there's all these 'sevens' everywhere – like the seven seals, for example."

"Yes, it is certainly not straight-forward," said Yevgeny with a sigh.

"So what do you make of it all?"

Yevgeny thought for a minute, then he got out his Bible, something he rarely left home without.

"All right, see if this helps you a little," he said. "Now, there are three crucial 'sevens': the seals, the trumpets and the bowls. Each group of seven is associated with disasters on the earth in increasing proportions. Let's start with the seals. The first four are grouped together. As the Lamb opens these four seals the Four Horseman of the Apocalypse are revealed, traditionally known as War, Famine, Pestilence and Death. And it says they were given power over a *quarter* of the earth to kill people by means of the sword, famine, plague and, intriguingly, wild animals. Later on, the trumpets are associated with disasters involving a *third* of the earth, and even later still the bowls usher in *total* destruction."

"Yes," said Dima. "I had noticed that."

"The fifth and sixth seals sort of go together, too. The fifth one informs the church that they will face martyrdom, but that the number of people who will be martyred has been limited by God. Simple, really. But the sixth seal is a controversial one."

Yevgeny turned to the relevant page and read.

" 'I watched as he opened the sixth seal. There was a great earthquake. The sun turned black like sackcloth made of goat hair, the whole moon turned blood red, and the stars in the sky fell to earth, as late figs drop from a fig tree when shaken by a strong wind. The sky receded like a scroll, rolling up, and every mountain and island was removed from its place.'[1] Now, it sure sounds like the end of the world, doesn't it?"

"Yes. Are you implying that it's not?"

"Well, a *lot* of stuff continues to happen past this point, so it can hardly be the end of history. And we can't be talking about the destruction of the sun and moon, either. We're getting ahead of ourselves, but the fourth trumpet involves them both. And the third and fifth trumpets involve other stars falling from the sky. So you can't really say that the sixth seal means the end of the world."

"Well, why say it at all, then?" asked Dima, perplexed.

"The answer comes from recognising that the events associated with the sixth seal are all straight out of the Old Testament. John is practically quoting a whole lot of verses from the prophets of Israel and Judah. They used this sort of cosmic disaster language all the time when they were referring to the destruction of cities and countries."

Dima must have looked dubious. Yevgeny started flicking through his Bible.

1 Rev. 6:12-14.

"Let me give you some examples," he said. "Let's see… in a passage about imminent judgment coming upon the city of Babylon, Isaiah chapter 13 verse 10 says: 'The stars of heaven and their constellations will not show their light, The rising sun will be darkened and the moon will not give its light.' Then, in chapter 34 verse 4, in a passage talking about judgment coming upon the nations surrounding Judah, Isaiah says: 'All the stars of heaven will be dissolved and the sky rolled up like a scroll; all the starry host will fall like withered leaves from the vine, like shrivelled figs from the fig tree.' Notice the similarity to Revelation?"

Dima nodded as Yevgeny flicked forward to Ezekiel. "Another one. Ezekiel chapter 32 verses 7-8: 'When I snuff you out, I will cover the heavens and darken their stars; I will cover the sun with a cloud, and the moon will not give its light. All the shining lights in the heavens I will darken over you; I will bring darkness over your land.' That's in a judgment upon Pharaoh and the land of Egypt. And… where is it?… Ah, yes. Joel chapter 2 verse 10: 'The sun will be turned to darkness and the moon to blood before the coming of the great and dreadful day of the Lord.' Now *that's* in a passage that Peter said was fulfilled on the day of Pentecost!"

After a few moments' thought, Dima asked, "OK, so these prophets predicted serious cosmic disasters, which presumably didn't happen, even if the accompanying judgments did. Isn't it possible that they still had expected the cosmic disasters to really happen and were disappointed?"

"I think an extended case-study will help at this point," said Yevgeny, with a smile. "Jeremiah is a great example of why that isn't the case."

He flicked through his Bible until he came to Jeremiah.

"Now, where is it? Somewhere near the start... Ah, yes, here it is. In chapter 4, Jeremiah announces that a major disaster will come upon Jerusalem from the north. But in verse 23 he says this: 'I looked at the earth, and it was formless and empty; and at the heavens and their light was gone.' Jeremiah uses words that appear in Genesis chapter 1 *before* God created anything, so what he envisages here is a *reversal* of creation: an 'uncreation', if you will. Now, later on in the book, Jeremiah has serious doubts about the correctness of his prophetic ministry. Here, in chapter 20 verses 7 and 8 he says: 'O Lord, you deceived me, and I was deceived; you overpowered me and prevailed. I am ridiculed all day long; everyone mocks me. Whenever I speak, I cry out proclaiming violence and destruction. So the word of the Lord has brought me insult and reproach all day long.' Then in verse 10: 'I hear many whispering, "Terror on every side! Report him! Let's report him!" All my friends are waiting for me to slip, saying, "Perhaps he will be deceived; then we will prevail over him and take our revenge on him!" ' In other words, they were looking for a chance to denounce Jeremiah as a false-prophet!"

Yevgeny took a moment to catch his breath.

"But, as you know, Jerusalem *was* destroyed by the Babylonians just a little while after that, and Jeremiah basically says, 'I told you so!' He *doesn't* complain to God, 'O Lord, why did you not darken the heavens?' And his opponents *don't* respond by saying: 'You're still a false prophet because the sun still shines during the day, and the moon still shines at night, and all the stars are still in the sky, despite the fact you said they wouldn't!' No, everyone knew that the cosmic disaster language Jeremiah had used was simply a way of underlining the enormity of the destruction of Jerusalem. It's quite similar to today when we say that some political event – like the fall of the Berlin wall, for example – was an 'earth-shattering' event. This is not meant literally. It's metaphorical."

"Well, I guess that's reasonable. So how does all that apply to the sixth seal?"

"Well, it seems that John, by means of these allusions to the Old Testament, is talking about major political upheavals, like the sort of thing that happened when the Roman Emperor Nero killed himself. Since there were a few people who thought they deserved to rule Rome, the Roman Empire was plunged into civil war for an entire year. Now look at what comes straight after John's cosmic disaster language: 'Then the kings of the earth, the princes, the generals, the rich, the mighty, and every slave and free man hid in caves and among the rocks of the mountains. They called to the mountains and the rocks, "Fall on us and hide us from the face of him who sits on the throne and from the wrath of the Lamb! For the great day of their wrath has come, and who can stand?" '[1] Again, there are Old Testament allusions here, but the point is clear: major political upheavals."

"Fair enough," said Dima with a nod.

1 Rev. 6:15–17.

"Good. Now there's quite a gap between the sixth and seventh seals, but when the seventh one is finally opened, instead of the cataclysmic end of the world that you might expect there is a rather anticlimactic half an hour of silence. Then the trumpets are handed out to seven angels who then proceed to sound them. Again, there is a big gap between the sixth and seventh trumpets. When the seventh trumpet is finally sounded there's some singing! Again, not really the end you would expect. Then there is a whole lot of detailed stuff about a woman who gives birth to a son who is then pursued by a dragon. Then we have the beasts from the earth and the sea. Finally, we come to the seven bowls, and what really appears to be the end of everything, but we're only up to chapter 16 with 6 more chapters to go including the enigmatic 1000 years."

"Thank-you," replied Dima, somewhat sarcastically. "That *has* cleared it all up for me."

"I haven't finished yet," said Yevgeny with a laugh. "The big question is how are these three groups of seven – the seals, the trumpets and the bowls – related. Are they *chronological*, meaning did John expect the end of the world to be preceded by successive waves of earthly disaster of increasing magnitude? It's hard to argue this given that certain events are definitely *not* in chronological order, such as the birth of the Messiah in chapter 12 and the fact that five of the seven heads of the beast from the sea in chapter 13 stand for kings already dead. Others have argued for a sort of 'concertina chronology'. That is, the seven bowls occur during the period covered by the seventh trumpet, and that the seven trumpets occur during the period covered by the seventh seal. It's like John focuses in more and more on the end, providing more and more details. And I guess that's possible, but it doesn't really avoid the problem of the events that are out of order.

"Personally, I prefer to think of John's presentation as *artistic*. I read this in a commentary back during my studies at the Christian University, and I liked it so much I wrote it down here in the back of my Bible: 'John is like an expert guide in an art gallery, lecturing to students about a vast mural. First he makes them stand back to absorb a general impression, then he takes them close to study the details. In John's symbolic language seven is the number of completeness, and the sevenfold visions – seals, trumpets, and bowls – are his general views of the totality of divine judgment. The unnumbered visions are his close-ups, his studies of detail.' The commentary was written by G. B. Caird, and I would highly recommend it to you, except that it's only in English."[1]

"That's fine. I have an English-Russian dictionary."

"Of course you do. If you're interested, I'm sure Dr. Williams would allow you to borrow it from their library."

"I'll make sure I ask him about it. Well, you're right. You have helped me a little. But it still seems pretty grim: all that death and destruction."

"True. But it has a purpose. You need to place yourself back in time and imagine how the early church would have received this vision. I think it is extremely interesting that in the last four decades of the first century, the following

1 G. B. Caird, *The Revelation of Saint John*, (Hendrickson Publishers, 1993 (reprint ed.)), 106.

disasters had occurred. There had been some serious earthquakes in 60 AD. In 62 AD The Roman army had suffered a humiliating defeat on the eastern frontier at the hands of the Parthians. More specific to the church, there had been the persecution of Christians that followed the fire of Rome in 64 AD. I've already mentioned Nero's suicide in 68 AD, which initiated a year of political chaos and battles as four rival claimants battled it out for the imperial throne. Then from 66 to 70 AD there was the four-year horror of the Jewish war that ended with Jerusalem in ruins. Mount Vesuvius erupted in 79 AD creating a pall of darkness so widespread that people feared the imminent end of the world. Finally, there had been a serious grain famine in 92 AD. Now, if you had lived through all of that, what would you make of the events accompanying the seven seals?"

Dima stopped for a moment, thinking.

"Well," he answered, eventually, "it would sound pretty much like everyday life."

"Precisely!" exclaimed Yevgeny. "But with one significant fact: all these events occur because God wants them to, and only as a result of Jesus' death on the cross. They are all part of God's divine plan of salvation, even the martyrdom of some in the church. John is trying to tell his churches that God is in control."

Ephesus – May, AD 93

It was a warm, sunny day when Loukas set out for Smyrna. He had chosen to go on foot, for while the hills were many and very steep in places, the Romans had built excellent roads through them enabling pedestrians to achieve quite a rapid pace if they so chose. He had decided against taking a ship; it was just too uncertain what with the possibility of shipwreck. The scroll he carried to read in the other six churches of Asia was too important to take any such risks.

On his journey Loukas was going to be accompanied by Artemas and Hermas, two young men who had also become Christians through the ministry of Ioanneis. The three were good friends and Loukas was looking forward to long discussions as they travelled along the road. A few people from the church had come with them as far as the gates of the city to send him off, most notably his brother Markos, their father Theseus, his fiancée Iounia and her father Stephanos.

Stephanos was the first to give the three travellers each a strong squeeze around the shoulders with his long arms. As he hugged Loukas, he spoke softly in his ear.

"Loukas, my son-to-be, thank-you for reading Ioanneis' scroll to us. I know the church as a whole was quite unresponsive: there was a lot to take in, and there is much to think about as the days grow darker. But I know they will take it to heart. I have already had some come to me asking for my legal assistance should they be arrested for refusing to worship the Emperor."

Loukas frowned at the thought, but Stephanos continued, "Have no fear! We will take on the Beast from the land! And we will be victorious in the end for it has been foreseen."

"Thank-you, my father-to-be," replied Loukas with a smile. "Look after Iounia for me."

Stephanos laughed heartily. "Indeed! That is still my job right up until your wedding day. And then I will demand the same from you!"

He gave Loukas' shoulders another squeeze and stepped back.

Theseus stepped forward, somewhat awkwardly. Loukas had been afraid of his response to the scroll and had not been surprised to see him hurry from the church meeting room – his own house! – as soon as Loukas had read the last words. In the couple of days since then Theseus had avoided speaking to Loukas, but Loukas had caught him glowering in his direction every once in a while. Clearly, the impact of the scroll had taken a personal toll. But now, here he was, smiling shyly at his son.

"Loukas, forgive me," he began. "I am afraid I have taken out my *grief* on you, the messenger, rather than reserve it for the One who sent the message. These last days I have been *wrestling* with what has been asked of me. I might even have to *abandon* all commerce with Rome and her subjects! And I a *merchant*! I have asked myself how is that possible? Does God want me to give up *altogether*?"

There was a brief pause. Loukas could well believe such thoughts had been passing through his father's mind; they had been passing through his own, since he was the son of a merchant and had expected to take over the family business one day.

"But, last night as I lay tossing and turning in complete and utter sleeplessness something occurred to me," continued Theseus. "It is not just I who will be prevented from participating in commerce with Rome; everyone in the church must as well. So it will be up to Christian merchants like me to become suppliers for Christians *everywhere*, to help them through the storm to come, bartering food and goods between those in the countryside and those of us living in cities. And this has *revolutionised* me! It has given me a *mission*! Where before I saw merely profits, now I see needs. So thank-you for your faithfulness in carrying out Ioanneis' instructions. I see now that you were afraid of my reactions – and *rightly* so! – but you read the scroll regardless. Thank-you."

Loukas, with tears in his eyes, gave his father a long hug. "Of course," he replied, "I look forward to returning to Ephesus after this reading tour is over and assisting you in this great task."

"I will await your return with *great* anticipation," Theseus said with a smile. "May the Lord Iēsus Christos our Saviour go with you and protect you on your journey."

"Indeed," replied Loukas, as his father stepped back to stand next to Stephanos.

Then Markos stepped forward. "I don't see why I can't come with you," he began. "I'm old enough, surely!"

"Yes, you are," replied Loukas, "but someone has to stay with Mother and Father, you know that."

Markos shrugged. "I guess so."

"And it won't be for long, anyway." He gave his brother a playful punch on the arm then received one back graciously. As Markos returned to his father's side, they both rubbed their arms where the punches had fallen: it would be something to remember the other by, at least for a little while.

Finally, it was Iounia's turn. Without saying a word, she simply stood and stared into Loukas' eyes. Gently, he brushed her hair with his hand, moving some wayward strands away from her face. Then, he picked up her hand and placed it on his heart.

"I'll be back before you know it," he said.

"I know," she replied. She bent forward, and kissed him on each cheek, tasting the saltiness of his tears. "I'll be praying for you."

"And I you," he said.

With that, she pulled away. When she returned to stand next to her father, Stephanos placed his arm around her shoulders and she rested her head on his chest, as if she could bear its weight no more.

Loukas' arm felt heavy, too, as he lifted it in a final wave of farewell. Then, he, Artemas and Hermas set off along the paved road that went straight as an arrow down the grassy hill away from the city of Ephesus and everything and almost everyone that Loukas held dear. The parting was made so much more difficult by the fact that no one quite knew what would happen to them all as persecution increased. Loukas did not know what he would return to find; he could but trust that God truly was in control.

Between Ephesus and Smyrna – May, AD 93

At first, the going was quite easy. Once it had descended the hill upon which Ephesus was built, the road meandered gently up the Cayster Valley for some distance. Loukas,

Artemas and Hermas strolled quickly along the smooth flagstones that made up the typical Roman road surface. There were a few other travellers on the road: mostly farmers pushing crude wagons full of produce heading back into Ephesus. Occasionally, a city official riding a horse would pass, the speed of the horse depending on the urgency of the rider's business. Twice during that first day's travel they were stopped at check-points manned by soldiers. However, they were only going through the motions of ascertaining people's reasons for being on the road, and they were quite satisfied with Loukas' cover story: he was searching for a new date supplier on behalf of his father. Theseus' need of one was, at least, true.

As night was falling, the three friends sought refuge in a tiny hamlet some distance from the road. Artemas had relatives living there – an uncle on his mother's side – so they were gladly welcomed in and fed a reasonable meal before being given a blanket each and shown a place to lie down for the night. At first, Loukas had trouble getting to sleep. The floor of the sleeping platform was a lot harder than his mat at home. As he tossed and turned trying to find a position that did not result in one of his bones sticking painfully into the floor, his mind was concerned with the scroll he was carrying, and the affect it was having on the church in Ephesus. He thought about Stephanos and those who had come to him expecting to be arrested in the not-too-distant future. He thought about his father planning to operate a merchant business without having the special document from the Temple of the Revered Ones. They were doing these things because Ioanneis' scroll had foretold imminent disasters but had also set them a challenge: to stand firm against the Evil One in the heavens and his beastly minions on earth. When he finally drifted off to a sleep, his dreams were filled with beasts with hundreds of horns and claws dripping with human blood.

The next morning Loukas woke with a fierce headache, but a few splashes of icy, cold water from the trough near the door of the house helped to clear away most of the pain. Artemas' uncle gave them some milk and figs for their breakfast and some bread and cheese for the road. After eating with the family, they made their farewells, and descended to the road to continue their journey.

They had not walked far when Hermas, who had been strangely silent for much of the previous day, asked a question: "Loukas, you're a part of a guild, right?"

"Well," replied Loukas, "my father is – the guild of merchants – but I'm not officially a member yet. He hasn't put my name forward. I think he's waiting for my eighteenth birthday or my wedding, whichever happens first." When Hermas did not immediately say anything further Loukas asked, "Why do you ask?"

Hermas frowned. "Well, I'm a member of the weaver's guild. All apprentices are joined up straight away, whether you want to or not." He shrugged. "I guess everyone wants to, so it just sort of happens automatically. Even I wanted to. Until *you* went and read that scroll in church, that is…" He lapsed into silence.

Loukas was aware of the problem: attendance at temple feasts. It had not really been an issue with him since he was not a member of a guild; and anyway, his father practically ran the guild of merchants so such a situation would rarely come up. However, those in the church who were members of *other* guilds faced a serious problem. Guilds would often get together and have a meal. There would be a number of long-winded speeches that would still be received with warmth and appreciation. Perhaps there would be an award for the best artisan, who would be presented with an appropriately shaped clay figurine or special garment, followed by more long-winded speeches. As the evening wore on, and the wine continued to flow in liberal quantities, stories and jokes would be told to the accompaniment of much laughter and back-slapping. Those of a more serious disposition might prefer to conduct business meetings on the side; almost all of the most important deals were made at such gatherings. But the major problem for those members who also happened to be Christians was that these feasts were always held in pagan temples, and the meat on the tables had previously been offered to the god or gods associated with that particular temple. Furthermore, as part of the proceedings, attendees would be expected to participate in the worship of the deity in question.[1]

This problem was hardly new. Stephanos would occasionally reminisce to Loukas about the day when a letter had been read out in church. It had originally been addressed to the church in Corinth, but the letter had been widely disseminated in the decades following. In that letter, the great apostle to the Gentiles, Paulos himself, had forbidden Christians from participating in temple feasts: 'the sacrifices of pagans are offered to demons, not to God, and I do not want

1 See 1 Pet. 4:3-4 for a terse summary of such gatherings.

you to be participants with demons. You cannot drink the cup of the Lord and the cup of demons too; you cannot have a part in the Lord's table and the table of demons.'[1] At the time, there had been an outcry, since everyone – especially the richer members of the congregation – were members of guilds. However, most had come to terms with it, and had found ways to avoid the feasts, despite the cost to their careers within the guilds. Some had even felt it was allowable to attend such feasts as long as they refrained from eating or drinking. Stephanos, for one, had thought this went against the spirit of Paulos' words, and since he was a lawyer and Loukas' future father-in-law, Loukas had agreed wholeheartedly with him.

There had even been a few who had said it was fine to not only eat the meat as well, but also perform any rituals that were required. These were the followers of Nicolaus. The Ephesian church had rejected this teaching and excommunicated anyone who refused to recant; Loukas had heard that some of these excommunicants had settled in some of the other cities in Asia.

But recently things had got worse. When the temples being used to host these guild feasts were temples dedicated to one of the gods, it may have been frowned upon if you 'had other commitments' on the day of a feast, but when the temple was dedicated to the worship of the Emperors, then such a refusal was considered treason.

More than ten years ago, many of the wealthy families from Ephesus and some of the surrounding cities and towns of Asia had made a cooperative effort to honour the emperors

1 1 Cor. 10:20-21.

of the Flavian dynasty. They had sent a delegation to the Senate in Rome requesting permission to construct a temple dedicated to the worship of the then emperor Domitianus, his recently deceased predecessor and elder brother Titus, and their father Vespasian who had ruled Rome successfully for ten years after he had seized power from out of the chaos following the Emperor Nero's suicide. Not surprisingly, this delegation had been granted their request. Immediately upon their return to Ephesus work commenced on a temple complex that rivalled all other temples within the city walls, and nearly outshone the wonder of the world that was the Temple of Artemis. Once this temple was completed, it became one of the most popular places for guild feasts. Also not surprisingly, many of the Christians who refused to attend feasts at the Temple of the Revered Ones, as it was euphemistically known, were either fined, imprisoned or exiled, depending on the mood of the magistrate assigned to the case on the day. Stephanos had been kept quite busy defending his fellow Christians and trying to alleviate their sentences.

Now, Ioanneis' letter was predicting that the situation was about to deteriorate further: the routine sentence imposed upon those who refused to participate in worshipping the Emperor would be death. But the letter had also praised the Ephesian church for their rejection of the Nicolaitans. Clearly with the increased pressure, such teaching would become far more tempting.

All of this flowed through Loukas' mind as Hermas' silence continued. They had come to a ford, where the road crossed paths with a shallow river. Loukas and his companions had their feet cooled as they traversed the ford. Once on the other side, however, the road continued on, winding gently across the dry plains leading into Smyrna. They had a drink from the river just up-stream from the ford, and Loukas quickly filled up the water skins they had been carrying. Then, as he turned back to the road, he took a deep breath, in preparation both for the last stage of their journey and his answer to Hermas.

"I agree, it isn't fair. What they have done to us is terrible; what they will do to us soon will be a travesty. But we must remain faithful to our Lord and Saviour Iēsus Christos. Remember what I read? 'When the Lamb opened the fifth seal, I saw under the altar the souls of those who had been slain because of the word of God and the testimony they had maintained. They called out in a loud voice, "How long, Sovereign Lord, holy and true, until you judge the inhabitants of the earth and avenge our blood?" Then each of them was given a white robe, and they were told to wait a little longer, until the number of their fellow servants and brothers who were to be killed as they had been was completed.'[1]"

"Yes," replied Hermas, testily. "And it doesn't make me feel any less scared you reminding me…"

"But it should!" interrupted Loukas. "Don't you see what it means? Our Lord *will* come and judge those who perpetrate these crimes against us! He *will* avenge the blood of the martyrs!"

There was a lengthy silence as they continued to trudge along the road, the cool water of the ford long forgotten.

1 Rev. 6:9-11.

"Well," said Loukas eventually, "I for one am prepared to die if that is what it takes to remain true to Iēsus; for I know that Iēsus in return will remain true to his word through the prophet Ioanneis: Rome will fall!"

The further away from Ephesus they had gone, the less people they had seen on the road, and they were still many hours' walk from Smyrna. Fortunately, there was no one within earshot to hear Loukas' words, words that could only have been perceived as treason by anyone whose allegiance was to Rome.

St. Petersburg – September, AD 2005

Dima had almost finished preparing dinner, *pelmeni* – a traditional Russian dish of minced meat wrapped in a hard pastry – boiled in chicken stock, when Natasha came home from a day out with friends. He knew she was about to unlock the front door of their apartment because he had heard the beep that the *domophone* made when she placed her key in the lock of the downstairs security door. So he served up two big bowls of *pelmeni* and placed a large dollop of sour cream on top.

"I'm home," she called out from the entryway.

"Perfect timing," replied Dima. "Dinner's ready."

After Natasha had changed from her street shoes into slippers, they both sat down at their tiny dining table and began to eat.

"So you had fun?" asked Dima.

"Yes," replied Natasha. "I really love the Hermitage."

"What did you see this time?"

"Well, Sveta wanted to photograph a few of the Rembrandts, so we started there. Of course, there was quite a crowd around 'The Return of the Prodigal Son' but we waited our turn and she got a good picture." Natasha ate some more of the *pelmeni* before continuing. "I just wanted to see the French Impressionists again."

"But you see them every time!"

"And why not? They're brilliant, especially the Van Goghs. Anyway, from there we went down to the Roman statues and wound our way through to the exit. Then we had coffee in a café on Nevsky."

"Speaking of Roman statues, Dr. Williams called."

"And what did 'Ed' have to say?" asked Natasha.

"Well, he just wanted to let us know that they are up to chapter 14 now."

"What's so special about that? It's not like they're anywhere near finished yet."

"No, that wasn't the point. It means they've just done the number of the Beast. Remember his little example of textual variants? Well, our scroll has 666 not 616."

"That's good, is it?" asked Natasha uncertainly.

"Yes," nodded Dima excitedly. "And Dr. Williams said he thinks our scroll is very early, probably dating back to the beginning of the second century at least." As Natasha cleared away their dishes, Dima continued. "He said that our scroll matches up extremely closely to the UBS 4 text. There have been a few differences, but on the whole, our scroll is almost word for word the same as the scholarly reconstruction."

"What does that mean?"

"Basically, it means that our scroll could well be one of the earliest scrolls of the book of Revelation. Its text could be the original text, the one that all the other copies were derived from."

"I'm not sure I understand," replied Natasha.

"I didn't either until Dr. Williams explained it to me. Remember when he said that as scribes copied the text they introduced changes, either inadvertently or deliberately?"

"Yes."

"Well, if you start with the UBS 4 text, you can explain how all the other variants came about. And our scroll's text is pretty much the same as the UBS 4 text."

"Is that why he thinks it's so old?"

"Yes, I think so. He also said that the box we found the scroll in is very old, perhaps carved during the first century, but that doesn't necessarily make the scroll that old."

Natasha quickly washed the dishes, stacking the wet things in a drying rack conveniently located above the sink.

"When will they finish?" she asked Dima as he prepared coffee.

"He said it would be soon, assuming that the scroll is intact. He also said he was going to give us a copy on a DVD. He's going to put on all the scans and their translation into Russian and English."

Natasha chuckled to herself. "You're a bit excited about that, aren't you?"

Dima nodded. "You can tell, can you?"

"Yes."

"I can't wait to have a good look at it. To think, we – along with my great-great-grandfather – may have found the original scroll of Revelation! I wonder how it came to be hidden away in that hole in Ephesus? After all, it should have been read in all seven of the cities mentioned."

"Maybe, it only got as far as Ephesus."

"Maybe," said Dima sadly. "I guess we'll never know."

Smyrna – June, AD 93

Once again, Loukas found himself standing at the front of a church gathering with the eyes of everyone firmly fixed to him. Once again, he took a deep breath, and began reading:

" 'The revelation of Iēsus Christos, which God gave him to show his servants what must soon take place…' "

It had taken them two days of strenuous walking, but they had finally trudged through the gates in the walls surrounding Smyrna a few days before. Loukas had been to Smyrna a couple of times previously, on business for his father, so he knew who the leaders in the church were. They, of course, knew Ioanneis through his itinerant preaching ministry and were only too glad to hear how he was doing in exile. Over the intervening few days between Loukas' arrival and the Sunday gathering there had been intense anticipation for what Ioanneis had written in the scroll. However, the only person Loukas allowed to look at the scroll was the scribe appointed to make a copy, a young man by the name of Polycarp.

As Loukas began reading the section explicitly directed at the congregation sitting before him he could sense a stillness come over them.

" 'To the angel of the church in Smyrna write: These are the words of him who is the First and the Last, who died and came to life again. I know your afflictions and your poverty – yet you are rich! I know the slander of those who say they are Jews and are not, but are a synagogue of Satan.'[1]"

There was much nodding of heads at this point. Clearly, these people had been suffering for their faith, and it was the Jews living in the city – ones who did not recognise Iēsus as the Messiah – that were causing trouble. Loukas knew well enough that Jews were exempt from participation in the worship of other gods, and that included Emperor worship. Until very recently, the Christians had tried to appear as though they were still a sect of Judaism. But this had become very difficult to maintain, especially when Jews were actively separating themselves from Christians, even to the point of denouncing individuals to the civil authorities as ones practising a *superstitio* – an illegal religion, one not officially recognised by the authorities. This had been true in Smyrna, from what Loukas had heard, resulting in some persecution. One practical upshot of all this had been the expulsion of many Christians from their respective guilds resulting in them being unable to practice their trades. When Ioanneis referred to the church as poor, he meant it in a monetary sense.

" 'Do not be afraid of what you are about to suffer. I tell you, the devil will put some of you in prison to test you, and you will suffer persecution for ten days. Be faithful, even to the point of death, and I will give you the crown of life. He who has an ear, let him hear what the Spirit says to the

1 Rev. 2:8-9.

churches. He who overcomes will not be hurt at all by the second death.'[1]"

There was a reflective silence at this. Loukas could see tears in the eyes of many people. But there were some smiles, too. And he could also see that a few, those who were smiling through their tears, understood the significance of 'ten days'; it meant that the persecution had been *limited* by Iēsus, that it would not last forever. He would not allow the church's enemies, inspired and directed by Satan himself, to triumph over his people. So he had placed bounds upon that persecution. Knowing this would make it a little easier to bear.

The other factor in bearing the approaching persecution was the reward for perseverance. The crown of life! No second death! This congregation well knew, stemming from Paul's letters and the Gospels, the church's teaching on the final judgment: that all people would be resurrected at the end of history to face the ultimate Judge, and that those who were judged against would perish forever. Even martyrdom was bearable knowing that you were safe from that second, and permanent, death.

Having given the people a chance to ponder these things for a while, Loukas continued reading. Again he could sense them respond in wonder to the description of God on his throne and the Lamb looking as though it had been slain. He knew they understood the significance of the Seals by the nodding of heads and the occasional whispered comment as someone asked their neighbour for clarification.

1 Rev. 2:10-11.

But as Loukas read about the sealing of the 144,000 –
12,000 from each of the 12 tribes of Israel – followed by the
vision of the uncountable multitude of people from every
nation, tribe, people and language, he could hear the
murmured questions and when he looked up from the scroll
he could see their puzzled expressions. He did not stop
reading, however. He wanted the people to hear the scroll
read out straight through so that they would get the whole
picture clear in their minds before stopping to deal with any
problematic details.

He was not surprised that the stunned silence that
immediately followed the concluding words of the scroll was
eventually broken by a question: "So who are the 144,000?"

Loukas' voice was feeling rather sore after such a long
reading session. However, he well knew from the scroll that
these people would very soon be facing vicious persecution
and that many of them would indeed be killed for their faith
in Iēsus. Consequently, this was a vitally important part of
the picture for them. And not just for them. Loukas looked
over to where his two travelling companions were sitting,
and caught Hermas' eye.

"You might have been wondering why there was such a
long time between the sixth and seventh seal being opened."
There were a few nods. "Well, this was to provide you with
an answer to the question asked by the kings of the earth and
all the powerful people hiding in the caves from the disasters
of the first six seals. Remember they asked, 'For the great day
of God's wrath has come, and who can stand?'[1] Well, the
144,000 are those who can stand. They are those who have

1 Rev. 6:17.

been sealed by God so that they do not succumb to those disasters. But they are sealed for a different fate."

Loukas suddenly realised he was preaching. It was not something he had done before. He had always thought of himself as a merchant, like his father and his father before him. He had certainly not considered a leadership role in the church, not at his young age. Yet, here he was, exhorting a congregation of believers! It caused him to pause briefly, wondering how much Ioanneis had known in advance.

"But you have to recognise something important. This is one of those situations where what Ioanneis *heard* and what he *saw* differed. He heard the angels reading out a military census, like one straight out of the histories of the nation of Israel. But what he *saw* was the uncountable multitude from every nation, tribe, people and language."

Loukas started rolling the scroll back to the beginning, something he would have to do anyway at some point, looking for the place in the scroll he was talking about. Eventually, he found it and read out for all to hear again: " 'These are they who have come out of the great tribulation; they have washed their robes and made them white in the blood of the Lamb.'[1]" He looked up from the scroll. "In other words, the Scriptural image of the army of Israel has been transformed into an army of martyrs. Those of you who suffer martyrdom will be there! And listen to these promises." He continued reading. " 'Therefore, they are before the throne of God and serve him day and night in his temple; and he who sits on the throne will spread his tent over them. Never again will they hunger; never again will

1 Rev. 7:14.

they thirst. The sun will not beat upon them, nor any scorching heat. For the Lamb at the centre of the throne will be their shepherd; he will lead them to springs of living water. And God will wipe away every tear from their eyes.'[1]"

This time there were no puzzled glances, just a solemn nodding of heads with tears in many eyes. Now Loukas could see they understood; and again, he had a sense that this church's lamp stand was safe. They would suffer persecution, but they would endure and gain the crown of life. Satan would have his way for a short time, but he would be defeated in the end.

Loukas glanced across at Hermas and saw that he, too, was crying freely. But he was also smiling through his tears.

∽

St. Petersburg – October, AD 2005

"It's done!"

These were the words that emerged from the telephone receiver when Dima received a call from Dr. Williams one chilly autumn afternoon. Almost without waiting to hang up the telephone, Dima threw on a coat, grabbed his backpack, and rushed out the door.

Sitting on the Metro train, he reached into his backpack for the earphones of his portable CD player. He pushed the tiny button that would start the CD playing but nothing happened. It was then that he realised he had left the

1 Rev. 7:15–17.

apartment too quickly to have remembered to bring a CD as well.

Oh well, he thought, *at least it also picks up FM radio.*

He pulled out the CD player itself and switched it over to FM. But all he could hear was a faint static; FM stations cannot be picked up in the Metro, since it is so far underground. He put the CD player away and whiled away the time reading the advertisements on the walls of the train, mentally translating them into English to keep himself in practice.

Eventually he arrived at Narvskaya station. Impatiently tapping the arm of the escalator he slowly rose to the surface of the city and then hurried through the darkening streets to the Christian University. It was after 5pm but the front door was unlocked. He made his way up to Dr. Williams' office and knocked on the door.

"Come in!"

He opened the door and entered the office.

"Ah, Dima, good to see you."

"Thanks for calling. You said it was done?"

"Yes," replied Dr. Williams, "the scanning is finished. And the manuscript was entire: every word was there right to the end. Truly amazing! For a scroll to be that old and complete is a miracle."

"So you do think it's old, then?" asked Dima excitedly.

"Dima," Dr. Williams said solemnly, "every day I feel more and more certain that this scroll is the very first one ever written, the original manuscript from the very hand of John!"

Dima could not contain his grin.

"I've been in contact with a palaeography expert," continued Dr. Williams, "and he was so interested he's flying in to St. Petersburg at his own expense as soon as he can get his visa organised."

"Goodness!"

"Yes, so he should be able to give a more definitive dating. Until then, I'd date it to the early second century at the latest."

There was a pause in the conversation. Finally, Dima said, "You mentioned you had something to give me?"

"Oh yes, I'm making up a DVD data disk for you." Dr. Williams indicated with a casual wave of his hand the computer screen sitting on his desk. "I'm putting on it all the scans so you will be able to see every last inch of the scroll, and I've included the translation of the scroll into English and Russian. Lyuda did the Russian translation, you know, the girl helping me with the preparing of the scroll. Anyway, it's all on the disk, just as soon as it finishes burning. The scans take up quite a lot of memory, hence the need for a DVD rather than a CD, and why it has been working away for what feels like hours."

Suddenly, there was a chiming sound followed by the noise a computer drive makes as it ejects a disk.

"Ah, it's finished. Perfect timing. Now we can head home." Dr. Williams reached underneath his desk to where the computer was and retrieved the disk. Taking a permanent marker he carefully wrote on the upper surface of the disk: 'Scans and translations of the papyrus scroll of Revelation (Ephesus: April 1885).' "That way you won't get it confused with any other DVD data disks you may have lying around at home. Now, where did I put the case?" He looked around his desk, but could see nothing. Then he frowned. "Oh that's right, Sasha gave me the disk from his supply cabinet and he didn't give me a case. Darn! How can you take it home without it getting scratched?" He continued to look for a case in one of the drawers of his desk, but was somewhat hampered by the fact he was still holding the disk in one of his hands.

Dima had an idea.

"I know," he said. "I brought my CD player with me and forgot to put in a CD."

"Excellent," exclaimed Dr. Williams, anticipating the direction of Dima's train of thought. "You can just put the disk in the player for the trip home and then you can transfer it to a proper case. I assume you have something suitable?"

"I think I'll be able to find something," replied Dima, opening his backpack to retrieve the portable CD player.

"Well then, here it is." Dr. Williams handed the disk over to Dima, who placed it carefully in the player and then closed its lid.

"Right," said Dr. Williams cheerfully. "Let me accompany you out." He switched his computer off, placed a few books and what looked like student essays into his own backpack and then came out from behind his desk. Dima clipped the CD player to his belt, under his coat.

"Will that be OK?" asked Dr. Williams, watching.

"Yes, safer than my backpack," replied Dima. "I don't want to take any chances."

"Fair enough. OK, let's go."

Dr. Williams ushered Dima out of the office, locked the door after them, then together they walked down the corridor to the stairwell.

"Where are you headed?" asked Dr. Williams.

"The Metro," Dima said.

"Ah, same with me! My home is down the Yellow line and the Metro really is the easiest way to get home, especially when it starts getting cold and dark."

As Dr. Williams said this they reached the main entrance and stepped out into the dark and rather chilly autumn evening. People were making their hurried way along the street, most heading for the Metro station. Dima and Dr. Williams joined them.

"I'm on the Green line, myself," said Dima, eventually.

"Yet here we are on the Red line!" exclaimed Dr. Williams, as they walked into the ground-level atrium of Narvskaya station. It was not as cold inside and as they descended the escalator and the temperature rose Dima undid the buttons of his coat so that he would not get too hot. Once they got down to the platforms they found a place about half-way along the platform and placed their backpacks on the ground between them to wait for the next train. Judging by the number of people waiting Dima thought that they would not have to wait long. Sure enough, within a few minutes a train arrived. When the doors opened they could see that the carriage was quite crowded, but there was room for more, so Dima and Dr. Williams, having picked up their backpacks, squeezed on. The doors shut with a bang and the train quickly accelerated into the tunnel.

Dima happened to be standing facing the map of the St. Petersburg Metro system. He quickly located the station they had just left and mentally tracked his way home, making the switch from the Red line to the Green line at Ploshad Vosstaniya. But then he remembered the short cut. It is possible to avoid several stations by changing to the Blue line at Technologichesky Institute and then changing to the Green line at Nevsky Prospect. What made it worthwhile was that the change at Technologichesky Institute involved simply walking across the platform since at this station – unlike at any of the other crossover points in the St. Petersburg Metro system – the Red and Blue lines travel in parallel in the same direction. As the train was just then leaving the station immediately prior to Technologichesky Institute Dima leaned over and spoke to Dr. Williams.

"I'm going to take a short cut home. I'll speak to you soon."

Dr. Williams raised his eyebrows, glanced at the transport map, then nodded.

"Well, goodbye then, Dima."

"Goodbye, Dr. Williams."

"Please, call me Ed."

"OK, goodbye Ed."

At that moment the train began to pull into Technologichesky Institute. Dima was pleased to see another train pulling in at the platform directly opposite from his own train; he would not even have to wait, so long as he could get across quick enough. But in the end he made it easily: the doors of his train opened first; he was able to get out amongst the initial bunch of people; and then he sauntered across to the opposite platform arriving just as the doors of that train were opening. After waiting for the emerging passengers to disembark, he got on the train.

Right, he thought. *Blue line to Nevsky Prospect.* In case he might have dropped something during the brief run across the platform, he went through a mental check-list, touching his pockets as he went: backpack, apartment keys, CD player, wallet, travel pass, wrist-watch; all there.

The doors closed with a bang and the train moved quickly off. The station he needed to get off at would be the second stop, so he stayed close to the doors. This train was also very crowded as people made their way home after a long day of work. In the middle of the carriage a salesman starting shouting, hawking some world maps to a captive audience. Dima had seen him at other times on the Metro, always selling something different each time. In fact, he had bought a couple of packets of bandaids off the guy a few months before. Put simply, the man was good at what he did. He had a strong voice, able to be heard above the roar of the train, his spiel was always convincing, and every time Dima had seen him he always made a sale. Even today, there were a few people who had not realised their need for a brightly coloured map of the world, displaying the principal exports of countries by means of humorous cartoons, until this salesman had drawn their attention to it. They pulled out some money from the deepest recesses of their clothing and handed it over to the man as he made his way up the carriage towards Dima, squeezing past people as he came. A good salesman to the end, he made eye-contact with almost everyone. Dima shook his head when the man looked at him. *Not this time*, he thought.

Sennaya Ploshad came and went. Nevsky Prospect was next.

The salesman, having concluded his business with those members of the carriage that required his product of the moment, moved to the door and stood next to Dima sorting out the money he had acquired and extracting a few more maps from the backpack he carried over one shoulder in preparation for moving to the next carriage when the train pulled in to the station.

The train began to slow. Dima, balanced carefully with his feet apart, still ended up swaying a little as the train came to a complete stop. The doors opened, and he and the salesman were the first to get out. Briefly disoriented by the crowd of people waiting to get on, Dima moved through them away from the edge of the platform, had a quick look around, located the way to the Green line and started off. There was the usual crowd of people. The junction of the Green and Blue lines is always busy, and at rush hour exceedingly so. There were thousands of people moving purposefully, many sitting on a few benches that lined the walls, even a couple of buskers.

Dima walked up a short flight of stairs and entered the connecting passageway. He was in a steady stream of people all moving in the same direction, all wanting to connect to the Green line. Suddenly, the man in front of him stopped walking and reached out to the wall for support. Dima, wondering if the man was drunk or unwell, had to pull up short. Someone careered into Dima causing him to almost lose his own balance and he too reached for the wall.

It was all over quickly. The man in front had clearly recovered for he continued walking briskly away. As Dima turned to apologise to whoever had crashed into him, he was surprised to see the man, wearing a dark beanie and a heavy dark green coat, disappearing into the crowd back the way they had come. This immediately raised Dima's suspicions. He did his little check-list again: backpack, apartment keys, CD player…

The CD player was not there. Neither was his wallet, but that only had a few rubles in it – and he always kept his credit card in an inside pocket of his backpack – so that did not really matter. But his portable CD player, with the DVD-ROM of the scroll safely inside it, had somehow been unclipped and taken out from underneath his coat all without him even noticing. The whole incident must have been a set-up.

At once Dima set off after the man in the beanie who was still just in sight. They were both working against the flow of pedestrians so the other man had not got too far away. People frowned at Dima as he dodged in and out of their path, but he did not care. He kept his eyes locked on that beanie until it disappeared down the short flight of stairs Dima had ascended only a short time before. When Dima reached the top of the stairs himself he could not immediately locate the man. But then, off to one side heading for a platform, he saw him and jumped down the stairs in hot pursuit.

The man in the beanie seemed very cool about the whole business. He did not turn around even once to see if he was being followed; he just continued on his way as if he was a good, law-abiding citizen on his way home from work. It made Dima seethe as he attempted to follow as quickly as he could. The man disappeared through a large archway opening onto the platform, but Dima was fairly close behind so that by the time he arrived on the platform he again caught sight of the beanie ducking and weaving as the man moved up the platform between the people waiting for a train to arrive. Dima followed, and felt the wind start to pick up behind him. A train was arriving. Dima kept away from the edge and tried to narrow the distance between them, without taking his eyes off the man to make sure he did not try and escape through another archway.

However, when the train came to a stop many passengers got off, congesting the already-crowded platform still further. Dima only just caught a glimpse of the man in the beanie getting onto the train through the middle doors of a carriage. Knowing the train would not wait for him to get to the same door, Dima jumped through the doors at the nearest end of the same carriage. Seeing the man standing in the space near the middle doors, Dima made his way through the carriage towards him. But without really glancing in Dima's direction, the man casually got off the train. Dima could see him through the windows, moving directly passed Dima.

The usual announcement came over the train's intercom: "Watch out. The doors are closing." As quickly as possible, Dima made a jump for the doors and was able to get his body wedged between them. The doors, unable to close completely, must have signalled the driver of the train in some way. After a few moments, the doors reopened and Dima was able to get off the train.

But the man was not there. When the doors had reopened, he had nonchalantly got back on the train, down the other end of the carriage. Dima stepped back onto the train himself. The man did not move. Neither did Dima, knowing what would happen if he tried to get to the man through the carriage.

Again, the warning announcement sounded and the doors began to close. Knowing he would very soon be trapped in the train with his pursuer, the man in the beanie jumped through the doors. The doors closed on his body, but he managed to push the doors apart slightly with his hands and then to squeeze through. Dima moved towards the doors nearest him but he was just not quick enough. They had closed with a bang when the man had got through. Instead, he was left stuck on the train watching the man disappear into the gloom as the train rapidly accelerated away.

∽

St. Petersburg – October, AD 2005

"I've been inspired to preach on Revelation, this week," Yevgeny started his sermon by saying. "For various reasons…" (he looked at Dima and Natasha, sitting near the front of the small room in which their church met) "…I have been reading the book of Revelation recently, and have found it to be enormously challenging. It contains a message that is just as relevant today as it was when it was first read in the churches of Asia Minor.

"Before we get to the passage I particularly want to look at today, I need to say something about the structure of the book as a whole. You can't read through Revelation without noticing the three groups of seven: the seven seals, the seven trumpets and the seven bowls. Each series of seven is accompanied by disasters on the earth, disasters that get progressively worse as each group of seven arrives. A quarter of the earth is affected by the seven seals; a third by the trumpets, and the bowls usher in a complete destruction.

"But you have to remember we are talking about the first century, here, and how they would have viewed this text. This book was first and foremost written to seven churches – another seven! – located in the Roman province of Asia Minor, in the country we now know today as Turkey. In those days, the disasters of the seven seals would have sounded terrible, but very much like everyday life with just a small amount of hyperbole thrown in for effect. The people hearing the scroll read for the first time would immediately call to mind the many disasters that had befallen the known world during the previous decades.

"However, when we come to the seven trumpets, which is the passage I wish to look at today, we have to ask ourselves, 'What is the intensification for?' In other words, why do the disasters now involve a *third* of the earth?"

Yevgeny took out his Bible and turned to Revelation chapter eight, and read verses six through to twelve.

"As you have just heard," he continued, "all of these disasters involve a third: a third of the earth, trees and grass burned up; a third of the sea turned to blood, resulting in the destruction of a third of the sea creatures and a third of the ships; a third of the fresh water turned bitter; a third of the sun and the moon was darkened; a third of the stars ceased giving light.

"So far, the author gives us no clue as to the reason for the intensification. It is just simply stated. Now, I won't read most of chapter nine. Suffice to say that the fifth trumpet summons demonic locusts with scorpion stingers that torture people, and if that wasn't bad enough, the sixth trumpet summons an enormous army that kills a third of mankind. I pick it up from verse twenty:

" 'The rest of mankind that were not killed by these plagues *still did not repent of the work of their hands;* they did not stop worshipping demons, and idols of gold, silver, bronze, stone and wood – idols that cannot see or hear or walk. Nor did they repent of their murders, their magic arts, their sexual immorality or their thefts.'

"This, then, is the point of the trumpets. If the seven seals were a description of God in control over everyday life, then the trumpets signify God allowing evil to intensify *in order to bring people to repentance.* This is, in fact, why this particular group of seven is ushered in with the sound of a trumpet. In the Old Testament trumpets have various uses. For example, they are used in battle as a signal for the army of Israel to attack. Joshua used them to bring down the walls of Jericho according to God's instructions.[1] Similarly, Gideon sounded trumpets and the Midianites, who far outnumbered the

---

1 Josh. 6:4, 8, 9, 13, 16, 20.

Israelites, fled in terror killing each other as they went.[1] But we don't find the trumpets doing that here in Revelation. Instead, the other main use of trumpets in the Old Testament was as a warning. Let me read Ezekiel 33 verses one to five:

" 'The word of the Lord came to me: "Son of man, speak to your countrymen and say to them, 'When I bring a sword against a land, and the people of the land choose one of their men and make him a watchman, and he sees the sword coming against the land and blows the trumpet to warn the people, then if anyone hears the trumpet but does not take warning and the sword comes and takes his life, his blood will be on his own head. Since he heard the sound of the trumpet but did not take warning, his blood will be on his own head. If he had taken warning, he would have saved himself…' " '

"Similarly, in Joel chapter two verse one, we read: 'Blow the trumpet in Zion; sound the alarm on my holy hill. Let all who live in the land tremble, for the day of the Lord is coming. It is close at hand…' And what is even more fascinating, Joel's trumpet is warning of an approaching army of locusts, just like Revelation's fifth trumpet!

"So this is what the trumpets mean in Revelation: they sound the alarm. Mankind is supposed to hear the trumpets and realise that these terrible plagues are all part of God's judgment on human sin. But they are not his final judgment, for there is still a chance for repentance. However, in chapter 11 verses fifteen onwards, when the seventh trumpet sounds the time for repentance is over and the time for the final judgment is come. As it says in verse 18 of that chapter, 'The

1 Judges 7:16-22.

nations were angry; and your wrath has come. The time has come for judging the dead... for destroying those who destroy the earth.'

"Now, as I said at the beginning of this sermon, the message of the book of Revelation is as relevant now as it was back in the time when it was written. When you look around at mankind, do we still not see many people involved in idolatry? Of course, the idols have changed in appearance. They are no longer made of gold, silver, bronze, stone and wood. For some people, their idols simply are gold and silver. Peoples' ever-growing greed for money is one thing that is destroying the earth and Revelation speaks about a destruction for just such people. Other people make idols of their possessions, like their car, their computer, their satellite navigation system. Whatever comes between you and God is an idol, and these verses make it clear that such things are sinful.

"And of course, there are still murders. Here in Russia we have been plagued by Mafia hits and terrorist acts on an almost weekly basis. And our streets are notorious for their pickpockets!" At this point, Yevgeny winked at Dima. "These are acts which must be repented of. And as for sexual immorality, one can only presume that this has certainly *not* decreased since the first century.

"Of especial interest in the list that John provides for us are two items which have been coming into their own in recent days: the worshipping of demons and the practising of magical arts. Apart from a perverse few, demons are not explicitly worshipped. However, we as Christians know that behind much of the New Age Movement lurks Satan, the prince of demons, disguised as an angel of light. And you only have to walk into any bookshop to see which magical arts are being practised in this supposedly scientific age.

"My point is this: mankind is still sinful and in need of repentance. The message of the seven trumpets is that God wants people to repent. He allows evil to intensify in order to bring people to their senses. He delays the final judgment to give all people the chance to realise their sinfulness and repent. As it says in Second Peter chapter three verse nine: 'The Lord is not slow in keeping his promise, as some understand slowness. He is patient with you, not wanting anyone to perish, but everyone to come to repentance.'

"But this appeal is a personal one. Do not wait for the multitudes to repent before you come to God. You may miss out. The seventh trumpet may sound before you confess your sins to God and accept Jesus' sacrifice on the cross. Instead, heed the warning and be saved. Let us pray."

After the service, Dima made his way through to Yevgeny, sitting quietly in the front row. He sat down next to him.

"I hope I'm not interrupting anything," Dima said softly.

"No," replied Yevgeny. "I was just praying for those people present who may not have taken that first step of faith. I really believed God wanted me to say what I said today, that there would be someone who would listen and respond."

"Maybe someone still will, so I'll make it quick. I only wanted to say that I have finally got a copy of the scroll at home now."

"Oh, that's excellent. I was sorry to hear you had had your CD player stolen."

"That's OK," replied Dima with a shrug. "It wasn't exactly the latest piece of equipment. This just gives me the excuse to go out and buy an MP3 player!"

"Fair enough," said Yevgeny with a laugh. "So what do you think of the scroll on DVD?"

"It's pretty interesting. I've had a good look through the scroll, trying to read parts of it. I'd really like to learn Greek so that I can read it properly."

"Well, you have to remember it's New Testament Greek, not Greek as spoken in Greece today."

"Oh, really? I didn't know that."

"Yes," said Yevgeny. "It's actually called Koinē Greek, and was the everyday speech of the common man, not the Classical Greek of the scholars and philosophers. It's much rougher and unrefined."

"Anyway, if you'd like to have a good look, I can lend you the DVD."

"Sure! I'd love that. And Dr. Williams believes the scroll really is old?"

"Yes," said Dima with a smile. "He thinks it could well be the original manuscript, the one from which all other copies were derived."

"That would make it well worth a look. Wouldn't it be funny if this copy explained who the 666 referred to!"

"Yes, that would be funny," replied Dima with a laugh. "But I've looked up the spot and it doesn't."

"Ah, well, it was worth a try."

At that moment another member of the congregation came up to Yevgeny. He looked as though he had been crying, so Dima thought it best to take his leave; Yevgeny had ministry to do.

෴

Between Smyrna and Pergamum – June, AD 93

They had a hard time getting away from the church of Smyrna. There had been quite a bond formed between this little group of Christians and Loukas and his companions through the reading of Ioanneis' scroll. Perhaps they felt that as soon as Loukas left, persecution would start immediately. As far as Loukas was any judge, that was certainly possible. He thought of the part in the scroll where an angel swears by God the creator and says, 'There will be no more delay! But in the days when the seventh angel is about to sound his trumpet, the mystery of God will be accomplished, just as he announced to his servants the prophets.'[1] This was the point in the scroll that correlated with the present moment in history; this was the boundary between what was past and what was to come. The sixth trumpet had sounded its warning; the majority of the peoples of the earth had not responded with repentance. And this is where Ioanneis then went on to describe the martyrdom of some in the church. Actually, it was not hard to foresee that as the resistance of those in the church to the worship of the emperor increased, opposition would increase all the more. What had really made an impression on Loukas was the effect that Ioanneis claimed martyrdom would have on the rest of the world. It

1 Rev. 10:6-7.

was all in the contents of the little scroll: the persecution of the church would be the secret weapon by which God would win his victory over the church's persecutors and to achieve his purposes of redemption.

As usual, Ioanneis had not spelled it out word for word. He had used an allusion to the prophet Ezekiel when he was given a scroll to eat and it was sweet to the taste.[1] Going beyond this, Ioanneis' little scroll was also bitter to swallow, indicating that the contents of the scroll was not necessarily pleasant. And martyrdom seldom was.

So Loukas tried as best he could to encourage the believers to be strong in the face of this approaching persecution, knowing too that his friend Hermas was listening in. Eventually, they made their final farewells and set out through the city heading towards the city gates and the road that led to Pergamum. As they came to the Agora, Artemas decided they needed some additional supplies for the road ahead. After all, Pergamum lay due north of Smyrna, and would involve an additional day's walking compared with their journey from Ephesus to Smyrna; it made sense that they carry with them some provisions that would ease their journey in the event of unforeseen difficulties.

"Hermas, can you see where they sell cheeses?" asked Artemas, trying to peer through gaps in the crowds of people milling about the Agora.

Hermas, being almost a head taller than Artemas, scanned the tables that were visible to him.

1 Ezek. 2:9–3:3.

"Over there!" he cried, pointing to the eastern side of the Agora. Immediately, he set off in that direction, with the others following as best they could.

They chose some small, round and quite hard cheeses suitable for the road. Unlike softer cheeses, these did not have to be kept cool and could therefore withstand the warm temperatures of pedestrian travel during summer. From a nearby shop they purchased some bread rolls, also disconcertingly hard. Such provisions would give their teeth a good working-over, but would keep them from feeling hungry should they be forced to spend a night in the open. And the bread could always be softened with the addition of a little water.

Suitably laden, they exited the Agora through the central northern archway, and followed the flagstone roadway towards the northern gates of Smyrna. The street was itself quite busy, with many people hurrying towards the Agora to do their early-morning shopping, or – Loukas had to quickly step out of the way of a few men carrying large bags full of wares – even to set up their own stalls. Because of the crowds Loukas did not see the Roman patrol watching those passing in and out of the city gates until they stepped out of the shadows thrown by the gates themselves and stopped him and his companions in their tracks.

"Halt," said the decurion, with a weary voice. He and his group of ten men had been on guard-duty since the middle of the night and they were well overdue for being relieved. Quite a few of his men clearly needed to be relieved in other ways, too; their expressions of quiet concentration masked a deep desperation only given away by a tightness about their eyes. It was getting on his nerves, not least because he too had been feeling the pressure building within. But no one was to leave until the next squad of soldiers arrived. All of this was at the forefront of his mind as he spotted the three young men travelling suspiciously unburdened, going against the majority flow of traffic. "Just a couple of routine questions."

Loukas was suddenly very conscious of the scroll nestled in its leather pouch in his shoulder bag. "Certainly, sir," he replied, in what he hoped was a suitably deferential tone.

The decurion, with a pained look that made Loukas feel rather uncomfortable, asked, "What has been the purpose of your visit to Smyrna?"

"I have been scouting out trade opportunities for my father," Loukas replied.

"Who is your father and where is he based?"

Loukas had not been expecting his cover story to be challenged so he was at a loss whether to tell the truth at this point or not. In the end he felt it would be unwise to lie, especially when the lengthening silence would imply a lack of veracity anyway. "Theseus of Ephesus," he said, eventually.

At that, one of the other soldiers looked up from his inward concentration. "Hey, I know of him. I had some excellent dates from him once."

Loukas smiled, relieved that this backed up his story nicely. "I know for a fact, sir, that my father works hard to guarantee your satisfaction."

"I well believe it," said the soldier. "I've had some horrible ones in my day, but your father's dates were as succulent as an Asian peach!"

"That's enough, Gaius," said the decurion with a frown. Turning to Loukas, he said, "Very well. You may proceed. You are heading to Pergamum, I believe?"

At first, Loukas was concerned that somehow the decurion must have had spies present at the reading of the scroll. But then he realised that since he was leaving from the northern gate, there were only a few cities he could be heading to if he was serious about looking for suitable trading opportunities, and Pergamum was the nearest one.

"That's right," he replied.

"Well, I wish you a quick and easy journey."

"Thank-you, sir," said Loukas, and with that he and his companions walked through the gates of Smyrna. Behind him, he heard the soldier speaking, "Yes, indeed, those dates were delicious. I'm salivating just thinking about them…"

A little way before the road turned around the edge of a hill, Loukas risked a quick look back at the gates. It appeared that the squad of soldiers was in the process of handing over to their relief. Loukas could see several of the soldiers hurrying off to some nearby barracks. Clearly, they had successfully avoided arousing any suspicions.

"That was close," said Hermas with a worried look on his face.

"Possibly," replied Loukas. "But I can't see that we pose them any threat. After all, they don't know about the scroll, and even if they did, they wouldn't understand it."

"That's true," said Hermas, only partially mollified.

"Well, let's get on," said Loukas cheerfully, turning back towards Pergamum. "We've a long road ahead."

They continued around the bend and were soon well out of sight of the walls of Smyrna and of the decurion who had rushed up to one of the lookout posts in order to keep the three men in view for as long as possible.

∿

St. Petersburg – October, AD 2005

Dima fingered the slip of paper in his hands nervously as the queue in front of him gradually lessened in size. He was standing in a post office, with a notice that had been placed in his letter-box informing him that a parcel had arrived from Nizhny Novgorod. So here he was in the post office waiting to receive it.

He guessed it would be from his grandmother, but he could not for the life of him think what she would be sending him. After all, what could she have that he could not buy here in St. Petersburg? Presumably then it must be something more personal; some of her delicious pickles or preserves in a jar, perhaps?

Finally, he was the first person in the queue, and then one of the ladies behind the counter called out, "Next!" He went over, handed her the notice along with his passport – to verify his identity and his right to the parcel – and she muttered something before disappearing into a back room. She returned with a small box wrapped in brown paper sealed at each end with what looked like black tar. She handed it through the small window with his passport sitting on top.

He took it over to a bench that lined one of the walls of the post office. Once he got through the black tar the paper came off easily, revealing a cardboard box with the flaps taped up with masking tape. Using his apartment key, he sliced through the tape and opened the flaps.

Inside was a book, bound in leather with gold filigree on the cover. In fact, it looked very much like another volume in Dima's great-great-grandfather's diary. With some excitement, Dima took it from the box and opened to the first page. Sure enough, there was Nicolai's elegant Russian script, the Cyrillic letters flowing beautifully yet almost indistinguishably from one to the next.

Oy, thought Dima to himself. *Natasha's going to like this!*

He checked the box to see if there was anything more, and discovered a piece of paper. It was a short letter from his grandmother:

> *Dearest Dima & Natasha,*
> *I came across this book of Nicolai's behind a bookcase that we had taken down because it needed fixing. Knowing your interest in my grandfather, I thought you would like to read it. From what I can tell, it comes from a time after the diary that you still have. Perhaps you will finally learn how he came to injure his leg!*
> *I look forward to seeing you again when you can spare the time. And if this will provide a suitable incentive, this year's pickles are even better than last year's!*
> *With much love,*
> *Babushka.*

The post office was fairly close to Dima's home, but he could barely stop himself from sitting down there and then and trying to read the diary. However, he knew that Natasha would find it difficult to forgive him if he did so. It was only fair, Dima considered, since she had found the original one. As he opened the post office door, and stepped out into the street, he had to admit that she had a much better chance of being able to decipher Nicolai's handwriting, especially if he ever broke into French again!

Natasha was already at home, having finished work earlier than Dima, and had already prepared some food. She met him at the door and gave him a kiss.

"Is that the parcel?" she asked. "Is it from your grandmother?"

"Yes, indeed. And it's more of Nicolai's diary."

"Oh!" exclaimed Natasha, all thought of the food cooking out in the kitchen forgotten. "Let me have a look!"

Dima put the box down on a low shelf, lifted the book out and handed it to Natasha. As he removed his shoes and placed some slippers on his feet, she began to read the first entry.

" *'Wednesday, 3rd March, 1886*

" *'I am continually struck by the extremes of this at once beautiful and hideous culture. Today, for example, I was strolling through the amazing streets of the Great Bazaar. It is always an experience that is completely bewildering to the senses: the overpowering wafts emanating from the spice markets; materials shaded in all the colours of the rainbow combined into the most intricate designs; the deafening effect of thousands of recalcitrant beasts of burden all being urged by their impatient masters to keep moving; and then, somehow through the din comes the haunting sound of a local stringed instrument being expertly played by an elderly man, seated in the shade of an even more elderly Persian rug. All in all, I can usually pass the day just wandering around, occasionally buying a trinket here, having a drink of hot tea there.' "*

"Oh, speaking of tea…" interrupted Dima.

"Oh, the pasta!" cried Natasha, dropping the diary hurriedly on the couch and running into the kitchen. She came back a few minutes later.

"It's all fine," she said. "Dinner is ready, then."

"Why don't you finish the entry first?" suggested Dima.

"Sure," she replied, picking up the diary again, and opening the book at the first page again.

" *'But then, around three in the afternoon, I heard a commotion approaching. A crowd of men were following hard on the heels of a town crier. As he went by I heard him announcing the execution of some poor scoundrel who had somehow managed to get on the wrong side of the Emir – not a hard thing to do, unfortunately. I had heard from some of my compatriots here what usually happened to these unfortunates, so I followed at a distance, not wanting to intrude on these local affairs. The crowd centred in on the Minari Kalian, or the Tower of Death, so named for precisely what I then witnessed. The crowd continued to expand, as more and more men came from the surrounding streets and bazaars. And then the culprit appeared at the very top of the tower, with an escort of two large and formidable guards. There was almost instantly silence. From where I was standing I could barely hear the charges being read out. And then, almost casually, the man was picked up by the two guards and hurled out over the edge of* the Tower. I consider myself fortunate not to have seen the landing; I consider myself most unfortunate that I, even at that distance, heard the landing.

" 'And then the crowd dispersed. I overheard one man say to his friend: "Not as good as last month. Last month the man screamed the whole way down. This one seemed resigned to his fate..."

" 'So there you have it: beauty and horror juxtaposed, and I for one am not sure that the beauty outweighs the horror.' "

There was a long silence.

"So, who wants some pasta?" asked Natasha with a forced smile.

"I'm not sure I have any appetite left," replied Dima, grimacing. He gave a quick shake of his head. "No, I'm OK. Let's eat."

They went into the kitchen after Natasha placed the new diary next to the TV.

Over the next few days Dima and Natasha read more of the diary together. They learned that when the railway was being built to Bokhara, the Emir of the time had considered it evil – the locals referred to it as the Devil's Wagon, apparently – so he had not allowed the Russians to build it too close to Bokhara. Consequently, this meant that the railway and the station were located some ten miles from the city. But once the locals had seen how the railway boosted trade in the region it had quickly caught on, so that New Bokhara, as the town that grew up around the station came to be called, soon became a bustling little trade centre, like a satellite orbiting the central bazaars of Bokhara itself.

They discovered that Nikolai had a fondness for silk, and often frequented the silk bazaar, sorting through the wares on display in the various stalls like a seasoned connoisseur. He had even ventured into the back courtyards of some of the old houses of Bokhara where the women would weave these silks in the shade of the mulberry trees whose leaves were just as important to the whole process.

Then, late one night, Natasha came across something quite intriguing.

"Dima," she exclaimed, "Listen to this." They were sitting up in bed, reading. Dima was wading through an unabridged version of Victor Hugo's *Les Misérables*, and while he was enjoying it, was grateful for a momentary distraction.

"What is it?" he asked.

"I think you will want to hear this. Listen. *'I think I may have found someone able to translate the parchment I found in Ephesus. I have often wondered as to the significance of the parchment, given that it was found in with the scroll, and yet seemed to be separate from it. But I have been unable to find anyone who can read it. No one in the bazaars has been able to do so – or at least has not let on – so that I am still mystified as to its contents. However, today one of the sellers of trinkets of antiquity mentioned that a Muslim scholar of some repute had arrived recently to study some of the ancient texts found in the mosques of Bokhara. Tomorrow, I will take the parchment and seek him out.'* Well, what do you make of that?" she asked.

While Natasha had been reading from the diary, Dima had replaced his bookmark and returned *Les Misérables* to the bedside table. This was clearly something important. "What parchment?" he asked.

"I don't know. He says it was separate from the scroll, yet found inside the box. What could it be?"

"I have no idea. But what if it, too, dates from the first century? I mean, it could well be from the author of Revelation himself! Remember, Dr. Williams thinks we found perhaps the original manuscript. What if this parchment contains more – perhaps a commentary on the book of Revelation, perhaps the interpretive keys, maybe even the name of the beast…"

"Now, now, don't get carried away!" interrupted Natasha, laughing. "I think you're getting ahead of yourself. Wouldn't it make more sense to see if Nikolai was successful in getting it translated?"

"Of course. Does he?"

"How should I know? I stopped reading so that I could read that bit out to you. But I can keep going now, if you like."

"Please do."

She was quiet for a few minutes as she quickly scanned ahead.

"Hmmm, nothing yet," she murmured after a while. "Just some more stuff about the silk bazaar."

Dima was waiting impatiently. Eventually, though, Natasha stopped reading.

"That's it," she said sadly.

"What do you mean?"

"I've reached the end of the book. He never mentioned that parchment again, at least, not in this volume. Maybe Nadezhda will find another?"

Dima was rather disappointed.

"Well, I wouldn't count on it. Maybe we should go and look for it ourselves. I mean, if we could find that parchment, who knows what value it may have to the Revelation scroll?"

"Well, then," said Natasha with a sigh, "I guess we're off to Nizhny Novgorod again…"

∽

Pergamum – July, AD 93

"Well, well, if it isn't Lucius the merchant's son!"

Standing on a beautiful, cobbled street in the centre of Pergamum, Loukas froze and turned slowly to face the speaker. He and his friends had been travelling for the last few days through the hills and valleys of Asia – and across two major rivers – as they had wound their way northward along the road that connected Smyrna to Pergamum. They had made good time, but it had taken its toll. They were exhausted and in need of much rest. As soon as they had entered through the city gates Artemas and Hermas had headed off to the Agora for food for their evening meal. Loukas had wandered off to find the house of Antipas. Although Antipas was no longer alive, his widow was known to offer shelter to those visiting the church from out of town. So Loukas was on his own when he turned around to see Sergius Maximus coming towards him.

"Sergius Maximus! Greetings!" replied Loukas in what he hoped was not a guilty tone.

"We did not run into each other on the wide streets of Ephesus," said Sergius Maximus with a smile. "Clearly what was required were the narrower streets of Pergamum to bring us together again!"

"So it seems."

"So what brings you to my new home town?"

With an effort Loukas stopped himself reaching for the scroll nestled so vulnerably in its bag. Instead, he shrugged and said, "The usual: collecting trade payments, that sort of thing…"

"Well, it is good to see a familiar face. I haven't been here long enough to make any real friends, so I am making do with acquaintances. Even those from Ephesus."

He turned to look at Loukas more closely before asking, "Have you just come from Ephesus?"

Loukas again thought it better not to lie too much. "Indirectly," he replied.

"Hmmm," said Sergius frowning a little. "So you don't know anything about the problems there?"

Loukas' heart missed a beat. "Problems?"

"Well, nothing much. Just a few people demonstrating rebellion against Rome by refusing to worship the Emperor – may He reign over us forever. I wouldn't even mention it except some of them have come from well-born families. Very surprising, really."

Loukas did not reply. He was suddenly overcome by anxiety for his friends at home. Who had been the ones to refuse? What had happened to them? He wanted to ask

Sergius Maximus, but he knew full well that to do so would bring immediate suspicion upon himself, thereby destroying his chance to spread the scroll to the remaining churches.

"By the way, I am heading to the library. Are you interested in seeing it? It is as wonderful as I had been led to believe. I have been gladdened to see that the citizens of this fair city have been slowly rebuilding their collection. I spend many long hours reading at the feet of Athena herself. Perhaps seeing her will bring wisdom to your business dealings? She has brought much wisdom to me, and don't I need it in this job!"

Just then he caught sight of a man running down the road towards him. He groaned. "Speaking of the job, that looks like Crispus. He appears to have tracked me down before I could disappear into a quiet corner of the library…"

"Sergius Maximus!" called the man whose name was apparently Crispus as he ran up to them waving a sealed scroll. "A messenger has just come from Smyrna bringing this letter for you and rumours of unrest for all who have ears to hear."

"Crispus!" Sergius replied sternly. "Enough loose talk! I don't want you listening to gossip and then passing it along to everyone you happen to meet. You know that I want you listening to gossip then passing it along to me alone!" Turning to Loukas he said, "I think I had better bid you farewell. I hope to see you again before you leave this wonderful city of mine."

Loukas, who had not actually contributed to the conversation for quite a while, was only too eager to get away, so he bowed to Sergius Maximus and hurried off in the direction of Antipas' widow's house. In fact, he could not even trust himself to speak. In the deepest recesses of his mind, Loukas could not prevent the thought that Iounia was one of those in trouble.

He found the house with not too much trouble. When Artemas and Hermas came in with some food and wine, he quickly told them about his encounter with Sergius Maximus.

"May God be with them," said Hermas mournfully, after Loukas lapsed into silence.

"Well, we knew it was coming," replied Artemas.

Yes, thought Loukas. *We did know it was coming, thanks to Ioanneis' scroll. And yet, in some ways, it is intensifying* because *of the scroll…*

Putting all thoughts of Iounia out of his head, Loukas quickly made contact with the leaders of the church. When they heard what he carried, the church did not even wait for their regular Sunday meeting. Knowing that the authorities were becoming aware of the spread of civil rebellion, which Loukas knew only too well was the direct result of the scroll in his possession, the church had decided to meet secretly and immediately to hear the reading of the scroll.

So it was that later that very night, Loukas stood up in front of the assembly and read from the scroll. Things were going well until he got to the section addressed specifically to them.

" 'To the angel of the church in Pergamum write: These are the words of him who has the sharp, double-edged sword. I know where you live – where Satan has his throne.'[1]"

1 Rev. 2:12.

Almost as a group everyone's eyes drifted in the direction of the Altar of Zeus. Loukas thought back to their approach to the city earlier that day. From quite a distance away, the acropolis of Pergamum could be seen, the pillars of the various temples standing out white against the brown of the rocky hillside and the blue of the sky. The smoke, too, had also been visible from a distance, rising up from the various sacrificial altars of the many deities worshipped by the people of Pergamum. As they had got closer, they had been able to distinguish the four terraces, each one cut into the side of the hill. The largest theatre in the world – with 80 rows of seats, capable of seating 10,000 men – took up a significant part of the first terrace, with an Agora on the left. Higher up the hill, on the third terrace, they had been able to see the Temple dedicated to Athena. The fourth terrace had been harder to make out, the palaces located there hidden somewhat by the curve of the hillside. But the second terrace had been the one that really stood out: standing to the right of the theatre, the Altar of Zeus was an imposing structure located at the crest of the ridge looking down on the valley below. With its majestic columns, fourteen metres tall, it dominated the entire acropolis. And it even looked like a throne: the altar was located within a colonnade that made up three sides of a square, the fourth side remaining open towards the valley. It was not at all hard to picture Satan seated on this 'throne' feasting on the blood and smoke and sexual immorality that made up the cultic rituals.

" 'Yet you remain true to my name,' " continued Loukas. " 'You did not renounce your faith in me, even in the days of

Antipas, my faithful witness, who was put to death in your city – where Satan lives.'[1]"

This time all eyes swivelled to focus on Antipas' widow, whose eyes were shining with tears and righteousness both at the same time.

Loukas took a deep breath. Even someone who had not heard the scroll before could sense the rapidly approaching 'but…'

" 'Nevertheless, I have a few things against you.' "

There was an immediate susurration of anxious whispering.

" 'You have people there who hold to the teaching of Balaam, who taught Balak to entice the Israelites to sin by eating food sacrificed to idols and by committing sexual immorality.'[2]"

This brought looks of bewilderment to the faces of many in the church. Balaam? There was no one of that name teaching in the church. However, a few – those who were more familiar with the Jewish Scriptures and who could link it to the reference to food sacrificed to idols – knew where the finger was pointing. To make it abundantly clear to everyone, Loukas continued reading.

" 'Likewise you also have those who hold to the teaching of the Nicolaitans.'[3]"

There was an immediate sensation. Several people jumped up indignantly and started talking loudly, so Loukas had to raise his voice to continue.

1 Rev. 2:13.
2 Rev. 2:14.
3 Rev. 2:15.

" 'Repent therefore! Otherwise, I will soon come to you and will fight against them with the sword of my mouth.'[1]"

That was as far as he could get.

"How dare you criticise us!" someone shouted from the side of the room.

"But idols are nothing!" someone else shouted. "So the great teacher Paulos wrote."[2]

"He also said do not participate with demons!" someone else retorted.[3]

"Brothers, brothers!" The leader of the church, a man by the name of Silas, was attempting to restore order. "We are here to listen to this letter from Ioanneis himself. Have you so quickly forgotten his love for us? If he writes this, then it must be for our own good."

"What does he know?" The man who had called out from the side of the room stepped forward. His name, Loukas learned afterwards, was Rufus. "Ioanneis has never been a member of a guild, so he has no idea of the pressure we have been under. Nicolaus showed us the way through."

Rufus turned around and faced the people. "We all know that Zeus is not a real god! What does it matter if we eat meat that was offered on his altar?"

There were some cheers at this, but also quite a few shaking of heads.

"And the Emperor:" continued Rufus, a lot quieter, as if he did not wish to be overheard, "we know he is only a man. How can it possibly matter if we just go along with the

1 Rev. 2:16.
2 1 Cor. 8:4.
3 1 Cor. 10:20.

crowd and say with our lips that he is a god? No one really believes he is! And if it means we are able to continue living and working…"

"No," shouted Hermas. There was a stunned silence, and all eyes turned to face him, including Loukas, who was wondering what his friend wanted to say. Hermas was immediately embarrassed, for he had not meant to speak aloud. He had just wanted Loukas to continue reading the rest of the scroll, for as they had discussed together on the road, the answer was in there.

"No," he said again, this time more quietly. "There is another way through. Yes, there will be persecutions. There have been in the past" – here, he glanced at Antipas' widow – "and undoubtedly there will be more to come. I for one know this only too well, since I am a member of the guild of weavers. I know what it will mean for me if I do not participate in their feasts. But compromising our faith is not the answer! The answer is… well, it's in this scroll if you will only listen to it."

There was a long silence. Loukas gazed with pride at his friend who had clearly absorbed the contents of the scroll and was prepared to live it out, despite knowing what it could cost him. Then, taking up the scroll, he made as if to start reading again.

Suddenly, Rufus started walking through the crowd to the door at the rear of the room. Many of his fellow Nicolaitans were quick to follow. There was a deep irony, though, as Loukas continued reading from where he had left off.

" 'He who has an ear, let him hear what the Spirit says to the churches.' "

As the last of the dissenters departed, Loukas looked around at those who remained and smiled at them warmly. " 'To him who overcomes, I will give him some of the hidden manna. I will also give him a white stone with a new name written on it, known only to him who receives it.'[1]"

Loukas knew that the people gathered in that small room would soon be living in fear of what Rome would do to them should they obey what Iēsus through his prophet Ioanneis was asking them to do. And he knew that they would be asking themselves, 'Was potential martyrdom worth such rewards?' But what rewards! Instead of the polluted idol meat, Iēsus was offering them manna from heaven; and the white stone was an engraved invitation to the messianic banquet!

Yet there was more to it than mere rewards. Ioanneis was trying to tell them something more: something about the effect those martyrdoms would have on their very persecutors. Loukas kept reading…

On the train to Nizhny Novgorod – November, AD 2005

Dima was silent as he stared out the window of the speeding train at the desolate white of the snowy landscape rushing past. Occasionally, an isolated *dacha* could be seen, smoke unwillingly emerging from its chimney, dissipating rapidly in the harsh, freezing wind. Natasha sat next to him,

1 Rev. 2:17.

reading a book. Dima had brought a couple of books with him too, but he had had enough reading. The more he read, the more frustrated he was becoming.

He had wanted to understand what the eleventh chapter of Revelation was all about. Dr. Williams had allowed him to borrow a copy of G. B. Caird's commentary on the book of Revelation, the one Yevgeny had so highly recommended. Then, to get a differing opinion, he had also got hold of a copy of *The Morning Comes And Also The Night*, by Byron MacDonald. After reading a little of both, Dima decided it could not have been more of a differing opinion. It was hard to comprehend how two people could approach the same passage of the Bible and yet arrive at such different conclusions.

Admittedly, that particular chapter of Revelation could not be more difficult to understand at first glance. It starts out with John being told to measure the temple of Jerusalem, but not the outer court, since it has been given over to the Gentiles who will trample it and the rest of Jerusalem for 42 months. Then comes the two witnesses, who prophesy for 1260 days – which is the same as saying 42 months if you go by months of 30 days. They are protected by God, who kills any who try to harm them with fire from heaven, while they themselves have miraculous powers: they can prevent rain from falling on the earth, and they can turn water into blood and also strike the earth with every kind of plague.

Then after they finish testifying the Beast that comes up out of the Abyss kills them. But what Beast? This creature is not properly described until chapter thirteen, so John is getting ahead of himself slightly. Then, after three and a half days, the two witnesses are resurrected and are whisked off to heaven in full view of their enemies. This ushers in an earthquake that kills 7000 people which concludes what John calls the second woe.

Simple, really, thought Dima sarcastically.

Dima had started with Byron MacDonald. Recognising the similarity of the description of the miraculous powers of these two witnesses with certain key Old Testament figures, he notes that perhaps these two men are actually Moses and Elijah, Moses representing the law and Elijah the prophets. But he does not push this point, emphasising rather that the two men fulfil the prophecy of Zechariah chapter four. But there is no doubt in his mind that the two witnesses are two particular individuals.

More importantly, these two witnesses have one job to do: to testify to the Jewish people and to warn the nations of the world of the impending judgment of God; and they are the only ones able to do this, since all the Christians have previously disappeared in the Rapture – whatever that might be, since that word does not appear in the book of Revelation. Perhaps because of their miraculous powers, many Jews respond. (This comes from a jump backwards to Revelation 7 and the 144,000 described there.) Others around the world, watching on TV and the Internet, also respond, but are persecuted. Byron MacDonald makes an amazing claim at this point: "These are part of the reason Revelation is written with such detail given of these seven years. Revelation will become their survival guide, as parts of it speak directly to them…"[1] Dima could not help thinking what the poor people who had first received this book from John must have thought of those parts that were apparently intended for people undergoing persecution in some far future time after the Rapture of the church.

Byron MacDonald then appears to link all the plagues associated with the seven trumpets as emanating from the two witnesses, despite the fact that, apart from the seventh trumpet, these occur before the two witnesses arrive on the scene.

Then, after the 1260 days / 42 months / 3 and a half years, Satan is finally removed from Heaven, cast down to earth as it says in Revelation 12:9. And since the 144,000 have all responded, the two witnesses suddenly lose their divine protection and are summarily killed. The inhabitants of the earth celebrate, but not for long, since the two witnesses are resurrected and an earthquake strikes Jerusalem killing 7,000 people. And when Satan tries to attack the 144,000 Jewish Christians, God moves them all off into the desert, as it says in Revelation 12:13-17.

Dima was mainly dizzy from all the jumping around in Revelation. If Byron MacDonald was right, then John had not been very logical, let alone chronological, in his presentation of future events.

But *was* Byron MacDonald correct? Was there an alternative approach? Well, if G. B. Caird's commentary was anything to go by, there certainly was.

1 Byron MacDonald, *The Morning Comes And Also The Night*, (Xlibris Corporation, 2001), 178.

Like Byron MacDonald, G. B. Caird was quick to recognise references to the Old Testament. However, unlike the other writer, he then tried to see if the Old Testament echoes threw any light on such a cryptic passage. Who are the two witnesses? Well, John explicitly refers to them as "two olive trees". This image comes from Zechariah 4, and is explained in verse 14 of that chapter as "the two anointed ones", Zerubbabel the anointed king and Joshua the anointed priest. But who in New Testament times can be described as a Christian king and a Christian priest? All believers, according to Rev. 1:6, 5:10; but especially Christian martyrs, according to Rev. 3:12, 21 and 20:6.

This identification is further supported when John also refers to them as "two lamp stands". The lamp stands had already appeared in the first chapter of Revelation, and were explained there as referring to the seven churches and by extension the whole church. Instead of seeing this as singling out two particular churches out of the seven, Caird concluded that the two lamps are a proportion of the church in all parts of the world.

In stark contrast to the literal approach of Byron MacDonald, G. B. Caird interpreted the "fire from their mouths" as the word of their testimony as they defend themselves in the Roman court of law. The reference to stopping rain alludes to Elijah (1 Kings 17:1), and the turning water to blood alludes to Moses (Ex. 7:17). These actions are not supposed to be seen as vindictive. They are supposed to lead people to repentance just like the plagues associated with the seven trumpets.

What, then, is "the great city"? John *explicitly* tells us he is using figurative language when he calls it Sodom – a symbol of vice – and Egypt – a symbol of tyranny. And while the place of Jesus' death was literally Jerusalem, *figuratively* John is referring to Rome since the Romans were responsible for the crucifixion. Rome, then, is the current embodiment of Babylon most especially when it attacks the Christian church through martyrdom.

But of greatest importance is that the witnesses are resurrected: God vindicates them in the sight of their enemies. And this vindication *is* the consequent earthquake, an Old Testament symbol for the overthrowing of an ungodly political order, that destroys part of the city, and which leads to the conversion of many people, mentioned in Revelation 11:18.

So G. B. Caird saw the section detailing the fate of the two witnesses as fitting into the wider context of the seven trumpets. After six trumpets had sounded, the peoples of the world had not responded in repentance despite God allowing evil to intensify on earth. So John interrupts his sequence of trumpets to explain to the prospective martyrs how indispensable is their witness to the consummation of the redemptive purposes of God. In other words, chapter 11 would have taught the original recipients of the letter that the persecution of the church is the secret weapon by which God intends to win his victory over the church's persecutors and to achieve his purposes of redemption.

Dima put the books down with a sigh. Basically whenever Byron MacDonald interpreted something literally G. B. Caird interpreted it metaphorically. So who was right?

Dima's gut reaction was that G. B. Caird was. It just held together better. It made more sense within the context of the book as a whole. And he could imagine someone in the first century reading Revelation and finding in it the reason for standing firm in the face of persecution.

Suddenly, in a moment of recklessness, Dima stood up and opened the window. There was an immediate icy blast that started the pages of Natasha's book fluttering.

"What are you doing?" Natasha cried out, as Dima flung the Byron MacDonald book out the window with as much force as he could muster. When it was gone, he slammed the window shut and sat back down, rubbing his hands together in an attempt to get the circulation going again.

"I made an interpretive decision," he replied, cryptically.

It was then that he remembered that the book that was even now collecting snow in some rail-side ditch had been borrowed from Dr. Williams. With a grimace, he realised he would have some explaining to do when they returned to St. Petersburg.

❧

Between Pergamum and Thyatira – July, AD 93

Loukas and his friends set off from Pergamum as soon as it was light. They had been staying in a small room of one of the richer members of the church. This man, Terlios by name, operated a vineyard not far from the walls of the city. So as soon as the gates were opened, Loukas, Hermas and Artemas climbed up onto Terlios' wagon with the chief steward of the vineyard and headed through the gates of

Pergamum to all intents and purposes Terlios' vineyard workers. Thus disguised they went completely unnoticed by the Roman guard.

Once the wagon arrived at the vineyard, they waved farewell to the steward – also a member of the church – and set off in the direction of Thyatira. They had a good way to go before night fell, so they set off cheerfully enough along the wide and well-made Roman road. Loukas walked a little ahead of the other two. He was lost in his thoughts, pondering the varying reactions of people to the scroll of Ioanneis. He had been saddened by the reaction of the Nicolaitans but not surprised. After all, these people were only trying to find a way through the difficult times. It was just unfortunate that the way they had settled on completely compromised their faith in Iēsus. But on the other hand there were people like Terlios: prepared to uphold his belief in the ultimate lordship of Iēsus to the exclusion of all others, especially an upstart human with divine pretensions. Terlios would not compromise. He was prepared to die if the Romans so chose to punish him for refusing to offer worship to Domitianus.

Thinking about Terlios reminded Loukas of his father. He wondered briefly how he was coping with the mammoth task of organising trade between fellow Christians unable to trade using the normal channels. Suddenly, he wished he was back in Ephesus, helping his father in the work, able to encourage his family through the persecution to come.

And Iounia. How he missed her! Picturing her brought a smile to his face and tears to his eyes.

"Halt!"

The voice was harsh and commanding. With a start, Loukas realised he had walked straight into a Roman patrol. He had been so lost in his reverie that he had not been keeping much of an eye out for potential trouble. As he turned to his friends he became aware that they were not there: he was on his own and he was carrying the scroll.

"Who are you and where are you from?" The leader of the patrol was a burly man with dark bushy eyebrows. He looked as though he had seen much fighting, with noticeable facial scars.

"Please, sir, my name is Loukas and I am from Ephesus." Again, Loukas figured it was safest to stick with the truth as much as possible.

"Really?" the man answered with a sneer. "You are a long way from home then. This road will neither lead you to or from Ephesus, so where are you bound and what is your purpose?"

At this point Loukas was unsure whether to lie or tell the truth, but for every split second he delayed answering he knew it would look more and more like a lie.

"I am heading to Thyatira. My father wishes me to investigate the market there. He is seeking new sources of merchandise."

Loukas could tell the man was listening attentively to what he said but was paying still closer attention to the way he said it.

"Very well," said the burly man.

Loukas must have made some sort of involuntary response of relief. Perhaps he relaxed his shoulders or made a barely audible outward breath. Whatever it was the leader of the patrol noticed.

"Wait," he said, softly. "You say you are headed to Thyatira, and you are on the road from Pergamum. You say you are from Ephesus, so you must have been through Smyrna. I need to search your belongings."

He was looking closely at Loukas' face as he said this, but Loukas had regained his composure and was giving nothing away. If the Romans wanted to search them, his face and relaxed body stance said, they were welcome to. Inside, though, Loukas' mind was racing, trying to remember which part of the letter the scroll was currently wound to. He had not really checked it when he had received it back from the Pergamum church's scribe, just placed it back in its special cover and then into his bag.

"Be my guest," he replied calmly, placing his bag on the ground and stepping away.

The patrol leader opened the bag and immediately pulled out the scroll in its cover. It was, after all, the only item of interest in the bag.

"Well, well, what is this and why do you have it?" The man seemed incapable of asking just one question at a time.

"Just some light reading for the journey," replied Loukas hoping that would answer both questions at once. After a slight pause, he said: "You can take a look if you wish."

"I intend to," said the man, sharply. He pulled the scroll roughly out of its cover and unwound the scroll a little thereby revealing a column of characters.

"Well, let's see. It's in Greek which makes it easier." Loukas had guessed from the man's dark complexion that he was not a Roman who would be more familiar with Latin. Desperately trying not to appear too concerned, Loukas wondered what the man would be able to read. He did not have to wait.

" 'Then I saw another beast coming out of the earth. He had two horns like a lamb, but he spoke like a dragon…' "

There were titters from the other members of the Roman patrol.

" 'He exercised all the authority of the first beast on his behalf, and made the earth and its inhabitants worship the first beast whose fatal wound had been healed…' But this is nonsense!" he exclaimed, as the patrol started laughing. The burly man wound the scroll on a little further before reading again. " '…No one could buy or sell unless he had the mark, which is the name of the beast or the number of his name. This calls for wisdom. If anyone has insight, let him calculate the number of the beast, for it is a man's number. His number is six hundred and sixty six.'[1] This doesn't call for wisdom! It is nonsense pure and simple." He began to put the scroll back in its cover, but appeared to want to get rid of it faster, so just handed it all over to Loukas.

"Well, kid," he said in a voice that was more kindly than he had used before, "I am afraid I don't think much of your choice of reading material. On your way!"

With that, he and the rest of the patrol continued on their way towards Pergamum leaving Loukas standing alone on the road, carefully rolling the scroll up before placing it back in its cover again. Turning to face Thyatira, he silently offered heartfelt thanks to God for protecting him and the

1 Rev. 13:11, 17–18.

scroll. He was also glad that Ioanneis had not written the scroll in plainer terms. After all, if the leader of the Roman patrol had known what Ioanneis had meant, Loukas could well have been arrested on the spot.

Loukas was just wondering whether he should continue on his own when Hermas and Artemas appeared somewhat sheepishly from behind a thicket of trees near the left side of the road.

"Loukas! Are you all right?" asked Hermas.

"Yes, I'm fine. What happened to you two?"

"Well," said Artemas, "We heard the patrol coming, but you were too far ahead of us. If we had called to warn you they would have heard us and known we were there."

"We're sorry, Loukas," said Hermas.

"Don't worry. It has turned out fine for us all. Perhaps if they had stopped all three of us things may have turned out differently. As it was, they appear to have found a travelling salesman with a scroll of nonsense."

"Do you mean that Roman read Ioanneis' scroll?" asked Hermas with his eyes wide.

"He wasn't a Roman, but yes, he did," replied Loukas. "He even read the part that speaks directly about him: a part of the beast from the earth. And he read the number."

Artemas and Hermas were unable to speak.

"It's all right," laughed Loukas. "Not everyone knows who six hundred and sixty six refers to! He didn't know what he was reading. If he had he would never have let me go on my way. However, we do need to be more careful. We can't afford to be picked up by someone with a better head for numbers."

By this time they were walking again towards Thyatira. They would not get there that night, but Loukas knew a place where they might be able to stay the night. It was already getting dark when they finally stumbled wearily into a little road-side hamlet, whose only reason for existence, it appeared, was to provide service to hungry travellers. It was only because he was looking for it that Loukas located the small outline of a fish carved into a mud brick in the wall of a ramshackle house on the outskirts of the hamlet.

"Here we are," he said to his friends. "We will be safe here."

He knocked on the door. After a moment, he caught a flicker of movement in a window to his right, but turning towards it he could see nothing more. Then the door opened quickly.

"Come in, come in," said a man quietly. "Quick, before anyone sees you."

Loukas, Hermas and Artemas hurried inside, and found themselves in a very small house with an old man and his wife.

"Loukas, son of Theseus, we have been expecting you," the old man said gravely.

"Abram Bar Iudah, it has been a long time," replied Loukas with a smile. "Greetings to you, and to your family. May I introduce to you my friends Hermas and Artemas."

"Welcome to our humble home," said Abram, warmly giving each of them in turn a double-handed shake.

"You say you were expecting us?" asked Artemas.

"Yes, indeed," replied Abram seriously. "I am afraid you are being sought by the authorities."

"The Romans?" asked Hermas. "They had Loukas today but let him go. They can't be seeking us too carefully."

Abram looked shocked to hear their news. "Well, perhaps they didn't know it was you that they are seeking, but they are seeking you nonetheless. You see there have been outbreaks of what the authorities are calling civil rebellion. These outbreaks have so far been localised to Ephesus and Smyrna, but it appears that there have been more and more cases of people who are refusing to perform the rites before the statue of the emperor. And the Romans are looking for whoever is responsible for spreading such sedition. And that *is* you three, unless I am very much mistaken."

There was a stunned silence. Eventually, Loukas spoke: "We are not even half way and already it looks as though it will be impossible to finish."

" 'Whatever is impossible for man is possible for God,' " quoted Abram with a smile.[1]

Loukas smiled, too. "You are right. We are in God's hands, indeed." Then turning to his friends, he exclaimed, "By the way, did you know that Abram used to live in Jerusalem?"

The smile slowly faded from the old man's face.

"Yes, it's true. I used to live in Ephesus, too, you see. So Loukas and I go way back. And, yes, I was in Jerusalem before…" Abram's voice cracked, and he could barely force the words out. "… before the sun was darkened and the moon faded away and the stars fell from the sky. But we had the word of Iēsus himself, that the unthinkable would happen *again*: that Jerusalem would fall. So we fled when we had the

1 Luke 18:27.

chance. But I cannot bear to recall the glory of the city and its temple and know that not one stone now rests upon another…"

Loukas placed his arm around the old man's shoulders. "Abram, my brother, there will be a new Jerusalem one day. Let me describe it to you." Then taking out the scroll, Loukas wound it through to near the end and began reading:

" 'Then I saw a new heaven and a new earth, for the first heaven and the first earth had passed away, and there was no longer any sea. I saw the Holy City, the new Jerusalem, coming down out of heaven from God, prepared as a bride beautifully dressed for her husband. And I heard a voice from the throne saying, 'Now the dwelling of God is with men, and he will live with them and be their God. He will wipe every tear from their eyes. There will be no more death or mourning or crying or pain, for the old order of things has passed away.'[1]"

Abram's eyes were still full of tears, but he was smiling again.

"So this is the scroll that is causing so much trouble. I think you had better wind it back to the beginning and start again…"

Loukas sighed. It looked as though it was going to be a long night.

1 Rev. 21:1-4.

Nizhny Novgorod – November, AD 2005

"It's just not here!"

Dima slapped his hand on a bench located in one of the small sheds adjoining his grandmother's *dacha*. Assorted papers and broken bits and pieces of what must have once been a highly complicated engine went flying. Ice crystals dropped off the windows of the shed, and outside, birds startled by the sudden noise flew off through the forest calling anxiously.

Natasha sighed. "I think you are right," she said, resignedly. "We really have looked everywhere this time."

"So what do we do now?"

Natasha looked around at the disordered piles of books and old Communist newspapers, boxes of ancient car-parts and empty jam jars.

"Let's go inside and get warmed up. I think it might even be time to eat."

Dima was rubbing the hand he had slapped the bench with. The cold had made it hurt rather more than he had anticipated, so Natasha's suggestion was very agreeable.

They left the shed, Dima locking the door with a large and very rusty iron padlock, then made their way through the snow-covered garden to the back door of the *dacha*. Dima's grandmother, Nadezhda, was in the kitchen as they came in, cooking up some soup with some of the year's last fresh vegetables. It smelt good, but was, more importantly, piping hot.

"Is it ready?" asked Dima, impatiently.

"Nearly, dear," replied Nadezhda, with a smile. "Now, I can tell from your expressions that you did not find what you were looking for?"

"Yes, that's right," replied Natasha, getting in before Dima slapped something else. "I'm afraid there is no sign of the missing piece of parchment."

Nadezhda ladled some soup into three bowls and Natasha carried them over to the table where Dima was sitting, dejectedly resting his head in his hands. When the three of them were seated at the table, Nadezhda prayed a blessing over the food and they began to eat.

"I certainly don't remember any such thing," said Nadezhda sadly. "Still, I didn't know about the scroll, either. I guess they were deliberately kept hidden from prying eyes."

"That's a good point," said Dima, taking a slice of rye bread from the plate in the centre of the table. "If the authorities had got their hands on them they would have destroyed them immediately."

Nadezhda nodded, but she was frowning.

"*Babushka*," asked Dima, "what's wrong?"

Nadezhda was silent for a while, aimlessly stirring her soup. Dima's words had stirred some unpleasant memories. Eventually, she spoke. "I'm not sure if you knew this, but I was brought up as a Christian."

Dima almost dropped his piece of bread into his soup. "Really? I had no idea."

"Yes," replied Nadezhda, sadly. "It's true. We were Christians; at least my parents were until things started getting very difficult for them. I can only dimly recall attending a church service in our town. I must have been only five or six at the time, and I didn't really understand any of it. And then they closed the church. It was turned into a salami factory, I think. But my father would tell us children stories from the Bible as he put us to bed. There we all were – four of us in the bed, squeezed in top to tail – eyes wide as we heard about David's narrow escapes from an insane King Saul; or about the men of Jerusalem rebuilding the walls with one hand while carrying a bow in the other. Of course, the best stories were about Jesus. I loved hearing about the way he would heal people, how he would eat with the outcasts, and especially how he cared for little children.

"But then, when my father disappeared…" She stopped, the sudden thickening of her throat preventing further speech. Blinking back the tears, she took a deep breath and continued. "Well, let's just say it took all of my strength to hold onto what my father had told me. I grew up a good communist to all intents and purposes. We worked on a collective farm, singing patriotic songs as we swung our scythes. But deep within, I cherished a tiny spark of rebellion: I still believed in Jesus. I never once saw a Bible during all those years. But I remembered the stories my father had told, and they kept me going."

She paused. Dima and Natasha were staring at her, their soup and bread quite forgotten.

"I had no idea," said Dima eventually.

"No, well, I tried a few times to tell my children those same stories, but my husband – your grandfather, Dima – didn't like it. It wasn't that he was an atheist; he was just plain scared. Scared that I would disappear one day like my father had."

Natasha suddenly smiled at Nadezhda. "But now that times have changed? You attend church now, don't you?"

"Yes, that tiny spark was not entirely extinguished, and it has been fanned into a flame these last few years. And Dima, I have been praying for your father and also for little Vityenka." Dima had a difficult moment connecting this particular diminutive to his far-from-diminutive Uncle Victor.

They continued eating the soup for a few minutes in silence.

Finally, Dima spoke. "I wish you had had a copy of Revelation, *Babushka*. It would have helped you through those long years of persecution."

"Really?" asked Nadezhda. "I didn't know it was about that."

"Yes," replied Dima. "It's all about remaining firm in the face of strong opposition; that, in the end, God will have the victory over the persecutors and that those who stay true to Him will be vindicated and rewarded."

"Well," said Nadezhda after a while, "I guess that is true for me. The authorities were overthrown, and now I can attend church again in peace. And seeing *your* faith, Dima, is a reward in itself."

Dima blushed.

"And as for that missing parchment: if anything turns up I will let you know."

"Thanks, *Babushka*," replied Dima with a smile.

Thyatira – July, AD 93

It had taken Loukas and his two friends a lot longer than normal to get to Thyatira. Unable to use the main road for fear of entanglements with Roman patrols, they had had to make their way across country, using tracks when there were tracks that were heading their way, breaking out over the rocky countryside when there were none. It had been hot, thirsty work, but there had been a few streams along the way in which they had quenched their thirst and dampened their clothing in order to mitigate the effects of the sun.

As the day wore on, and their breakfast with Abram and his wife was nothing but a dim memory, hunger became more of a problem. Then, just as the sun was preparing for its descent behind the rim of the world, they came up over a rocky hill, and looked down upon the town of Thyatira, still quite a distance away across a wide fertile plain chequered with small farms and fields.

Thyatira was a growing city. It had had a difficult history, however. Because of its vulnerable location in a wide valley devoid of defensive possibilities, Thyatira had been overtaken by whichever army happened to be in the ascendancy at the time. As such, it had passed from one empire to the next. In some ways, this had not affected the every-day life of the people; they were happy to buy and sell from anyone. Consequently, trade was far more important than politics, and this had led to the establishment of many trade and craftsmen guilds that had more recently flourished under the *Pax Romana*. In particular, the Thyatiran metallurgists were renowned for having mastered the art of making fine brass, by combining copper with pure zinc metal, the distillation of which was a closely-guarded trade secret.

There was some traffic on the road leading into the city, people returning from their fields, mostly. Loukas, Artemas and Hermas joined a group and made their way through the gates without attracting any unwanted attention. Once inside, Loukas made his way to the house of a family friend, one of his father's old trading partners. He had been welcoming, but not overly so; they had been given some food and shown a place to sleep.

Once they had eaten, Loukas sent Hermas off to make contact with the church. While they waited, Loukas sat quietly, wondering how the scroll would be received this time. Having read the scroll many times, he was well aware of the strong words he would soon be reading out to the church. He also wondered whether he would recognise 'Jezebel' if she happened to be there.

Hermas came back after a while to inform them that the church would come together the very next day. Knowing that he had a lot of reading to do, Loukas went to bed.

He need not have wondered: in the end it was blatantly obvious who 'Jezebel' was. They had been taken early to the house where the church was to gather, so they had had a good opportunity to see everyone as they came in. Those who had already arrived were talking quietly amongst themselves, every so often glancing Loukas' way, although they were probably looking more at the scroll he held carefully in his lap.

Suddenly, without any noticeable signal, a hush had come over the crowd, and a small, worried-looking man had entered, followed by a beautiful woman, dressed in some of the richest clothes Loukas had ever seen. The man had made his way over to where the men were sitting; the woman, after giving Loukas a piercing and decidedly uncomfortable stare, glided up the back to the place where the women sat, where she was given the prime seat.

This appeared to be the impetus to begin. One of the elders stood up to pray and then he had nodded to Loukas. Loukas had the scroll ready, so he began to read.

" 'The revelation of Iēsus Christos, which God gave him to show his servants what must soon take place…' "

It was very strange. Loukas felt that everyone in the room was focused not on the scroll, but on the beautiful woman's reactions to the scroll. If she nodded and smiled at the description of Iēsus, then they did too. But Loukas could sense the delay.

In fact, he was finding it difficult to read. He kept wanting to look up and see if *she* was watching him. He knew the words quite well now, so when he did look up from the scroll, of course she *was* watching him. Perhaps she was the only one in the room doing so; everyone else was watching her. But her gaze was disconcerting. It was worse than the sun that had beat down on them all day yesterday as they had traversed the rocky hills. There was something in the way her beautiful mouth curled up at the edges in the semblance of a smile. She really was beautiful; he could not deny it, despite all his feelings for Iounia.

There was only one point where the members of the church reacted without reference to the beautiful woman. It was in the description of Iēsus, when Ioanneis described his feet 'like bronze glowing in a furnace'. Ioanneis had used the very word that the Thyatiran metallurgists had coined to refer to their special brass. Loukas sensed a murmur of pleasure from a few, presumably metal workers who well knew the brightness of this particular metal when it is heated in a furnace.

Then, just to drive the point home further, Ioanneis used the same word again in the part of the letter written just for them:

" 'To the angel of the church in Thyatira write: These are the words of the Son of God, whose eyes are like blazing fire and whose feet are like burnished bronze. I know your deeds, your love and your faith, your service and perseverance, and that you are now doing more than you did at first.'[1]"

At each compliment, *she* had nodded her head knowingly, as though she was taking credit for them personally.

" 'Nevertheless, I have this against you…' "

Loukas felt his voice falter slightly. He took a deep breath and continued.

" 'You tolerate that woman Jezebel, who calls herself a prophetess.'[2]"

1 Rev. 2:18-19.
2 Rev. 2:20a.

There was an audible indrawing of breath on the part of many members of the congregation. But the woman herself did not bat an eyelid. Her smile remained fixed on her face, although Loukas was aware that the nodding had stopped.

" 'By her teaching she misleads my servants into sexual immorality and the eating of food offered to idols. I have given her time to repent of her immorality, but she is unwilling. So I will cast her on a bed of suffering, and I will make those who commit adultery with her suffer intensely, unless they repent of her ways. I will strike her children dead. Then all the churches will know that I am he who searches hearts and minds, and I will repay each of you according to your deeds. Now I say to the rest of you in Thyatira, to you who do not hold to her teachings and have not learned Satan's so-called deep secrets, I will not impose any other burden on you. Only hold on to what you have until I come.'[1]"

Loukas had been quite prepared for a walkout, such as had occurred in the church in Pergamum. He had not been prepared for a wall of silence. The beautiful woman just sat there, staring at Loukas, that perpetual smile goading him to respond in some way. He tore his eyes away and willed them to focus on the words of the scroll.

" 'To him who overcomes and does my will to the end, I will give authority over the nations – He will rule them with an iron sceptre; he will dash them to pieces like pottery – just as I have received authority from my Father. I will also give

---

1 Rev. 2:20b-25.

him the morning star. He who has an ear, let him hear what the Spirit says to the churches.'[1]"

Somehow, Loukas kept reading. He knew that many of the people listening to him would reject the message, simply because this woman would reject it. She called herself a prophetess, but clearly she was not speaking any words from God, not if God had inspired Ioanneis to write the scroll. And Loukas trusted Ioanneis.

There must be some in the church that were listening, and for that faithful remnant, Loukas read on. Afterwards, when Loukas finished reading and had begun to wind the scroll back to the beginning, the beautiful woman had simply stood up, and quietly left the room, this time followed by the small, worried man, and quite a few other members of the congregation.

One of the elders of the church, a man by the name of Apollos, came over to Loukas and his friends. "Thank-you, Loukas," he said softly. "Thank-you for reading Ioanneis' scroll. It has much to say to us."

Loukas glanced over in the direction the woman had left; Apollos noticed.

"Yes, that was our prophetess," Apollos said with a sigh. "Her name isn't Jezebel, by the way. It's Dorkas, and she's from the wealthy Hargas family. Dealers in purple cloth, which explains the wealth. But her followers refer to her as 'The One Who Hears', which is all very mysterious, and not a little pretentious, if you ask me. Basically, she claims to receive special knowledge from God."

"What sort of knowledge?" asked Hermas.

1 Rev. 2:26-29.

"Well, all sorts of things. She has revealed hidden sins in a few people in the church, some of which were later confirmed. That was a bit scary, actually. Had even me worried that God would bring to light some horrible sin that I hadn't done." Apollos was smiling as he said this. "She has occasionally shared an encouraging word during our gatherings."

"That doesn't seem too bad," Loukas said, frowning. "Perhaps Ioanneis went too far?"

At this Apollos shook his head. "Oh no," he replied. "Ioanneis was absolutely correct. At least one of her deep secrets is truly not from God: she has been teaching that participation in the guild feasts is allowable for Christians."

"Oh, not that again," exclaimed Artemas. "The Nicolaitans were teaching that in Pergamum."

"So I have heard, and this scroll confirmed it. Yes, I think she is considered one of their leaders."

"So, she is not actually encouraging sexual immorality?" asked Hermas.

"No," answered Apollos. "But just as Jezebel seduced Ahab and the rest of Israel into worshipping the Canaanite gods, this woman is seducing members of the church into worshipping Satan through their participation in these temple feasts. And idolatry is a form of immorality when the church is supposed to be the bride of Christos."

There was silence for a while, and then Apollos spoke again. "However, this letter from Ioanneis has also convicted me. We have allowed Dorkas to remain within the church, even though we knew that what she was advocating was not right. I believe the time has come to confront her directly. If she is willing to repent, then so be it. But, if she will not listen to the voice of Iēsus speaking to her through a *true* prophet then she will be excommunicated. I have no wish to suffer intensely with her in her bed of suffering…"

Loukas smiled quietly to himself. It looked like the immediate future of this church would not be easy, but they would make it in the end. The heresy of syncretism would not continue to find a foothold here.

⁊

St. Petersburg – January, AD 2006

It was the opening seconds of New Years Day. Dima, Natasha and Marina were standing out in the cold, their winter coats wrapped tightly around their bodies, hats pulled down warmly over their ears, as a little way off Yevgeny stooped over to light the fuse of some fireworks. He was apparently successful, for he came jogging over to them, before quickly turning around to watch. All around them the sound of Russians ushering in the New Year could be seen and heard. And then, their own contribution was added to the light and noise: one after the other, more than a dozen brilliant balls of fire were shot high into the air above them before exploding into a million pieces of shimmering light accompanied by an electrifying and almost deafening sizzle. The last few seemed to speed up and the climax came as three went off almost simultaneously.

Dima realised he had been shouting "Hoorah!" as each firework had exploded, and suddenly he felt a little embarrassed. But no one seemed to have noticed. In fact, now he came to think about it, they had all been doing the same thing. Turning to Natasha, he gave her a big hug and a kiss. Then, he gave Marina and Yevgeny a hug and the traditional New Year greeting: "*S Novym godom!*"

With a shiver, Natasha exclaimed, "That's enough. Let's get inside!"

Everyone agreed. The temperature was around minus fifteen – not horribly cold, but cold enough. With the occasional flash of firework-light illuminating the path, they made their way across the snowy area in front of Dima & Natasha's building. Within a few minutes they were removing their coats inside their apartment, ready to drink something to warm themselves up again.

Once everyone had a cup of tea or coffee made to their exacting specifications, Yevgeny posed a question to everyone: "What are your plans for this new year?"

There was a brief silence as everyone started thinking of something deep and profound to say. From outside could be heard the muffled bangs as the impromptu and unofficial fireworks display continued.

Marina was first.

"I am looking forward to the birth of our first child," she said, simply.

This was news; Natasha leapt up, shrieking excitedly, to give Marina a special hug while Dima solemnly shook Yevgeny's hand.

"Congratulations," he said to Yevgeny.

"Thanks," he replied. "I, too, am looking forward to that occasion. It will bring many changes to us as a couple, but nothing we cannot face with God's help and presence. It is also hard to separate a man from his work, so I am also looking forward to seeing what God will do in our church. We have much to be thankful for, but still many challenges to face."

Natasha was back in her seat by this time. "Well, we are not expecting any additions to our family just yet," she said, looking sideways at Dima with a smile. Then she looked rather serious. "Actually, I have been thinking about my parents recently. My father is drinking again, and my mother has basically kicked him out. They really need to become Christians, but I just can't see it happening, and I don't know what I can do. So I have been praying for them, and I want to visit them when I can." However, Natasha's parents lived in a town a few days train-ride from St. Petersburg, so a visit was a serious undertaking, one that did not occur too frequently.

"We will also pray for them," said Yevgeny, as Marina nodded beside him. "And for you."

It was now Dima's turn to speak.

"You all know that I have become rather obsessed by the book of Revelation." There was some laughter. "Well, I want to try and find a way of making the book more accessible to the church here in Russia. I'm not sure if I will write a book, or start a web site, or what. But I know that in the past, the church would really have benefited from having a proper understanding of Revelation. And who knows if the church may need it sometime in the future."

"Indeed," said Yevgeny, heartily. "And that reminds me! I have a little Christmas present for you." He got up, went over to his satchel and pulled out a present wrapped in cheery

Christmas paper. "Here, I thought you might find this interesting."

"Thanks," replied Dima, taking the present. He tore off the paper and found himself holding a book: *The Late Great Planet Earth* by Hal Lindsey.

"It's a bit of a classic," said Yevgeny. "Hal Lindsay wrote this book in 1970, in which he predicted that the return of Jesus would happen within about 40 years after 1948. As you may have noticed, Jesus didn't return in 1988, so Hal Lindsey has revised his book quite a few times since. What you are holding, though, is his first version, which makes for very interesting reading."

"Wow," said Dima, "How did you get hold of it?"

"Amazon.com," replied Yevgeny with a shrug.

"Well, thanks again," said Dima. "I look forward to reading it."

"And now," said Yevgeny, solemnly, "let's commit this year to God."

They all bowed their heads as Yevgeny prayed. All in all, it was a good way to start the year.

Pergamum – July, AD 93

Sergius Maximus sat with his head resting on his hands, deep in thought, staring at the document in front of him. It was yet another missive from Ephesus detailing the increasing signs of rebellion. Another apparent atheist, a man from a town not far from Ephesus, had refused to perform the sacred rites at the altar of Domitianus. The local authorities were holding him, awaiting further instructions. Well, he would write back and say the same as he had said every other time during these last few weeks: give the man one last chance to recant, and if he still refuses to pay homage to Caesar, then let him be executed as an example to other potential trouble-makers. Of course, the actual deed would need to be delayed until the proconsul could make his way to Ephesus to oversee proceedings, but without a recantation the end result was assured.

But something was troubling him. Looking back over his records, he could see a pattern. The first problems had occurred in Ephesus, and interestingly enough they had started not long after he had himself passed through the city. Then soon after that, Sextus Flavius, an old friend from their school days in Rome, had written from Smyrna to report a problem that had just occurred there. True, the details had been different, but the end result had been the same. In Smyrna, one of the Jewish leaders had denounced a number of people who had been attending the Jewish synagogue. This man had claimed that these people were not in fact Jews, and therefore should not be considered exempt from the sacred rites. When these people had been brought to the local temple, they had also refused to worship the emperor even when faced with death. Sergius had written back to Sextus commending him on his handling of the situation.

And now it was even happening here in Pergamum! Admittedly, a few of those who were brought before the courts recanted and performed the sacrifices, but there were still a few who had not. And they had been Roman citizens! But the proconsul had been quick to react. The sound of the heads of these atheists hitting the ground after being severed from their necks by the sword stroke of the executioner had been ringing in his ears for many days.

What was going on? Was there some hidden rebellion that was slowly making its way northward up the coast of Asia? Was there anything that could connect the three cities, something that would explain the pattern?

"Sergius Maximus!"

He jumped. A scribe had entered the room without him noticing and was standing in front of him.

"Yes, what is it?" he replied, somewhat more sharply than he had anticipated.

"The proconsul has summoned you," said the man, his face pale.

Sergius Maximus blinked, suddenly fearful. He had been looking forward to his new posting, but the proconsul had turned out to be a difficult master. Proconsuls in general were always worth avoiding; they were only ever in their position for a year, during which time they tried to gather as much wealth as they could for themselves. This particular proconsul was no different in that respect. But he was also a hard man, dangerously bordering on cruel, liable to respond quickly and sometimes rashly. It was never a pleasant experience to be in the same room with him, especially if you were the one he was conversing with. He wondered what had happened that had necessitated his immediate presence.

"Very well, I am on my way," said Sergius Maximus.

He got up, straightened his robes, and neatened the loose curls of his hair as well as he could. It paid to remove any possible distractions, just in case they resulted in a harsh word at the worst possible time. Then, he followed the scribe out of the room and along a corridor. They went outside, through an atrium in which a garden had been planted. As they passed by, Sergius Maximus caught the scent of some flowers that were making the most of the hot summer day.

Eventually they came to the offices of the proconsul. Here, the scribe stopped, obviously unwilling to enter if it was not truly necessary, and indicated the open doorway with a small gesture. Sergius Maximus took a deep breath and stepped within.

He found that he was not alone with the proconsul; there was a soldier standing in front of the man. So far so good: this could only serve to *dilute* the proconsul's attentions somewhat.

"Ah, Sergius Maximus! It has been too long," said the proconsul, languidly. He was reclining, lazily feasting on some roasted meats, his chubby fingers dripping with fat.

"Indeed, sir," replied Sergius Maximus. The other man, he now saw from his uniform, was a decurion. "You summoned me?"

"Yes, yes," the proconsul's eyes flicked sideways at the decurion. "I wanted you to hear the latest news from Smyrna."

The soldier took this as his cue. He began haltingly, but gained confidence as he continued to speak.

"Well, sirs, we have been hearing a little about the recent rebellions." Sergius Maximus was suddenly very alert. "At first we thought it was just confined to us, a local difficulty involving the Jews. But then we heard about Ephesus, and then more recently about the executions here in Pergamum.

And it reminded me of something I saw recently. Actually, it reminded me of someone.

"A couple of weeks ago, before the seditions began, I was on duty at the city's north gate. It was near the end of our night's shift that we stopped three young men for routine questioning. One of them said they were scouting out trade opportunities for his father, and that they were headed to Pergamum. One of my soldiers recognised the name of the trader in question – someone big in dates, apparently. I'm not sure what triggered my suspicion at the time. Maybe it was the slight pauses the boy made before answering the questions; maybe it was the way the three of them kept glancing at each other. Whatever it was, once they went on their way, I ran up onto the city walls and kept them in sight for as long as possible. When one of them looked back towards me, well, it was all I could do to keep myself from running after them and bringing them back for further questioning. But, when I stopped to think about it, guilty looks and thoughtful pauses just weren't reason enough to miss my breakfast."

The proconsul, clearly one who enjoyed the delights afforded by food, nodded heartily. Encouraged by this, the decurion continued.

"And then when we started hearing about the rebellions in Ephesus and Pergamum, well, it made me think."

"Why?" asked Sergius Maximus with a frown, "What had the boy to do with Ephesus?"

"Well, that's where he said he was from."

Sergius Maximus was suddenly thoughtful: someone from Ephesus, in Smyrna, on their way to Pergamum, all before the troubles started. It sounded very promising.

"Decurion," he asked sternly, "You said one of your men recognised the merchant's name. Do you recall it now?"

"Yes, sir," replied the soldier. "It was Theseus. It sort of stuck in my mind, what with my suspicions and all. And, of course, the original Theseus founded Smyrna!"

"Proconsul, I have no further questions," said Sergius Maximus. "This man can be relieved."

"Certainly. Soldier, to barracks. I will send for you if the need arises."

The decurion bowed to both men, first a long and respectful bow to the proconsul followed by a slight dip in Sergius Maximus' direction. When he had left the room, the proconsul asked, "Well, what do you make of it?"

"Sir, that soldier let slip through his fingers dangerous men. If my suspicions are correct then it appears that those are the very men who have been deliberately inciting rebellion, first in Ephesus, then in Smyrna and finally here in Pergamum. Who knows where they might be now."

"Did he, indeed?" replied the proconsul slyly, more concerned with the known omission of the decurion than the unknown rebels. "I will have him confined on a starvation diet. We'll see if he comes to regret that fateful breakfast! Thank-you, Sergius, you have been most helpful as usual. It was surely worthwhile having you transferred from Patmos."

It was then, with the mention of the name Patmos, that a light went on in Sergius Maximus' mind. Lucius, the son of a merchant! From Ephesus, and yet he had been here in

Pergamum not seven days ago! He had said that he had come from Ephesus, and you could not easily get here from there without passing through Smyrna. Could this be the one? He had been alone, but any companions could have been elsewhere in the city at the time.

All this passed through his mind in a flash.

"Sir," he said to the proconsul. "May I be excused? I need to set a few things in motion."

"As you wish. I leave this in your capable hands. If further sedition can be prevented then I can assure you, you will be rewarded. Oh, and send in that flunky as you go, would you?"

"Certainly, sir."

Sergius Maximus bowed, then took his leave. When he saw the messenger, it was Sergius' turn to make the small gesture. The man's face grew even paler, but he quickly went in to the proconsul. It clearly did not pay to keep the great man waiting too long.

As he hurried back to his room, he was mentally planning his next moves. First, of course, he would have Pergamum searched, in case Lucius was still in the city. He doubted this very much, though. This messenger of rebellion clearly had a plan of attack, a route whereby he would stir up the masses against the emperor. But where would he have gone? Further north? He would have to send out messages in a number of different directions just in case, with Lucius' name and description, as well as a description of his travelling companions. Oh, yes, he would need the decurion's help for that. He could also check if his description matched that of

Lucius. Perhaps it would be best to get to the decurion before the proconsul had started disciplinary actions…

Second, he would send a message through to Ephesus to arrest the date merchant Theseus. Maybe *he* would have something helpful to say.

❦

St. Petersburg – January, AD 2006

A week after the New Year celebrations, Dima and Natasha's phone rang.

"Can you get that?" Dima called out. He was trying to tape around the edge of their windows to stop the frigid air from coming in. He heard Natasha pick up the phone.

"*Allo…* Oh, hi Zhenya. How are you?… Yes, he's here. Is something wrong?… What?!?… No, I'll get him…Dima?"

But Dima was already by her side. He took the phone.

"Zhenya, it's Dima. What's wrong?"

"*Dima, someone has released the scroll on the Internet!*"

"What do you mean? Dr. Williams was planning on doing that at some point, I think, but he didn't mention anything the last time I saw him."

"*No, you don't understand. This isn't an official thing. There's been a leak.*"

"A leak?"

"*Yes, somehow someone must have got a hold of the scans. They have placed them on a web site, and they are providing 'commentary'. But, I use the word loosely…*"

"Zhenya, what is the site? I've got to check it out?"

"*You'll love this: www.ephesusscroll.com. Catchy, yes?*"

Dima had a mobile handset, so still holding the phone he sat down at his computer and started up a web browser.

"OK, I'm typing in the address…"

After pressing the Enter key, the web site quickly appeared; their ADSL connection was money well spent.

"Oh, goodness," he breathed.

It was slow going, reading the English text of the web site, but he could quickly see that the scans were in fact exactly like the ones he had received from Dr. Williams.

"*Do you see what they are claiming?*" asked Yevgeny. "*In the middle of the home page: they say these scans were taken from the original scroll of Revelation!*"

"But how could they know that!" exclaimed Dima.

"*That's not the worst of it: they also say that this copy of Revelation has annotations made by the author himself: extra clues as to the meaning of some of the symbols.*"

"But that's not true! There are no annotations, not if this is our scroll." Dima was puzzled and angry at the same time. "Maybe it's not ours after all."

Then, he noticed the caption in the title bar of the web browser: 'Scans and translations of the papyrus scroll of Revelation (Ephesus: April 1885)'

"Oh no, it *is* our scroll. There is no way anyone would pick a date for the scroll in 1885. You would use the date the scroll was originally written or the date it was found, and anyone claiming to have found a scroll now would use a modern date, surely! No, this is our scroll, and I think it came from *me*."

"*What?*"

"Look at the caption, Zhenya. Those are the very words Dr. Williams wrote on the DVD of scans just before he gave it to me, the DVD that was in my player when it was stolen! Someone must have checked out what was on the disc before throwing it away…"

"*A thief in the Metro recognised the importance of the scans?*"

"Look, I know it sounds a little dubious. But how else do you explain all this?"

"*I guess.*"

"Does Dr. Williams know yet?"

"*I haven't told him.*"

"Well, let me do it," said Dima wearily. "I want to hear his reaction."

"*All right, good talking to you Dima. Bye!*"

"Bye!"

After locating Dr. Williams' number, Dima called him up. When he heard about the web site, he was stunned. After calming down a little, he started thinking about what they should do in response.

"*What gets me so mad is that we were nearly ready with our own web site,*" Dr Williams said. "*I guess the time has come to announce the existence of the scroll. We have been granted permission to put it on display at the Hermitage in one of their special exhibit rooms. We were just liaising with the Russian Orthodox Church about the opening ceremony…*"

"Won't people be a little incredulous, since this web site has already claimed finding the scroll?"

"*Well, we have the scroll – they don't! So I think in the end there won't be any problems. But in the mean time, we will have to respond to their wild claims that the scroll has been annotated.*"

"Indeed!"

"*By the way, who do they identify as the Beast?*" asked Dr. Williams.

"Oh," replied Dima. "I haven't looked. Hold on a second…" He was sitting back in front of his computer again, so he quickly clicked around on the web site for a while until he found the right spot.

"Ah, here it is. They claim that in the margin next to Revelation 13:1 John also wrote 'the Antichrist who rules the church from Rome' so I am guessing they are not inclined towards the Catholic Church."

"*Well, Dima, as you well know there is no such annotation. In fact, the word 'Antichrist' does not appear in the book of Revelation at all. That is just one of the inaccuracies inherent in the pre-millennial interpretation of Revelation: they piece together parts of the Bible like it was a jigsaw puzzle. But they end up taking things out of context and forcing them into contexts in which they do not belong. The concept of 'Antichrist' comes from the letters of John where it refers to false teaching. In fact, the second letter talks of* many *'antichrists' – many false teachers at work in the church. I always find it ironic that when these people teach about the Antichrist in Revelation it actually makes them antichrists!*"

Dima chuckled. "Actually, I am reading Hal Lindsey's *Late, Great Planet Earth* at the moment."

"*And what do you make of it?*"

"Well, I'd sort of like to get together with you and Zhenya, if you have time. I would like to talk about it face to face."

"*Dima, I would be delighted. Name a time and place.*"

Sardis – July, AD 93

The journey to Sardis was actually uneventful. It was almost anticlimactic given the problems they had had with Romans on the previous legs. But just after the sun had passed its highest point in the sky, Loukas, Hermas and Artemas turned a corner in the road, and there in the distance before them was the stronghold of Sardis, built on a high plateau of crumbling white rock that jutted out from the side of a very steep hill. Only a narrow spit of land connected the plateau to the hill, making this stronghold almost impregnable. It towered over the rest of the town, which spread out across the plain beneath, trade roads disappearing into the distance in many directions.

In the entire history of the city the stronghold had only been taken twice. The first to do so had been Cyrus the Persian ruler, capturing King Croesus alive in the process. Indeed, some thought that he had even *rescued* the king from an attempted self-immolation. The second, and to date last, person to take the city had been Antiochus the Third. In both times, the city had fallen because of the negligence of the watchers on the walls; thinking that their stronghold was *entirely* impregnable, their complacency had been their downfall.

As they slowly approached the walls of the city, Loukas could not help but look up at the citadel and marvel. As they got closer he could even make out the signs of the great earthquake that had struck Sardis more than 70 years before: here, a cliff-face with marble blocks scattered about the base; there, a deep crack in the rock, carefully bricked over to prevent further subsidence. The town itself, once they had passed without incident through the barely guarded gates, was bustling with activity. The Agora was in full swing, with people loudly proclaiming the superiority of their products. Men carrying large swathes of material were haggling from within the deep folds of what they were selling, their faces almost completely obscured by the layers of cloth. Loukas and his friends made their way through the crowd, until they came to a small stall selling a variety of food-stuffs. It was manned by a good friend of Loukas' father, a man that Loukas and his family called Probus, essentially a Latin nick-name derived from his reputation of being a good man. Loukas had often made the journey from Ephesus to Sardis in order to assist with trade between the two men, money and goods exchanging hands in both directions.

Probus smiled briefly when he saw Loukas, then quickly called behind him for his son. A young boy came out of the storage room behind the stall as Probus came out from behind the heavily laden wooden table to embrace Loukas. Without saying anything further, he hurried Loukas and his friends through the labyrinthine streets of Sardis until they came to a small doorway near the end of a quiet lane-way. With a none-too-subtle glance back up the street he quickly opened the door and physically pushed them into the darkened room within. Only after he had opened the shutters into a delightfully decorated inner courtyard, where Loukas could see two of Probus' younger children playing, did he finally speak to them. Even then, he spoke very quietly.

"Loukas, it is good to see you. I was afraid that I would not."

"Why were you so worried?" replied Loukas. "How could you possibly know that I was in any danger?"

Probus paused briefly, before moving aside a curtain that had been blocking off a side-room. There, lying on a floor mat, was Markos, Loukas' younger brother. He looked like he was barely alive, but Probus quietly assured them he was merely sleeping. Loukas longed to speak with him but the boy obviously needed to rest. Probus let the curtain to fall back before he continued.

"Markos has travelled from Ephesus almost without stopping, and arrived here in Sardis last night under cover of darkness. After telling me what has been occurring in Ephesus in recent days, he collapsed into bed and has not moved since."

"News from Ephesus," breathed Loukas, his eyes wide. "What did he say? How is my family? Iounia?"

Loukas could tell from the look on Probus' face that the news was not good.

"There have been many arrests," began Probus quietly, "though not your father, Loukas," he added when Loukas started. "He was taken in for questioning, but released a little later on. I think your family's wealth helped with that. However, since then a number of other people were denounced by their guilds when they refused to participate in guild feasts. Markos tried to explain why, but he was exhausted and he didn't make much sense, to tell you the truth. Something about a scroll with terrifying beasts, and – what was it? – seven letters from Ioanneis? And you, Loukas;

he said you were involved, and would soon be arriving here in Sardis, that is, if you had not already passed through. I assured him that I had not seen you.

"Then, this morning, I get a visit from a Roman official asking me questions about my involvement with your family, telling me to inform the local garrison the instant I ever lay eyes on you. So when you show up as bold as brass in the broad daylight of the mid-afternoon sun without so much as a cloak to conceal your face... well, I just don't know what to think."

Loukas looked a little ashamed. "Well, we have had some interactions with the Romans, but on the whole they have not been looking for me specifically," he said, slightly puzzled.

"Well, they certainly referred to you by name," replied Probus firmly.

"Please, sir," interrupted Hermas, hesitantly. "Did Markos mention who had been arrested?"

Probus shrugged. "Yes, but I don't recall the names..."

He was interrupted by a voice from the other side of the curtain. "Is that you, Hermas?" It appeared that Markos was awake after all, for the curtain was pushed aside and the tired young man stepped into the larger room.

"Markos, my brother!" cried Loukas, as he jumped forward to embrace him. "Are you all right?"

"Yes, Loukas," Markos replied, "I am fine. But" – he released Loukas, and turned to face Hermas – "I'm afraid I have bad news for you: your father was one of those arrested."

Shock registered on Hermas' face, to be quickly followed by determination.

"I need to return to Ephesus," he declared. Turning to Loukas, he said, "Do you mind? Can you continue on with just Artemas?"

"Of course I can," Loukas replied, feeling a sudden surge of fear in his stomach. "You need to be with your family."

Markos spoke again. "The church in Ephesus felt the same, which is why they sent me to try and find you. It is by God's grace that our paths have crossed so quickly."

"Are you to return to Ephesus, too?" asked Hermas.

"Yes, we can set off tomorrow. But I am very much afraid that I will be unable to go as quickly as my outward journey."

"Actually, this may work out better for Loukas and I," added Artemas. "If the Romans are looking for three travellers, then two travellers will be less likely to arouse any suspicions."

"That is true," nodded Probus. "But remember, that Roman asked for you by name. They will presumably have a description to match, if they are doing their job properly. Merely disguising yourself as a twosome may not be sufficient."

There was a thoughtful silence.

"Well, why are the Romans after you, Loukas?" asked Probus eventually. "What have you done now? And what has it got to do with guilds and arrests in Ephesus?"

"How quickly can you call the church together?" asked Loukas, by way of reply. "I have a scroll to read." He reached into his carry bag and pulled out the scroll in its protective cover. "This is the answer to all your questions."

❧

When Loukas stood up holding the scroll there was an immediate silence. The church of Sardis met in the house of a wealthy man, a God-fearer who had worshipped in the synagogue of Sardis before responding to the good news proclaimed by the Christians. As Loukas began to read, every eye in the place was fixed on his face.

When he had read the first four of the sections directed to specific churches, Loukas glanced up at Probus and saw a look of understanding there: the mystery of the seven letters of Ioanneis was now being explained. With a deep breath, Loukas launched into the fifth section.

" 'To the angel of the church in Sardis write: These are the words of him who holds the seven spirits of God and the seven stars. I know your deeds; you have a reputation of being alive, but you are dead. Wake up! Strengthen what remains and is about to die, for I have not found your deeds complete in the sight of my God. Remember, therefore, what you have received and heard; obey it, and repent. But if you do not wake up, I will come like a thief, and you will not know at what time I will come to you.'[1]"

There was some murmuring among the people present. The allusion to the history of the city had been hard to miss: just as the city had been taken twice through the negligence of those who should have been watching, so here Iēsus was

1 Rev. 3:1-3.

203

threatening to come upon them with judgment if they did not repent of their hypocrisy.

But what was their sin? Why were they considered almost dead in the eyes of God? Loukas could see these questions in their angry eyes. He kept reading. From his recent experiences he knew that most questions were answered by hearing the scroll as a whole.

" 'Yet you have a few people in Sardis who have not soiled their clothes. They will walk with me, dressed in white, for they are worthy. He who overcomes will, like them, be dressed in white. I will never blot out his name from the book of life, but will acknowledge his name before my Father and his angels. He who has an ear, let him hear what the Spirit says to the churches.'[1]"

It was only afterwards, when Loukas had read through the entire scroll and had then retired to Probus' house to rest, that he was able to learn more of the recent goings on in the church. Tullius, one of the church leaders, had come back with them.

"Yes," nodded Tullius solemnly, "it was hard to hear, but Ioanneis is right. We are barely alive as a church. In fact, I sometimes wonder if we even are a church."

Loukas was puzzled. "Really? From what I hear, you do much for the poor in your city."

"Yes, that would be our reputation for being alive."

"But you haven't followed the teachings of Nicolaus."

"Well, we haven't needed to! We are in no danger of falling into the hands of the Romans. Most of those in the church are still listed in the Jewish register, so they are

1 Rev. 3:4-6.

exempt from participation in the Imperial Cult. Even the guilds are happy to turn a blind eye in our direction, as long as we remain under the auspices of the synagogue. The Jews here in Sardis have a lot of power and influence."

"But what about the accursed Benedictions?" asked Artemas.

Tullius looked decidedly uncomfortable. "Actually, I think that may be the problem. You see, most of us have just gone along with it."

There was a moment's silence as Loukas and his friends considered what it would mean for Christians to utter the words 'May the Nazarenes and the Minim suddenly perish, and may they be blotted out of the book of Life and not enrolled along with the righteous'. Every week they would be bringing down God's curse upon themselves, and indeed, upon all Christians everywhere!

"All of you?" asked Loukas in a small voice.

"No," replied Tullius wearily, "there were a few who couldn't do it. And they were struck off the synagogue register as a result."

Suddenly the words of the scroll made more sense to Loukas. These few were the ones dressed in white. They may have been blotted out of the Jews' book of life – the synagogue register with its security from the threat of the Imperial Cult – but they had definitely not been struck out of the true Book of Life, the only one that could guarantee security when it mattered: before the great, white throne.[1]

"So now you know the truth," said Tullius. "And you know that we face a difficult choice: to remain within the

1 Rev. 20:15.

synagogue and risk Iēsus' threat of judgment, or to separate ourselves from the Jews and risk retaliation from the Romans when they discover we are adherents of an illegal sect that refuses to show obeisance to the emperors. And to be honest, I am not sure of the outcome."

"But what about you?" asked Loukas.

Tullius paused. "I want to be dressed in white. I want Iēsus to acknowledge my name before God and the angels. And if it means dying at the hands of the Romans then so be it."

Such talk brought a dark look to Hermas' face. Loukas happened to notice, and reached out to place his hand on Hermas' shoulder.

"Do not be afraid, Hermas," he said. "You will soon be with your family. Iēsus will give you strength, no matter what happens." Inside, though, he did not feel as positive as his words.

"When will you leave, Loukas?" asked Probus.

"We leave tomorrow as well. You will have to send someone to Thyatira to get a copy of the scroll. There is no time for me to wait for you to copy the original. I must get to Philadelphia and Laodicea as soon as possible. For my heart is in Ephesus and I am greatly troubled."

"God will go with you," said Probus solemnly.

"*Amen*," replied Loukas.

St. Petersburg – January, AD 2006

The day of the Revelation Symposium, when it finally arrived, was a cold one. The temperature outside was -26 degrees Celsius. But inside the small hall in which Yevgeny's church met, it was a mild 20 degrees, thanks to the hot water pumping through the wall radiators. Dr. Williams had been surprised to find more than twenty people sitting in chairs when he was led by Dima through the audience to a row of seats at the front in which Yevgeny was already sitting. Yevgeny stood up as they approached and welcomed Dr. Williams.

"Greetings, Dr. Williams," he exclaimed enthusiastically. "Thanks for coming out on this chilly day!"

"Call me Ed," replied Dr. Williams, absently. "I wasn't expecting a crowd..."

"Oh, sorry about this, but when Dima mentioned you were coming to explain Revelation, well, a few of us wanted to listen in, too." With an expansive wave of his arm, he indicated the collection of mostly young Russian university students. "So we set up this informal discussion group. Please, take a seat."

Yevgeny remained standing.

"Thanks, too, for coming," he said, addressing the group. "The interpretation of Revelation has become quite an item of interest in recent days, most notably thanks to Dima and Natasha's unlikely discovery of what may yet prove to be the original scroll of Revelation in their family's dacha. But, it must also be said, this renegade website has also brought the scroll even more to the fore. So, to get things started, I believe Dima has prepared something..."

Dima, who had also sat down in one of the chairs facing the audience now stood up as Yevgeny found his own seat.

"Yes, I have been reading a book from the early 1970's which I have found quite fascinating. The book is *The Late, Great Planet Earth* and was written by a man named Hal Lindsey. Basically, to summarise his position, he claimed that the Second Coming of Christ would occur within about 40 years of the birth of the nation of Israel. In 1948 Israel was re-formed, but it wasn't until 1967 that they captured Jerusalem, so it is possible that was the moment the clock started ticking. Anyway, as far as the end is concerned, there was only one further event required, and that was the rebuilding of the temple, which Hal Lindsey was expecting to occur at any moment.

"Now, obviously, that hasn't happened yet, the problem being, of course, that the Dome of the Rock – an Islamic mosque – sits on the presumed site of the future temple.

"But then it gets even stranger. When Lindsey starts talking about the lead-up to the Second Coming, he actually believes the Bible predicts that *Russia* will attack Israel. Now, I have to be honest and say that I became really lost at this point. Dr. Williams, could you perhaps explain what is going on here?"

Dima sat down again, and Dr. Williams slowly got to his feet.

"Well, Dima, that's an interesting place to start. Is Russia referred to in Biblical prophecies? That's a good question. But before I answer it, I think we need to take one step back and look at Hal Lindsey's method of Biblical interpretation." Dr. Williams shrugged, and reached for one of the books he had placed on a small table just next to his seat. "It isn't a unique approach to Scripture – there are plenty of others who have done the same thing. But not all openly acknowledge it." He was flicking through his own copy of *The Late, Great Planet Earth*. "Ah, here we are. It's near the start of his chapter on Israel. He briefly summarises what he calls his 'Keys to the Prophetic Puzzle'. And I quote:

" 'A definite international realignment of nations into four spheres of political power had to occur in the same era as the rebirth of Israel. Each sphere of power had to be led by a certain predicted nation and allied with certain other nations. The relationships of all these factors to each other is easily determined by the following clues: first, each one of the four spheres of political power is said to be present and vitally involved with the reborn state of Israel.

" 'Secondly, each one of these spheres of power is a major factor in the final great war called "Armageddon," which is to be triggered by an invasion of the new state of Israel.

" 'Third, each one of these spheres of power will be judged and destroyed for invading the new state of Israel, by the personal return of the Jewish Messiah, Jesus Christ.

" 'It should be obvious that these predicted movements of history are interrelated in their general time of beginning and ending. This is why the prophecies can be pieced together to make a coherent picture, even though the pieces are scattered in small bits throughout the Old and New Testaments.'[1]

1 Hal Lindsey, *The Late, Great Planet Earth* (Zondervan: 1970), 42-43.

"End quote. It is actually quite difficult to know how to respond. Firstly, note the certainty in his statements. Secondly, if he is to be believed, then what he is saying is 'easily determined' and 'obvious'! If Hal Lindsey was standing here today, I would be the first the say, 'No, it is far from obvious!'

"However, the biggest problem is with what I call 'jigsaw prophecy'. Lindsey even alludes to this himself when he talks about 'the Prophetic Puzzle'; the scattered pieces of prophecy, found all over the Old and New Testaments can be pieced together to form a big picture. Actually, I have another good quotation from a book by Byron MacDonald, but for some reason I couldn't find it in my library this morning."

Dima, for some reason, blushed and looked somewhat ashamed.

"Fortunately," continued Dr. Williams, "I had written it out some time ago: 'The problem is prophecy is like a jigsaw puzzle. Throughout the Bible it is given in some large pieces, but also in many smaller pieces. What has happened is that people are confused as to what the picture looks like, so they keep trying to fit the pieces to match a picture, and too often it doesn't work.'[1] Of course, once this particular author goes ahead and presents *his* picture of biblical prophecy, he argues that his picture is the correct one.

"Personally, I think they are all wrong. To me, it seems that these prophetic interpreters are bringing their big picture *to* the text rather than getting their picture *from* the text. It reminds me of those posters that when you stand close to them, you can see that they are formed from thousands of

[1] MacDonald, 57.

tiny photos. But if you stand far enough away, all the tiny photos blur into one image. Now, those posters are created using a special computer program. You feed in your big picture, and the program searches through millions of stock photos to create the final image. Basically, it doesn't matter what photos it uses. The program just shrinks them down and places them somewhere in the final image so that their predominant colour appears to match its new context.

"It is the same with jigsaw prophecy. They take these scattered bits of prophecy, *rip them out of their original contexts*, and force them into their prophetic reconstruction. There is a good example of this on page 169," he said, flipping through the book again. "Ah, here it is. He has a go at the United Nations for using part of Isaiah 2:4 on the wall of their building. But then he complains that the quotation has been taken out of context. What context, one may ask? Well, this is what Lindsey says: 'The meaning of the passage speaks of the time when the Messiah would reign over the earth out of Jerusalem and judge between the nations in a visible, actual, and historic kingdom of God on earth.'[1] In other words, the millennium as constructed by Lindsey! But if you allow this argument, then you could also say that even Isaiah was using the verse out of context!

"So, what Dima has described is Hal Lindsey's big picture, and it is very much a reconstruction based on jigsaw prophecy. He uses prophecies without *any* regard for their original contexts, just so long as they appear to fit into his scheme for the future. As far as Russia invading Israel is concerned, for example, he uses Ezekiel 38 and 39, Daniel 11,

1 Lindsey, 169.

verses 40 through to 45, and Joel 2 verse 20.[1] And he links this battle into Revelation chapter 16 verse 16 (despite the fact that Revelation 20:8 would actually be more appropriate if it wasn't on the wrong side of the millennium). Quite a jigsaw!

"But think about what this implies about those original prophecies. It means that only we who have *all* the scattered pieces can make any sense of it. For instance, I don't think Ezekiel understood the dry bones to refer to the Jewish state formed in 1948 and then some nationwide turn to Christ at a yet-to-occur time being represented by the breath of God's spirit coming upon the army of dead people.[2] But this is what Hal Lindsey argues.[3]

"Jigsaw prophecy gives us a very warped view of the Old Testament prophets. It makes them out to be crazy – at least that is how they must have appeared to those listening to them at the time. If Lindsey is right, how on earth could anyone have understood what they were talking about? These men must have appeared mad as they 'channelled' some particular piece of foretelling. It rips them right out of their own historical context.

"In contrast to this, I would argue that the prophets were highly intelligent men who believed God was leading them to say specific things to their contemporaries. They gave a commentary of past events showing where the nation of Israel had gone wrong. They spoke about such issues as justice and mercy in the present. And they spoke about the future *as it related to their audience*. To take their prophecies

1 Lindsey, 60.
2 Ezek. 37:1-14.
3 Lindsey, 61.

out of the original context is not just misleading, it is actually a travesty of biblical interpretation. I am sorry to have to belabour this point, but if you remember only one thing from today, may it be that you simply cannot neglect the original context of biblical prophecies.

"Now, getting back to the question of Russia, and its apparent role in bringing about Armageddon. Lindsey gets most of his material for this from Ezekiel chapters 38 and 39. But these chapters follow on directly from chapter 37 with its vision of the dry bones that come together to form an army which is then breathed on by God. Given that Ezekiel was a prophet living during the time of the exile, wouldn't his vision have been interpreted by those who heard his message as God's promise that Israel would become a nation again, but this time it would be different since the people would have God's Spirit within them? This is, after all, how God *himself* interprets the vision in verses 12 to 14.

"Then in that same chapter, God goes on to describe the newly reformed nation. It will be one nation, no longer divided into two kingdoms as it was before the exile. And the people will not defile themselves by worshipping idols. There will be a Davidic king again, and the people will follow God's laws and decrees. They will live in the land forever, and God will make with them an everlasting covenant of peace. And God will return to dwell in his sanctuary in the midst of the people. If I was living in exile in Babylon, listening to Ezekiel repeating this message, I for one would be heartily encouraged.

"But then when we come to the enemy from the north in chapters 38 and 39, at first it seems that the idyllic life of post-exilic Israel is doomed. A terrifying army comprised of many of Israel's traditional enemies will come against them. But, in fact, it is God's plan. For as they step into Israel, God simply wipes them out.

"Now the true meaning of these chapters is clearly revealed towards the end. In verses 21 through to 24, God says: 'I will display my glory among the nations, and all the nations will see the punishment I inflict and the hand I lay upon them. From that day forward the house of Israel will know that I am God. *And the nations will know that the people of Israel went into exile for their sin, because they were unfaithful to me.* So I hid my face from them and handed them over to their enemies, and they all fell by the sword. I dealt with them according to their uncleanness and their offences, and I hid my face from them.' In other words, God is giving *the nations* an explanation for the Exile. It was not because the gods of the nations were more powerful. It was because the people of Israel had been so wicked. So when the Babylonians destroyed Israel, it was only because God let them. This will be proven when the future enemy from the north comes upon Israel and is instead wiped out by God.

"The words of encouragement continue in verses 25 through to 29: 'Therefore this is what the Sovereign Lord says: I will *now* bring back Jacob from captivity and will have compassion on all the people of Israel, and I will be zealous for my holy name. They will forget their shame and all the unfaithfulness they showed toward me when they lived in safety in their land with no one to make them afraid. When I have brought them back from the nations and have gathered them from the countries of their enemies, I will show myself holy through them in the sight of many nations. Then they will know that I am the Lord their God, for though I sent them into exile among the nations, I will gather them to their own land, not leaving any behind. I will no longer hide my face from them, for I will pour out my Spirit on the house of Israel, declares the Sovereign Lord.'

"Again, when Ezekiel spoke these words to the people of Israel living in exile, they would have assumed that these promises of God were for *them*, that their exile was drawing to a close, and that there would once again be a nation of Israel, but that things would be even better than before, since God's Spirit would be on them, giving them the strength to obey God's law. (Elsewhere, incidentally, Ezekiel talks about God taking away their hearts of stone and giving them hearts of flesh with much the same meaning.)

"Now, then, if Ezekiel's prophecy would have been so relevant to his contemporaries, fitting so *completely* into the original context, why then do we get people like Hal Lindsey coming along well over 2000 years later claiming that the prophecies are actually for now? Well, I think it is mostly because these prophecies were not fulfilled literally and completely in post-exilic Israel. Once the Israelites returned from exile, things were actually rather difficult for them, as we read in the books of Ezra and Nehemiah. And in fact, quite a few enemies came into Israel later on and were rather successful at attacking the Israelites. They weren't struck down by divine intervention, despite God's promises through Ezekiel.

"Consequently, many people today assume that since these prophecies were not fulfilled literally and completely, then there must be a future fulfilment that *will* fulfil the prophecies literally and completely. And thus we get Hal Lindsey's detailed account of the War of Armageddon, and more recently the *fantasy* series Left Behind by Tim LaHaye and some other guy, though I have strenuously resisted reading those.

"But an insistence on a literal interpretation of prophecies does not allow for the free will of those involved. Many of the Old Testament prophecies did not come to pass because the nation of Israel was not obedient to God. In fact, we Christians would argue that many of the prophecies were fulfilled through the coming of Jesus, the Davidic King who ushered in a new covenant! As such, the prophecies can now be applied to the church. After all, did not God pour out his Spirit on the church? Did not Peter in his first sermon claim that the prophecies of Joel were being fulfilled on the day of Pentecost?[1]

"So, the short answer to your question is, 'No, I don't think the Bible predicts that Russia will invade Israel in the lead-up to the Second Coming of Jesus.' I apologise for my enormously long answer, but I think it has been worthwhile since we have dealt with some interesting underlying assumptions and methods of biblical interpretation in the process."

He sat down, and took a long drink from a glass of water sitting on the side table.

"Thank-you for that answer," said Dima standing up. "I found it very helpful." Then, turning to those gathered

1 Acts 2:1-21.

there, he asked, "Does anyone else have a question for Dr. Williams?"

There was a pause. Finally, someone up the back of the room called out, "So who or what is the Beast?"

Dr. Williams smiled.

"Ah, now that is a *good* question..." he said.

∽

Pergamum – August, AD 93

The hallways of Pergamum's Law Courts had been rather busy in recent days. Sergius Maximus barely noticed, however, as he hurried distractedly from the nearby prison cells where he had been taking down a detailed confession from a seditious and atheistic Christian to preside over a case involving another one somewhat further down the legal track. Yet no matter how hard he tried – and he had certainly utilised as many of the tricks of the torturer's trade that he had the stomach for – he was still no closer to understanding what had brought about such a steep increase in rebellion towards Rome and the emperors. He had almost reached his private chambers when a voice, calling from the other side of a pillared courtyard, cut through the general clamour of the place to gain his attention.

"Sergius Maximus! One moment, please!"

Frowning, he turned towards the voice to see his assistant Crispus pushing his way through the crowd of people who had come out to see Roman justice applied with impartiality. When Crispus finally got to him he was silently handed a rolled up document, sealed, he noticed as he broke the seal, with the sign of the garrison of Thyatira. He began reading the scroll cursorily but as he read he quickly became more and more interested. By the time he reached the end of the document, the court case he had been so eager to get to had been completely forgotten.

"When did this arrive?" he barked at his assistant.

"Not an hour ago. The messenger had arrived on horseback and had stressed its importance. I have been seeking you ever since."

Sergius Maximus stood in thought for a moment. He needed quiet to think, and the Law Courts were not the place for quiet. He also needed to re-read this document immediately, so he needed to find a replacement judge. Back-tracking down the hallway he entered a side-room where a couple of men were reclining on couches drinking wine.

"Rufus," he said. "I am sorry to disturb you, but I have immediate need of the quietness and sanctity that only Athena can offer. Could I trouble you to take my place in the session due to start, oh, about five minutes ago?"

"Sergius," replied one of the men, "it would be an honour."

He carefully placed his cup on the table in front of him, then somewhat unsteadily got to his feet. Sergius was a little annoyed to see him slightly the worse for drink, but the case was not too difficult. These people refused to offer the petty sacrifice to the emperors; they were to be given one last chance to say that Caesar was Lord; and if they still refused they were to be executed in a manner determined by their status and rank in Roman society. Rufus would be fine; he could do it in his sleep, let alone drunk.

Once he had ushered Rufus to the correct court room, he exited the Law Courts and threaded his way through the streets to the Library. Once there he quickly made his way to the reading room dominated by the beautiful Athena, goddess of wisdom. The place was as quiet as he had hoped. Reclining in the couch that faced Athena, he again opened the scroll and re-read the message:

> *From Gaius Fabius, Commander of the garrison of Thyatira,*
> *To Sergius Maximus, legal envoy to the Prefect of the province of Asia.*
> *Greetings, in the name of our Lord Domitianus. May the gods bless you with all wisdom and understanding, especially in these days of trials and tribulations.*
> *I am writing in response to your recent missive describing three men wanted in relation to the recent rise of sedition in the province of Asia. After the descriptions had been read out to the men, one patrol leader stepped forward, saying that he had met with one of those described, the one named Lucius, although he had called himself Loukas. He reported that he had encountered this Lucius alone on the road leading from Pergamum to Thyatira, and had questioned him as to his reasons for travelling. Being not entirely satisfied by the boy's reply, he had had his baggage searched. The boy had been travelling light. Apart from some food and a skin of water, all that he had was a scroll. The patrol leader read some of the scroll, but*

*did not find anything incriminating, so he let the boy
continue on his way.*

*However, in the light of your missive, he thought that you
would want to know some of what was in this scroll. He
assured me that at the time it sounded like nonsense, but
these are some of the details that he recalls. It referred to
a beast that came from the earth and made the world
worship another beast that had suffered a fatal wound.
He remembered something about the beast having a name
that was also a number. And the number was six
hundred and sixty six. Perhaps all this will mean
something to you, for it means nothing to me.*

*We have, of course, made a thorough search for Lucius
and his travelling companions, but have not found them as
yet. This has been especially vexatious given the recent
sudden increase in sedition in the city of Thyatira. Please
inform me if there is anything specific you wish me to do.
All praise to Domitianus!*

So Lucius – or should he say Loukas? – had been carrying
a scroll. Could it be that this was the source of the sedition?
A scroll?

And then it hit him: Lucius must have received the scroll
from one of the prisoners on Patmos. Someone in exile had
written a letter that was spreading rebellion around the
province of Asia like wildfire. Lucius was nothing more than
a messenger boy. The timing certainly fitted.

So the scroll was the key. Sergius Maximus glanced back
at the commander's letter to remind himself of the few scraps

of details. Two beasts, one with a fatal wound, a name that was also a number. *Hmm, not much to go on*, he thought.

Wearily, he glanced up at Athena, as if willing her to provide him with inspiration. At that very moment, the sun must have come out from behind a cloud, for in that instant her head, shoulders and breasts were flooded with light. Sergius Maximus gazed up at her, breathless.

All very beautiful, but there was no flash of revelation to accompany the moment.

But then it occurred to him to try examining the problem from another angle entirely. The problem that was facing him every day was some people's refusal to worship the emperor. And Lucius' scroll refered to a beast that forces the world to worship some other beast. Suddenly, Sergius Maximus could see a parallel. What if that beast with the fatal wound somehow referred to the emperor? Calling him a beast was so horribly treasonous he was stunned that his brain had even suggested such a thing. But that would explain it, perhaps. By way of negative exaggeration, this scroll was persuading people *not* to worship the emperor, for who would want to worship a beast?

But what about the name that was a number? Clearly whoever had written the scroll in the first place had been cautious enough not to name Domitianus explicitly. But a number?

Well, he knew that every letter in the alphabet also stood for a number. If you knew the name you could certainly calculate its number. But to go back the other way was close to impossible. There were just too many options.

He grabbed a piece of parchment from a passing attendant, and began scribbling. He wrote the Latin letters of Domitianus' name down the side of the paper, with their correlating numbers beside them. Then, with his tongue between his teeth, he slowly added them up. But the answer was not the number from the scroll. If the scroll were in Greek, though, the numbers would be different. But after a few more minutes of scribbles and calculations he had discovered he was no closer. In fact, the resulting sums were all way too high. It would have to be a short name, then. But that would rule out Domitianus which didn't make any sense.

He sat there staring at the letters and numbers scrawled upon the page in front of him.

It was at *that* moment he had the epiphany. It had been the reference to a 'fatal wound' that had done it. When Nero had committed suicide, plunging the entire Roman Empire into a bloody civil war that had lasted some three years, the institution that was the Roman emperors had certainly suffered a significant blow. Only Vespasian, Domitianus' father, had been able to restore law and order to the empire.

Carefully, he wrote out the name Nero using Latin letters. That was not right, though. He tried it with Greek letters. Again, not right.

Frustrated, he swore under his breath. Yet he felt like he was *close*.

Could they have used some other alphabet? He nearly gave up completely when he thought of the numerous languages spoken in the region, although most had no alphabet. But then, the Christians had come out of Judea, had they not? Could it be in Hebrew?

Quickly, he sought out the attendant from whose grasp he had wrenched the piece of parchment earlier.

"Do we have any scrolls describing the language of the Hebrews?" he said, urgently.

The attendant's eyes glazed over, as if he was reading from some internal list, before finally speaking.

"Yes, but such scrolls will be stored in the basement somewhere."

"Fetch them immediately. And find me a specialist in Hebrew. And hurry!"

The man ran off. After perhaps an hour of restless torture the attendant returned with some scrolls under one arm, accompanied by a Jewish man, clearly reluctant to be present in the Library under the watchful gaze of the goddess Athena.

"Quick, man, what are the letters in Hebrew that would spell the name Nero?"

"Would that be from the Greek or the Latin?"

"I don't know! Try them both!"

"Well, that would be *nun*, *resh*, *waw* and *nun* from the Greek. The Latin form omits the final *nun*."

"And what are their numerical equivalents?"

The man paused for a moment. "Fifty, two hundred, six and fifty again, if you are including the final *nun*."

That was clearly not enough. A dead end after all. Sergius Maximus was about to dismiss the man and call it quits, when the man said, "Although, it is usual to include

'Caesar' as well. That would be *qoph*, *samech* and *resh*; or as numbers, one hundred, sixty and two hundred again."

Sergius Maximus snatched up the paper. 50 + 200 + 6 + 50 + 100 + 60 + 200. That was it. Six-hundred and sixty six. He had cracked the code!

Ignoring the Jew completely, Sergius Maximus turned to the statue of Athena and bowed low to show his gratitude. Then, he rushed from the library, ready to do battle with the forces of sedition now more clearly visible to his eyes. The rebellion was not specifically focused against Domitianus himself, although he had probably exacerbated the situation with his aspirations of divinity. It was directed against the worship of the emperors as a whole, against the cult of the Blessed Ones. He was sure that this information would assist him in persuading recalcitrant individuals to recant their seditious beliefs.

It was then that he realised he could probably have got the answer from one of the prisoners, if he had only turned up the heat a little more. Still, there was a certain amount of satisfaction in having done it on his own.

If only I could see the scroll for myself, he thought, wistfully. *If only Lucius could be found. Perhaps I should pay a visit to his family in Ephesus and wait for him to return...*

He hurried down the corridors of the Law Courts. There was much to organise before he would be free to travel anywhere. With a grimace, he realised he would have to start with the proconsul...

"So, the Beast," said Dr. Williams, almost to himself. "Well, the first thing that needs to be said is that there are actually two beasts in Revelation, not counting the Dragon! One beast appears briefly in chapter 11 verse 7 where it is described as coming up from the Abyss to make war against the two witnesses. In chapter 13, however, this same beast is described as coming out of the sea and in verse 7 is said to make war against the saints. It is further described in chapter 17. The *second* beast, though, comes out of the earth, and directs people's attention to the first beast. I think the stated origin of the beasts is important to their interpretation.

"Well, the usual approach of those who follow the prophetic jigsaw method usually call the first beast the Antichrist. But it is extremely interesting to note that the name 'Antichrist' does *not* appear anywhere in the entire book of Revelation. This isn't at all surprising since the name 'Antichrist' was given to the spirit of false teaching that had infiltrated the church. False teachers are referred to as 'antichrists' *plural*, and you can read more about *them* in the letters of John.

"Just to add to the confusion, prophetic jigsaw interpreters also link in Paul's teaching about 'the man of lawlessness' from Second Thessalonians as well as Daniel's Fourth Beast as described in Daniel 7. Now, the author of Revelation clearly intended us to think of Daniel's beast. After all, both beasts have 10 horns. But is he telling us these beasts are in fact the *same* beast, or that they are *like* one another in some way? After all, Daniel's on-going description of the horns is quite different to Revelation. In fact, the really bad news in Daniel is actually an *eleventh* horn that takes out three of the ten. Nothing like this occurs in Revelation.

"And if you look closely at the text, the first beast of Revelation is described in ways that refer to all *four* of the beasts in Daniel: the beast resembles a leopard (Daniel's beast number three), it has the feet of a bear (Daniel's second beast), and a mouth like a lion (Daniel's first beast). So, these allusions are definitely intentional. What the significance of these descriptions is, though, is less clear.

"Look, I don't really want to advertise the competition, but if you want a good summary of the sort of things said about the Beast following the prophetic jigsaw approach, you can't go past this renegade website claiming to have found the original scroll of Revelation, despite the fact that we have it here in St. Petersburg, and will soon be displaying it for all to see in the Hermitage itself!"

There was quite a stir from the crowd. Dima had only told Natasha about the upcoming exhibition.

"Yes," continued Dr. Williams, "it's all there: according to them the Antichrist *is* the Beast with the 10 horns. He is also *at the same* time the eleventh horn that takes out three other horns. This means, apparently, that when he comes to power seven world leaders will agree and three will oppose but will be over-ruled. He will become the head of the world government and the head of the world religion. Because Revelation 13 verses 3 and 14 refer to the beast having a fatal head wound, the Antichrist will apparently suffer an assassination attempt that will appear to be successful. But a supernatural miracle will occur restoring him to full health.

He will bring about a peace treaty in the Middle East, almost certainly between Israel and all the Arab nations surrounding her. However, at some point he reveals his true colours by deifying himself in the Jewish Temple in Jerusalem (the reconstruction of which must be part of that amazing treaty!) This act brings about the Tribulation with a capital T. Of course, the church gets taken out of the picture some time before all this by means of the Rapture with a capital R.

"Now, if you know your Bible you can probably work out which verses of which prophecy are being used to fill in these incredible details. But if you *really* know your Bible you will also know that in *each case* there is an alternative interpretation that would have made complete sense to the *original* hearers of the prophecies. For example, Daniel's four beasts describe world history leading up to Antiochus Epiphanies, who desecrated the Jewish temple in 168 BC, and who Daniel referred to as the eleventh horn.

"As for Revelation 13, is there an alternative? Is there a way of reading the passage that would have made sense to Christians at the end of the first century? And the simple answer is 'Yes, there is.' You have to remember that Christians living in the province of Asia Minor during the reign of Domitian *did* suffer persecution. We even have evidence from secular historical sources. A man named Pliny the Younger – we would probably call him Pliny Junior, these days – was, from AD 111 to 113, the governor of Pontus and Bithynia, a region in the north of modern-day Turkey, not far from the cities of the Seven Churches of Revelation. At some point during this period, he writes a letter to the Emperor Trajan in Rome. Allow me to quote you some of this letter:

" '...in the case of those who were denounced to me as Christians, I have observed the following procedure: I interrogated these as to whether they were Christians; those who confessed I interrogated a second and a third time, threatening them with punishment; those who persisted I ordered executed. For I had no doubt that, whatever the nature of their creed, stubbornness and inflexible obstinacy surely deserve to be punished. There were others possessed of the same folly; but because they were Roman citizens, I signed an order for them to be transferred to Rome.

" 'Soon accusations spread, as usually happens, because of the proceedings going on, and several incidents occurred. An anonymous document was published containing the names of many persons. Those who denied that they were or had been Christians, when they invoked the gods in words dictated by me, offered prayer with incense and wine to your image, which I had ordered to be brought for this purpose together with statues of the gods, and moreover cursed Christ – none of which those who are really Christians, it is said, can be forced to do – these I thought should be discharged. Others named by the informer declared that they were Christians, but then denied it, asserting that they had been but had ceased to be, some three years before, others many years, some as much as twenty-five years. They all worshipped your image and the statues of the gods, and cursed Christ.'

"End quote. Now, did you notice that Pliny Junior did not have any problem dealing with people who refused to repent of being a Christian. No, they were just executed, if only for being stubborn! His problem was with people who had once been a Christian but had changed their mind. Was it enough merely for them to repent? Or were they irretrievably stained for life?

"Now, what this passage demonstrates, then, is that there were people living in Asia Minor who *had been* Christians but who, when faced with Roman opposition, had recanted. In some cases, according to Pliny Junior, this moment of repentance had occurred up to 25 years previously. Now, if you subtract 25 years from Pliny Junior's years of being governor, you get the period 86 to 88 AD. Perhaps, Pliny Junior is not very accurate – after all, *he* wasn't involved in these earlier trials – but what this implies is that from at least as early as 86 AD people have been accused of being Christians by the Roman authorities. Pliny Junior only knows about those who repented, those who returned to emperor worship and therefore lived to tell the tale. But there would also have been those who resisted and were punished with either death or deportation to Rome.

"We also have Trajan's reply to Pliny the Younger: 'You observed proper procedure, my dear Pliny, in sifting the cases of those who had been denounced to you as Christians. For it is not possible to lay down any general rule to serve as a kind of fixed standard. They are not to be sought out; if they are denounced and proved guilty, they are to be punished, with this reservation, that whoever denies that he is a Christian and really proves it – that is, by worshipping our gods – even though he was under suspicion in the past, shall obtain pardon through repentance. But anonymously posted accusations ought to have no place in any prosecution. For this is both a dangerous kind of precedent and out of keeping with the spirit of our age.'

"Well, this answer beautifully sums up the Romans' ambivalent and frankly contradictory attitude towards Christianity: don't seek them out, which implies they don't really pose a danger to Rome; but when they are brought to your attention, kill them if they refuse to repent.

"So what these letters provide is evidence that the churches of Asia Minor had been suffering persecution from as early as AD 86, certainly all through the later years of Domitian's reign. How would the beasts of the thirteenth chapter of the book of Revelation be viewed in this context? Well, to give you a big picture, the beast from the sea is Rome and the beast from the land is the local civil authorities who were enforcing the policy of emperor worship.

"The first beast comes out of the sea. In other words, it is an *import*. Enacting this very concept, every year the new Roman proconsul would arrive by boat in Ephesus. The beast from the land, though, is a *local* product.

"In support of identifying the beast from the sea as Rome, in chapter 17 an angel provides an explanation for some of the descriptions. Notably, the seven heads of this beast are said to refer to seven hills, and of course, Rome was famous for its seven hills. The heads also refer to kings, five of whom are past, one is present, and one is yet to come. The beast itself also represents an eighth king, who belongs to the other seven. Things get complicated at this point, and there is much disagreement as to which Roman emperors are being referred to. Personally, I follow G. B. Caird who argues that, given the many repetitions of 'seven' in Revelation, that the 'seven kings' is representative of the whole series of emperors, and that the important one is the eighth one who will soon be persecuting the church. After all, the people who received this scroll would have had no difficulty in identifying the current reigning emperor. It is just we, who do not know precisely *when* Revelation was written down and distributed, who have the difficulty.

"There is also the matter of the fatal wound suffered by one of the heads. This is subsequently referred to as the beast's fatal wound, specifically the result of a sword blow, but that was healed. This appears to be referring to the suicide of Nero, which was followed by a year of civil war – and three terrible but fortunately short-lived emperors – that could have resulted in the end of the empire itself. But after Vespasian came to the throne there was a restoration of the *Pax Romana* which must have been viewed as miraculous by those who had previously enjoyed such peace and prosperity. It is no wonder that, upon his death, he was declared to be a god by the Imperial Senate. In fact, his last words were reported to have been, 'Dear me, I must be turning into a god...' You can sense the irony!

"So then, when we read what this beast is about to do, we can better imagine what those in the church of that time must have felt:

" 'The beast was given a mouth to utter proud words and blasphemies and to exercise his authority for forty-two months. He opened his mouth to blaspheme God, and to slander his name and his dwelling place and those who live in heaven. He was given power to make war against the saints and to conquer them. And he was given authority over every tribe, people, language and nation. All the inhabitants of the earth will worship the beast – all whose names have not been written in the book of life belonging to the Lamb that was slain from the creation of the world.

" 'He who has an ear, let him hear. If anyone is to go into captivity, into captivity he will go. If anyone is to be killed with the sword, with the sword he will be killed. This calls for patient endurance and faithfulness on the part of the saints.'[1]"

Dr. Williams paused for a while.

"Sobering words," he continued, eventually. "I'm not sure I would have had the strength to face such persecution. Anyway, now we come to the beast from the land, the local authorities of Asia Minor who were responsible for enforcing emperor worship. I'll leave it to you to read the text, but I think you will find that most of the details fit this historical context quite well. But I do want to speak a little on the mark of the beast. This is the text: 'He also forced everyone, small and great, rich and poor, free and slave, to receive a mark on his right hand or on his forehead, so that no one could buy or sell unless he had the mark, which is the name of the beast or the number of his name.'[2] And of course, the number is 666.

"The whole mark thing appears to be like how a master might brand his slaves so that everyone would know who they belonged to. There is certainly no evidence that this ever occurred *literally* in the first century. But, there is

1 Rev. 13:5–10.
2 Rev. 13:16–17.

evidence that people's ability to buy and sell was hindered if they had not participated in the various sacrifices offered to the emperors. People who *had* participated were apparently given a certificate – one would presume that it had the name of the reigning emperor on it somewhere – and anyone without such a certificate would have a hard time buying and selling anything, at least with someone who *did* have such a certificate and who would not want to associate with an enemy of Rome.

"So, all in all, it would have been extremely difficult for the Christians of the time. If they avoided attention from the authorities, they ended up being unable to buy and sell. If they did come to the attention of the authorities, then they were forced to choose between life and death by sacrificing to the emperors or refusing to do so. It is a wonder that any survived!

"But, then that is part of the reason the book of Revelation was written to these people. Not only does it instruct them on what to do, it also says that these persecutions will only be of *limited* duration. There will be an end, and there will be a judgment that will fall upon the persecutors..."

Between Sardis and Philadelphia – August, AD 93

The next morning dawned dark, the rays of the rising sun barely penetrating a mass of foreboding cloud to the east of the city. It looked as though rain was imminent and unavoidable. Loukas looked up at the sky gloomily, his mind still churning with the news of arrests in Ephesus. He was bitterly unhappy about sending his younger brother back into what was turning out to be a very dangerous situation for anyone associated with the Christian church, but there did not seem to be any viable alternative. It certainly would be no safer to stay with them, not now that the Romans were looking for them by name.

Just before Hermas and Markos headed off through the western gates Loukas pulled Hermas aside and entreated him to look after his younger brother. Hermas had assured him that he would.

"Our prayers go with you," Loukas had said, his voice almost breaking, as he had given Markos a tight hug. Then he watched until Hermas and Markos had made it safely through the city gates and had disappeared into the distance.

Then, as the rain began to fall in earnest, it was their turn to leave. Probus escorted them across the town to the Philadelphian gate, and then through the gateway. He accompanied them down the hillside, as the road followed a stream that was getting noisier by the minute. At the base of the hill he stopped, embraced them both, and then Loukas and Artemas continued on together.

They spent a tense morning, very carefully trying to stay out of sight of other travellers on the road. If they saw someone in the distance they got off the road as quickly as possible and hid in the trees until they had passed. If they found themselves approaching a place where the road ahead was obscured in any way, they left the road completely and cut across country to meet up with the road further on.

It was well that they did this. Once, as they were clambering over a wooded hillside, they spotted a Roman patrol waiting on the road below them, just around what would have been a blind corner. They proceeded as quietly as they could and the patrol was none the wiser.

The rain eased after midday, so they stopped for a snack of fresh fruit and bread on some rocks overlooking a valley, protected from passers by on the road by a dense thicket. A wan sun made an appearance, but did nothing to dry their thoroughly wet clothing.

After a brief meal they continued on their way. A couple of hours later, finding themselves unable to see around a bend ahead, they left the road again, taking instead a goat-track that wound back and forth as it made its way up and over the large ridge of rocky hillside around which the road turned. They got to the top successfully and were able to look over at the road far below. After surveying the dizzying descent of the goat-track, Loukas decided to follow the ridge around for some distance and then to rejoin the road again much further along. They back-tracked a little, so that they would be below the level of the ridge and therefore out of sight of anyone travelling on the road, and then began to make their way along the side of the hill, Loukas leading the way. But the going was difficult. The goat-track had been bad enough, but now there was no path to follow. They were forced to jump from rock to rock, scattering loose stones in places, grabbing onto large boulders to prevent themselves from slipping further down the side of the rocky hill.

Suddenly, behind Loukas, there was a noise of rocks falling and a cry of pain.

Loukas turned and saw his friend spread-eagled on the ground clutching his right ankle.

"Artemas! What happened? Are you all right?"

Between clenched teeth, Artemas replied, "A rock broke under my foot and I slipped. Owww! I think my ankle is broken."

Loukas quickly came over to Artemas and crouched down to examine his ankle. It was swelling fast, so it was difficult to judge whether the bone was broken or not.

"Can you put any weight on it?"

Artemas tried gently to put his foot on the ground. His sharp indrawn breath was answer enough for Loukas.

"Don't worry, Artemas, we'll get you to safety," he said with a confidence he did not really feel. He looked around. They were near the top of the rocky ridge, some distance from the goat track that had brought them to the top. Even if he could assist his friend back to the goat-track, across the rocks and boulders that had caused him to come to grief in the first place, they would still have to make their way down to the road. And then they were nearly a day's journey from Sardis, too far to travel even if they were able to walk at a normal pace. As for Philadelphia, he was not sure exactly how much further on it was. And, of course, the Romans were looking for him, and by name, too.

Then, to top it all off, it started raining again. Heavily.

Loukas sighed deeply. They still had two churches in which to read the scroll, and then he would be able to return to Ephesus and help his family and friends through the tribulation that was already breaking upon them. But that was looking more and more remote thanks to a fractured rock and a misplaced foot.

"Artemas," said Loukas eventually, "we need to pray."

Kneeling beside his friend, Loukas prayed. He prayed for wisdom and strength to be able to complete their task. He prayed for the healing of Artemas' ankle. He prayed for their families and friends in Ephesus. He prayed for the churches they had already read the scroll in and for the churches yet to hear it. He even prayed for the Romans, that they would turn aside from their persecution of the church and come to know the truth about Iēsus.

The sun could not be seen through the menacing rain clouds above them but it would be setting soon, and Loukas still did not know what to do other than to continue praying. Then, unexpectedly, from below them he heard a long whistle. He was briefly fearful that the Romans had spotted them, but the sound had not come from the direction of the road. Warily looking down towards the valley below them he could see a shepherd, surrounded by ten or so sheep.

"Is someone hurt?" the man called up to them.

"Yes, my friend slipped and hurt his ankle," called back Loukas.

"Wait there," replied the shepherd. He spoke something Loukas could not hear to the sheep, then he came bounding up the steep hillside as effortlessly as if he were strolling along a Roman road. Within moments he was at their side, bending over Artemas and examining the ankle.

"Yes," he said. "It is hurt, but the bone is not broken."

"Actually," said Artemas, "it is feeling a little better already."

The shepherd turned to Loukas. "My name is Iani. I think together we can take your friend somewhere more comfortable than this place for the night."

"Thank-you, Iani," said Loukas.

Iani helped Artemas to stand, then with Loukas supporting the other shoulder, they slowly made their way down the steep hillside. Iani directed them downwards on a slant so that the slope was lessened, but even so it was extremely difficult. Loukas winced each time that Artemas cried out in pain as his ankle was jolted. Then suddenly – just as the rain began to dwindle away – they found themselves on a different goat track, one heading down into the valley below, and the going became easier although the narrowness of the track meant that Loukas and the shepherd were still clambering from rock to rock.

Eventually, the slope eased off as grass became more abundant than rock, and they came to the place where the shepherd's sheep had patiently waited for their master, chewing grass and bleating quietly to one another.

"My hut is not far," said Iani with a smile. Then calling his sheep each by name they continued on their way. There was space now for them to walk three abreast so Artemas was able to be properly supported. They were also surrounded by the comforting sounds of sheep following their master home to the fold.

It was dusk by the time they came to a little hut sitting next to a roughly constructed sheep pen. The sheep appeared to know what to do. They filed into the pen – Loukas could just hear the shepherd counting under his breath – and then he closed the gate.

"All accounted for. Now, let's see to your friend," he said kindly.

He opened the door of the hut then almost carried Artemas inside and laid him on a mat that lay on one side of the hut. Then in a twinkling he had a fire going with water boiling and delicious-smelling food cooking. It all seemed to happen so quickly Loukas was amazed.

"I caught some fish earlier," replied Iani to Loukas' unspoken question. "There's a delightful stream not far from here. You can almost pull them out of the water with your bare hands."

While Iani was cooking the food, Loukas draped their outer garments over strings that stretched the length of the hut in the hope that they would dry out enough for them to be wearable tomorrow. Iani also treated Artemas' foot. By the light of a small oil lamp he examined it carefully before wrapping it in some strips of cloth.

"As I said, it isn't broken, but you shouldn't walk on it for a few days."

Even in the gloom Iani must have seen Loukas' face fall.

"So you are in a hurry, then?" he said. But before Loukas could reply, Iani continued: "The meal is ready. Let's eat."

Iani quickly served up the fish, accompanied by a stew in which Loukas could identify nothing but which smelled amazing. It had been quite a while since they had eaten anything so there was silence for some minutes while he, Artemas and the shepherd ate eagerly.

Finally, Iani broke the silence. "Tomorrow I will help you on your way. We should be able to get to the road easily enough. Then perhaps a wagon may pass and take you to your destination."

Loukas was hesitant about travelling by road again, but looking at Artemas sitting there eating his fish and stew with his leg outstretched in front of him he realised that they did not have much choice.

"Thank-you, sir, for your help and hospitality," he said. "We will do as you suggest."

"Well, then," replied Iani, "you must get some sleep. Especially you, my son," he said, touching Artemas gently on his head.

Quickly the man cleaned away the remains of their meal, before rolling out a second mat for Loukas.

"You will be safe here tonight," he said with a smile. "I will be outside – I have a cloak that will be quite warm enough for me, don't you worry about that – and if you need anything you have but to call."

With that, he left them alone. Artemas turned to look at Loukas and smiled despite the painful throb in his ankle. Loukas nodded, and lay himself back on the mat. As the glow of the fire slowly faded they fell into a deep and unexpectedly restful asleep.

❦

When Loukas awoke it was to the sound of sheep bleating playfully. He turned to see that Artemas, too, was awake.

"How's your foot?" asked Loukas.

Artemas sat up and gingerly put some weight on it. He grimaced. "Still sore."

Iani must have heard them talking for he came into the hut, carrying a couple of bowls.

"Good morning," he said cheerfully. "I have some fresh milk and dried fruits if you wish to break your fast."

"Thank-you again," said Loukas taking one of the bowls. Artemas added his own words of thanks.

"Sheep's milk, of course," said Iani, conversationally. "Also makes a good cheese."

Breakfast was completed quickly and it was time to go. Iani and Loukas – after putting his travel bag with the precious scroll in it over his shoulder – helped Artemas to his feet, and then they made their way outside.

"This way." The shepherd pointed with his free hand. "This path will soon take us to the road."

"What about your sheep, sir?" asked Loukas.

"They will be fine in the pen. But I will need to hurry back so that they, too, can break their fast."

It seemed that Artemas' ankle was improving. They were able to travel quicker than they had done the day before. After about thirty minutes Loukas could see the paving stones of the Roman road through a grove of trees just ahead. The deep anxiety that he had felt the day before came back with a jolt. What if a Roman patrol came along? What if the Romans had started to spread his name and description to the public and some civic-minded citizen turned them in? Their mission would be over and the scroll would fall into the hands of the persecutors.

The shepherd must have glimpsed some of this on Loukas' face. "Do not be afraid of men," he said with a twinkle in his eye. "Fear God and give him glory, because the hour of his judgment has come. Worship him who made the heavens, the earth, the sea and the springs of water."

Loukas looked at Iani in complete astonishment as the shepherd helped Artemas to sit with his back up against a tree not far from the road. Then, without saying another word, the man turned and disappeared into the trees. Loukas was left speechless, staring after him.

"Loukas, what is it?" asked Artemas, catching sight of Loukas' expression.

Loukas coughed, swallowed, then replied softly, "That was no man."

"What do you mean?"

"That must have been an angel, or, or, or... Iēsus himself!"

"Why do you say that?"

"Well, he just quoted from the scroll, the words of the first of the three angels." Loukas, with no thought of danger, took off his travel bag and brought out the scroll. He opened it, then scrolled through looking for the place. "Ah, here it is: 'Then I saw another angel flying in midair, and he had the eternal gospel to proclaim to those who live on the earth – to every nation, tribe, language and people. He said in a loud voice, "Fear God and give him glory, because the hour of his judgment has come. Worship him who made the heavens, the earth, the sea and the springs of water." '[1]

"There is no way a man could know the contents of this scroll without first hearing it, and there is no way that shepherd could have heard it yet. So he must have been an angel – and he came upon us at our very moment of greatest need."

"Then God is watching over our mission," said Artemas simply. "Even with my sore foot!"

1 Rev. 14:6-7.

"Yes," replied Loukas. He, too, sat down to wait for a wagon, all trace of anxiety gone. After all, had not an angel just told him not to fear man?

After some minutes of silence, Artemas spoke. "Loukas?"
"Yes?"
"You said there were three angels, didn't you?"
The scroll was still open on Loukas' lap.

"Yes, at this point in the scroll there are three. The first announces the judgment, with words about what we Christians are to do. The second announces the judgment over Rome, although he refers to her as Babylon, the traditional enemy of the Jewish nation. The third reinforces what we Christians are not to do: give in and worship the beast from the sea."

He looked down at the scroll. "The third angel finishes by saying: ' "This calls for patient endurance on the part of the saints who obey God's commandments and remain faithful to Iēsus." Then I heard a voice from heaven say, "Write: Blessed are the dead who die in the Lord from now on." "Yes," says the Spirit, "they will rest from their labour, for their deeds will follow them." '[1] We will remain faithful, even to death," Loukas continued, with tears in his eyes. "And despite all appearances God will bless us."

At that moment there was the sound of hooves on the cobbled flagstones of the road. Loukas looked up to see a farmer's wagon being pulled by two straggly donkeys coming towards them. He quickly put the scroll away, and then stepped out into the pathway of the wagon.

1 Rev. 14:12-13.

Before too long they were on their way again, Artemas riding in the back of the wagon surrounded by local produce. Loukas was up front with the farmer, the scroll safely in his travel bag, tears still standing in his eyes, but a look of determination firmly fixed on his face.

∿

St. Petersburg – February, AD 2006

"Dmitriy Nikolayevich? Nataliya Ivanovna?" It was a formally-dressed member of the Hermitage staff who stepped forward to meet Dima and Natasha just inside the security entrance in the Hermitage.

"Yes, that's us," replied Dima.

"Follow me, please," replied the lady, and she started off down the centre of the entrance hall. Their footsteps echoed around them as they walked between the pillars and occasional statues. Apart from their guide and a couple of bored guards manning the metal detectors behind them there was nobody else in sight, since it was after the museum's usual opening hours. But tonight was a special night and the guards had taken one look at their special passes and had waved them through to where their guide had been waiting.

They were soon walking up the magnificent steps of the Grand Staircase, the lights from the overhead chandeliers reflected in the ornate giltwork and highly polished mirrors that decorated the walls. Now that they were walking on the red carpet that lined the stairs their footsteps no longer could be heard echoing off the walls.

At the top of the steps they turned left, and began the rather lengthy walk through the labyrinthine halls and corridors to the special exhibition hall located in one of the furthest corners of the museum. Their guide led them quickly through the Field Marshals' room into a narrow, winding passageway lined with tapestries until they, rather unexpectedly, stepped out into one of the prettiest rooms in the entire building, the Pavilion Hall with its magnificent Peacock clock to the left and a stunning mosaic floor to the right. But they barely had time even to look at it since their guide continued on into the upper landing of the Council Staircase, turning immediately to the right. This took them past the dark yet strangely moving canvas of Rembrandt's The Prodigal Son. Other Rembrandts passed by in a flash, before they found themselves in the Small Spanish Skylight room, strangely named since this was in fact one of the larger rooms in the Hermitage, with some of the largest paintings in the entire museum. Their guide hurried them through the room, then into a long corridor with beautiful statues running down the centre. At the end of the corridor they turned right, into the Knight's Room, aptly named for the many suits of armour and weapons that lined the walls.

All of this had passed by Dima and Natasha in a flash, not just because of the break-neck speed their guide had set. Their minds had also been on other matters. For tonight was the night for the opening ceremony – the official unveiling – of the original scroll of the book of Revelation.

As they neared the Twelve Column Hall in which the exhibition had been set up, they could hear the expectant buzz of a small crowd. Then, coming through the final doorway, they beheld a number of people standing around in small groups, looking curiously at large white sheets that hung from the ceiling obscuring the walls. Dr. Williams must have been looking out for them, for he immediately came over and gave them both a warm hug.

"Dima, Natasha," he said, "so glad you could make it. We're just waiting on the delegation from the Russian Orthodox Church, now. And they should be here any minute."

"We wouldn't have missed this for the world," replied Natasha with a smile.

"Indeed," said Dima, "We have been waiting eagerly to see the scroll again."

Suddenly Dr. Williams looked over towards a different doorway. A large group of men dressed in traditional Orthodox robes were entering the exhibition room.

"Looks like you will need to wait no longer," he said, before hurrying over to greet the new arrivals. He then nodded to an elderly, official-looking man who was standing off to one side of the hall. The man immediately stepped up to a waiting microphone and asked for quiet.

"That's the curator of the Hermitage," Dr. Williams whispered to Dima, after rejoining them. The hubbub of the crowd quickly subsided.

"Welcome, ladies and gentlemen, to this special ceremony," began the curator. He continued by specifically singling out a number of important dignitaries, beginning with the high-ranking leaders of the Russian Orthodox Church standing off to his left. Eventually, the speech turned to the matter at hand. "Tonight," he said grandly, "we will unveil something of remarkable literary and theological value, a find that historical scholars dream of making, yet so rarely does it happen. And yet it did happen to two young people present with us today." He indicated Dima and Natasha, who were both immediately rather self-conscious as every eye in the room swivelled to look at them. "These two young people stumbled across a manuscript that, according to our in-depth research, was originally discovered in the ruins of Ephesus in 1885. As to how this manuscript came to be there, and when, that remains a mystery. The identity of this manuscript, however, is quite clear. It is a complete manuscript of the New Testament book of Revelation."

There were murmurings from the crowd at this, but it cannot have been a surprise. The Hermitage had been advertising its upcoming exhibition for a number of weeks now, with large signs in the foyer boldly proclaiming that a manuscript of Revelation would soon be on display.

The curator continued. "That it is a complete manuscript is wonder enough. The age of the manuscript has led our own scholars to deduce that it was originally penned at the latest in the early second century. It is certainly more than a possibility that the manuscript may well have been written earlier, even in the closing years of the first century *anno dominii*. Further studies are, of course, warranted, but initial findings suggest that this manuscript, indeed" – he paused dramatically – "could well be the original manuscript itself, written by John himself."

There were louder murmurings from the crowd at this point, for this had not been part of the advertising campaign. Dr. Williams turned to Dima and Natasha and whispered,

"He's only being cautious in a typically scholarly sort of way. He himself is convinced it's the original; he just doesn't want to stick his neck out too far!"

The curator's speech continued for quite a few minutes more, before concluding with further statements of thankfulness to one and all for coming. Finally, he said, "It is without any further ado that I declare this exhibition open!" And with a dramatic tug of a velvet rope, all the white sheets were whisked into the air. There, revealed in all its glory, was the scroll of Revelation, each carefully preserved section laid out in sequence around the walls of the Twelve Column Hall.

The guests were given permission to wander so Dima and Natasha, followed closely by Dr. Williams, began to stroll around the scroll. Dima noticed that underneath each section was a translation in Russian and English. To present a more multi-media effect, a number of Russian icons written on scenes from Revelation had been included on partitions in the centre of the hall. Dima was especially pleased to see a large photograph of the Revelation icon from the wall of the Dormition Cathedral located within the Kremlin walls in Moscow.

Then, quite to their surprise, they found themselves looking at a photo of themselves. In the far corner of the exhibition hall was a special display detailing how the manuscript had come to be put on display in the Hermitage. There were enlarged pages from Nikolai's diary that described the earthquake and the subsequent finding of the stone box. The photo of Nikolai holding the box standing next to the two unknown Turkish officers had also been blown up and put on display. There was a highly detailed map that showed Nikolai's progress – as much as was known – in getting the box back to Russia. And there were pictures of Dima and Natasha standing in front of the old dilapidated shed in which they had found the box so many months before. It appeared that the Hermitage staff had been doing far more than merely collecting background information when they had requested to examine the diaries and the location in which the box had been found. Dima and Natasha had been very willing to help, little realising that as a result they would be included in the up-coming exhibition. It was all very overwhelming.

Dr. Williams stood between Dima and Natasha and put his arms around their shoulders. "You should be proud of yourselves. Thanks to you, we now have at our disposal the very handwriting of John himself and the manuscript that he wrote to comfort and challenge the persecuted church of Jesus Christ."

"Thank-you, Dr. Williams," replied Dima.

"Oh, call me... well, call me what you like," said Dr. Williams with a smile.

"OK, thanks, Ed," said Dima. "I have enjoyed our many discussions, too, about the meaning of the text."

"So have I, so have I. And do you feel like you understand it all now?"

"Well," replied Natasha, "we have recently been discussing the harvest of the earth described in chapter 14."

"Hmmm, yes," said Dr. Williams, frowning. "That is a tricky part. Let's go have a look shall we?"

He released their shoulders and led them over to the wall of the exhibition hall where the fourteenth chapter was on display.

"Now, let's see... Ah yes, here we are: 'I looked, and there before me was a white cloud, and seated on the cloud was one like a son of man with a crown of gold on his head and a sharp sickle in his hand. Then another angel came out of the temple and called in a loud voice to him who was sitting on the cloud, "Take your sickle and reap, because the time to reap has come, for the harvest of the earth is ripe." So he who was seated on the cloud swung his sickle over the earth, and the earth was harvested. Another angel came out of the temple in heaven, and he too had a sharp sickle. Still another angel, who had charge of the fire, came from the altar and called in a loud voice to him who had the sharp sickle, "Take your sharp sickle and gather the clusters of grapes from the earth's vine, because its grapes are ripe." The angel swung his sickle on the earth, gathered its grapes and threw them into the winepress of God's wrath. They were trampled in the winepress outside the city, and blood flowed out of the press, rising as high as the horses' bridles for a distance of 1,600 stadia.'[1] Well, what do you notice?"

Natasha, looking at the Russian translation, answered, "There are actually two harvests."

"Excellent," said Dr. Williams, excitedly. "There are two harvests, the first one of wheat, the second one of grapes. This is very similar to Joel chapter 3, verses 12 and 13: 'Let the nations be roused; let them advance into the Valley of Jehoshaphat, for there I will sit to judge all the nations on

1 Rev. 14:14-20.

every side. Swing the sickle, for the harvest is ripe. Come, trample the grapes, for the winepress is full and the vats overflow – so great is their wickedness!' Now this sort of language is judgment language. In Joel, it is judgment of the nations. And similar language is used in Jeremiah 51:33 for judgment against Babylon. It is for this reason that many commentators believe that *this* is a judgment against the New Babylon and those who worship the Beast, just as was announced by the second and third angels earlier in this chapter." He waved vaguely off to their left. "But can you see anything that might call such an interpretation into question?"

There was a long pause as both Dima and Natasha searched the wall in front of them.

"Well," said Dima hesitantly, "the harvest doesn't follow the angels' comments at all. It follows a voice from heaven that says, 'Blessed are the dead who die in the Lord from now on' and the Spirit's reply, 'Yes, they will rest from their labour, for their deeds will follow them.'"

"Very good. What else?"

"I think it is interesting," said Natasha, excitedly, "that it says the reaping is done by the Son of Man sitting on a cloud. I'm sure I've heard that expression elsewhere in the Bible."

"Good! Yes, it comes originally from Daniel, but Jesus used it in his Mount of Olives Discourse. In that context, however, it is not a reaping of judgment. It is a gathering of Jesus' followers into the Kingdom of God. Consequently, some commentators think that John, here in the reaping of wheat, is describing the ingathering of the elect, and then secondly in the pressing of grapes, the judgment over everyone else."

"But," said Dima, "I'm starting to get the feeling that you don't agree with that."

"You're right," replied Dr. Williams. "To me, the parallel is too strong. For instance, the earth's harvest is said to be ripe; so, too, are the grapes on the earth's vine. No, I think John has one referent in mind here, underlying both harvests. And it *isn't* the final judgment upon Rome and those who performed emperor worship. After all, *that* comes up in the next chapter." He waved vaguely off to their right.

"What is he talking about, then?" asked Dima.

"I think John has left us some fairly glaring clues. Firstly, in verse 4 here" – he pointed to the place in the scroll – "John refers to those who were martyred for their faith as firstfruits. This is a word that describes the first part of a harvest that is offered as a sacrifice to God. So it really makes it easier to see the harvest that is described later in this very chapter as also referring to the martyrs.

"This leads us to the first of many references to wine in this chapter. Firstly, in verse 8, the second angel says, 'Fallen! Fallen is Babylon the Great, which made all the nations drink the maddening wine of her adulteries.' This is closely followed by God's response to this evil wine. He brews up a wine of his own, in fact. Here, in verse 10, the third angel describes what will happen to someone who compromises and gives in to emperor worship: 'he, too, will drink of the wine of God's fury, which has been poured full strength into the cup of his wrath.'

"So then when we finally get to the harvest of the earth, we can see that it is actually a picture of *how* God prepares the wine of his fury. It is actually through the martyrdom of the church that the destruction of the persecutors is prepared. Someone once said that the blood of the martyrs is the seed of the church, meaning that the church seems to grow most strongly when it is being persecuted. But that isn't what John is saying. For him, the blood of the martyrs is the seed of the *judgment* that will inevitably fall upon the persecutors. I think it is no surprise that the *following* chapters describe the final judgment of Rome."

There was a long silence. Finally, Dima said, "That must have been a difficult message to receive."

Dr. Williams nodded. "Yes, and John knew it. See here in verse 12: 'This calls for patient endurance on the part of the saints who obey God's commandments and remain faithful to Jesus.'

Standing in the Hermitage, looking at the unravelled scroll on display, it was hard to imagine what it must have been like.

❧

Philadelphia – August, AD 93

They had been passing vineyards for some time, so Loukas knew they were nearing the city of Philadelphia. It had been in his mind for some time now: how would they get into the city with the Romans on the lookout? He knew he would be endangering the life of the kind farmer who had picked them up, and driven them many miles, saving Artemas from hours of painful walking. So for his sake it made sense to take their leave before they reached the city, continuing the rest of the way on foot as best they could.

Suddenly, from just ahead of them, he heard a shout: "Loukas!"

Looking up with a start, Loukas saw someone standing beside the road. It was Melitos, a friend of Loukas' family who lived in Philadelphia. Loukas put his hand on the farmer's arm, and the man brought the cart to a stop. Loukas jumped down, giving Melitos a friendly hug.

"Melitos, well met!" said Loukas, warmly. "Were you looking for me, or have you just been sitting here watching the vines grow?"

"I have been sitting here for days, now, waiting for you," replied Melitos. "You sure took your time!"

"Sorry to keep you waiting. You knew I was coming?"

"Well, a slave in the Roman garrison heard about the warrant for your arrest…" He trailed off as Loukas was making subtle yet frantic gestures with his hands.

Loukas turned around quickly and addressed the farmer. "Looks like we can walk from here. Thank-you, sir, for your hospitality."

"You're welcome. But are you sure, though? The city is still some distance away."

"We will be fine," said Loukas, as he began helping Artemas down from the rear of the wagon. Artemas winced as his foot touched the ground, but with Loukas' arm around his shoulders he was able to walk over to Melitos.

"Right you are, then," replied the farmer, amiably. He clicked his tongue and the two donkeys started up again. He was soon out of sight, the wagon disappearing around a curve in the road.

"You were saying something about a slave?" said Artemas.

"Yes, Erdemos is his name. Since he's one of us, he was quick to share the news with the church elders. I was sent to wait for you, to warn you not to enter Philadelphia."

Loukas was dismayed. "But I have to! I have a message for the church, a message from Ioanneis – well, from God – and I have to read it to them."

Melitos nodded. "Yes, we have even heard of this scroll, too. But you don't have to come to the church. The church will come to you."

And with this, he put his arm around Artemas' shoulders and started to head away from the road. Loukas put his travel bag over his own shoulder and followed.

"So where are we headed?" he asked after half an hour. "This path does not lead to Philadelphia, unless I have become particularly disoriented this late in the day."

Melitos, puffing slightly from the extra effort involved in assisting Artemas, replied, "No, you are right. The city is too dangerous for you. We are going to a small village, actually not too distant from Philadelphia. There will be a place for you to stay there, and food for you to eat. In the morning I will return to the city to gather the elders of the church..."

Melitos continued explaining the details, but at the mention of food, Loukas stopped paying much attention. They had not eaten since breakfast and it was nearing sunset. The shepherd's milk and dried fruits had become a distant memory.

It was getting dark fast. But then as they came around the side of a hill covered in vines, they could see a flickering glow in the distance, and the delicious smell of a meat stew seasoned with garlic and onions wafted towards them. Even Artemas picked up the pace and before long they were seated on logs around a cheery fire, spooning chunks of meat into their mouths as fast as the temperature of the food would allow.

After the meal, they were shown to a small room in a hut where they gratefully collapsed onto some reed mats that had been laid out for them. Loukas was asleep almost immediately.

The next morning, true to his word, Melitos headed off to the nearby city to gather the church together. He reappeared after about an hour, and then over the next hour or so the elders of the church of Philadelphia along with some other members of the congregation made their way into the village in twos and threes. They gathered in the centre of the village, some sitting on the steps of the small houses, others finding as comfortable a spot as they could on the stony ground. Loukas sat off to the side, leaning against a tree, and when Melitos gave the signal that all were present, he began to read.

This was now the sixth church to which he had read the scroll out loud, and yet the words of the scroll still filled his soul with such fire. As he read the vision of the one like a Son of Man he could almost see Iēsus in his mind – although now he had the face of Iani, the shepherd.

Again, he felt a stir run through those assembled as he read the words written specifically for them.

" 'To the angel of the church in Philadelphia write: These are the words of him who is holy and true, who holds the key of David. What he opens no one can shut, and what he shuts no one can open. I know your deeds. See, I have placed before you an open door that no one can shut. I know that you have little strength, yet you have kept my word and have not denied my name. I will make those who are of the synagogue of Satan, who claim to be Jews though they are not, but are liars – I will make them come and fall down at your feet and acknowledge that I have loved you.'[1]"

What was almost surprising was that, unlike the other churches, Iēsus, through Ioanneis, had nothing bad to say about the church in Philadelphia. Yes, like the churches of Smyrna and Sardis, they had been suffering persecution as a result of the actions of the Jewish people in the city. Loukas had been talking with Melitos while waiting for everyone to arrive and had heard that the Synagogue leaders had spoken out against the Christians, threatening them with denunciations to the Roman officials if they tried to remain under the auspices of the Synagogue. But Ioanneis' scroll made it crystal clear: Iēsus holds the key of David, thereby emphasising his Messiahship. And by their rejection of Iēsus as the Messiah, the Jews of Philadelphia had forfeited the right to be called Jews. In fact, because of their slanderous accusations of the Christians, they had in fact become a synagogue of Satan.

Yet Iēsus had opened a door of evangelism for the church of Philadelphia, that would see these very Jews come and pay homage to the Christians. Loukas could hear the echoes of

1 Rev. 3:7-9.

the prophecies of Isaiah[1], but they had been wonderfully stood on their head. Instead of the Gentile oppressors of Israel coming to recognise Israel's supremacy in the Kingdom of God, it would be the *Jewish* oppressors of the largely Gentile church coming to recognise that the church is in fact the true Israel!

And then, of course, there was the promise that they would escape the coming persecution!

" 'Since you have kept my command to endure patiently, I will also keep you from the hour of trial that is going to come upon the whole world to test those who live on the earth.

" 'I am coming soon. Hold on to what you have, so that no one will take your crown. Him who overcomes I will make a pillar in the temple of my God. Never again will he leave it. I will write on him the name of my God and the name of the city of my God, the New Jerusalem, which is coming down out of heaven from my God; and I will also write on him my new name. He who has an ear, let him hear what the Spirit says to the churches.'[2]"

So it seemed like Philadelphia would be the place to ride out the coming wave of persecutions. *Perhaps*, thought Loukas, *I could persuade my family to move here, even temporarily. And Iounia, too…*

As before, certain passages appeared to resonate with those assembled to hear Ioanneis' scroll. The Philadelphians were visibly touched by the passage in which the third seal is opened and a voice describes the effects of a famine resulting from the failure of the wheat and barley crops, but that would

1 Is. 43:4; 45:14; 60:14.
2 Rev. 3:7-13.

leave the wine and oil harvests intact.[1] The loss of a grain crop could be endured, since there would be another harvest the following year. But the destruction of vines and olive trees would cripple a region's economy for years. And, of course, the Philadelphian economy was largely dependent on its vineyards.

But the passage that brought things to a temporary standstill was the Seven Bowls. Perhaps it was because there were many in the church who had suffered at the hands of the Romans, as a result of being denounced by certain Jewish citizens of the city. Even as Loukas was reading as each bowl was poured out, he could feel the tension rising. The first bowl brought sicknesses upon those who had worshipped the image of the Beast, an encouragement to those who had not compromised their faith by performing Emperor worship and had suffered accordingly. The second and third bowls turned all water to blood, in payback for all the blood of Christians that had been shed by the Roman Empire. The fourth bowl was poured on the Sun, but instead of putting it out, it made it shine hotter. But this did not bring about repentance, for the time of repentance was over. This was the final Judgment.

The fifth bowl was poured on the throne of the Beast – Rome, itself – plunging it into darkness. Then the sixth bowl was poured on the Euphrates River, drying it up thereby allowing the Eastern kings to attack the Empire.

" 'The seventh angel poured out his bowl into the air, and out of the temple came a loud voice from the throne, saying, "It is done!" Then there came flashes of lightning, rumblings,

1 Rev. 6:6.

peals of thunder and a severe earthquake. No earthquake like it has ever occurred since man has been on earth, so tremendous was the quake. The great city split into three parts, and the cities of the nations collapsed. God remembered Babylon the Great and gave her the cup filled with the wine of the fury of his wrath.'[1]"

This, then, was the earth-shattering event that Ioanneis' scroll was predicting: that at some time in the not-too-distant future, after a limited period of intensified persecution, Rome would fall. For all its sins against the Church, God would come in judgment and destroy the Roman Empire completely. For this small group of Christians this was welcome news, and there were plenty of noisy conversations that broke out at this point, as people discussed the implications.

It was also high treason. Again, Loukas was thankful that Ioanneis had at least *tried* to veil his language somewhat – referring to Rome as Babylon, for example. Even then, references to the 'seven hills' in the following section were not very cryptic! All the more reason why the scroll should not fall into the wrong hands…

As he waited for silence, Loukas caught the occasional exclamation:

"All that blood!"

"Kings from the East, he says. Well, I have heard that the Parthians are reforming again…"

"My uncle still lives in Rome. I had better write to him immediately!"

---

1 Rev. 16:17-19.

Then, just as most people stopped talking, one man was left speaking. "Why should we believe this? It's just Ioanneis' wishful thinking, isn't it…." The man trailed off embarrassedly.

"Not at all," replied Loukas, who had, after all, had a lot more time to think about these things than anyone else present. "Did not Iēsus himself declare judgment upon Jerusalem, predicting destruction within a generation? Well that certainly came to pass, and now he, through Ioanneis, is declaring judgment upon Rome – and soon!"

There was a reflective pause as everyone digested Loukas' words and then one of the elders of the church motioned for Loukas to continue reading. There were no further interruptions.

After he finished reading, the same elder came up to Loukas and thanked him for reading the scroll to the church.

"You will be leaving for Laodicea?" he enquired.

"Yes, as soon as possible," replied Loukas.

"But your friend, he is in no condition to travel. Perhaps he can stay here in Philadelphia and rest a while."

"Well, it would make it quicker," agreed Loukas. "And perhaps the Romans won't be looking for just one person travelling alone…"

"Then it is settled," said the elder. "Artemas can stay in my home. And then, by the time you return from Laodicea, he should be well enough to make the return journey to Ephesus."

Loukas nodded. He was not looking forward to walking to Laodicea and back with only the scroll for company.

St. Petersburg – February, AD 2006

Dima was washing the dishes when the phone rang.

"Tash!" he called, after it had been ringing for a while. "Can you get that? I'm busy."

"Sure," replied Natasha from the bedroom. She came out into their main room and answered the phone.

"Hello?" she said. "Oh, hi Dr. Will… I mean, Ed. Yes, we're all fine… What's that? An interview?… Well, I guess so… From England? And they are here now?… OK, then, tomorrow at two… Sure, I'll pass that on… Until tomorrow…" And she hung up. "Ed says 'Hi'. And there's a visiting writer for a Christian magazine staying at the University, and they want to interview us tomorrow."

"Really? Well, I hope we will be interesting enough."

"Hey, speak for yourself!" exclaimed Natasha, with a laugh. "You forget that the exhibition has been extremely popular. There have been long queues of people waiting to get into the Hermitage, despite the recent cold spell, and they're all there to see the scroll."

"Well," replied Dima, placing a clean glass in the drying rack above the sink, "that's true. I've been following a little of the international interest on some news sites."

"I wonder what questions we will be asked?"

"We'll find out tomorrow…"

Lying in bed later that night, Dima found it hard to fall asleep. He kept turning over in his mind what he might say. But as he was drifting off to sleep he kept getting the details of the seven seals and the seven bowls mixed up. And how many heads did the beast from the earth have? And how did you add up the letters to make 666? Not surprisingly his dreams, once he did fall asleep, were filled with apocalyptic imagery and difficult exegetical decisions.

But the next day, upon entering the office of Dr. Williams, Dima and Natasha were introduced to Andy Smith, a writer for the magazine *Christianity*. He turned out to be a short man, with wiry hair and a big smile. He shook each of their hands in turn with a ferocity bordering on physical abuse, leaving Dima surreptitiously massaging his hand throughout the interview.

After a few introductory questions, Andy started asking about the finding of the scroll. Dima and Natasha had had to recount this many times, so they answered him easily, taking turns with the details. Of course, this led directly to how the scroll had come to be located in their family's *dacha*. So Dima spoke about his great-great-grandfather's experiences in Turkey and his journey in bringing the scroll back to Russia.

"So you believe that this scroll is genuine?" asked Andy.

"Oh yes," interjected Dr. Williams. "Even if we had no information about how the scroll came to be found here in Russia, the evidence we have collected from the scroll itself is enough to prove both its age and provenance. We are dealing with a scroll that without a doubt comes from the correct time and place, Asia Minor towards the end of the first century A.D."

"Could it really be the actual scroll, written in the Apostle John's hand?"

"Well," replied Dr. Williams, "you are assuming that the Apostle John was the author. The book of Revelation makes no claim to apostolic authority. But if you are asking me whether this is the actual scroll as written by the man who experienced these visions, then my answer is 'Yes'."

Andy made some notes on his notebook computer, and then looked up at Dima. For some reason, Dima was suddenly hit with a sense of foreboding. Was this the moment that his dreams had been prefiguring?

"Dima, there have been many people claiming that the finding of the actual scroll of Revelation was no accident, that God wanted it revealed at this time, because we are entering the End Times."

Dima nodded. He had certainly been reading such things on a number of pro-premillennial websites recently.

"Do you agree with them?"

Dima swallowed. Yes, this was that moment. He took a deep breath.

"Well, Andy, no I don't."

Not knowing Andy's personal views on the matter, Dima paused for a moment, trying to gauge his response. But Andy was smiling, so perhaps it would be OK.

"No, I don't think we are entering the End Times," he continued, "because I think we *entered* the End Times when Jesus rose from the dead. The resurrection was the moment that started the End. And really the last event that had to occur before Jesus could return to end history was the destruction of Jerusalem that he had predicted would occur. And that happened in 70 A.D. Since then Jesus could come at any time."

"But then what is the book of Revelation talking about, if not the End Times?"

Glancing briefly at Dr. Williams, who nodded encouragingly, Dima replied, "Well, it is a book written to encourage Christians who are experiencing persecution. In fact, the book warns them that the persecution will get worse for a time, but that the persecutors will soon be destroyed by God's judgment. Of course, at that time Rome was the enemy of the church. Revelation 17 makes that quite clear: the Woman in that chapter is Rome, and the Beast she is sitting on is the Roman Empire. After all, the Beast is described as having seven heads, which is explained in verse 9 as referring to seven hills. And Rome was famous for having seven hills."

"That's right," continued Dr. Williams, as Dima paused for breath. "To use technical language, in chapters 17 and 18 John is demythologising the worship of Roma. He has already warned his Christian readers against participating in emperor worship. Now, he shines the light of truth on those who would worship the city of Rome. Apparently, prostitutes of the time wore purple robes, and would wear a headband with their name on it. John describes the Woman in *exactly* these terms, drunk on the blood of persecuted Christians. And he gives her the name 'Mystery, Babylon', where 'mystery' means symbolic, and 'Babylon' stands for the city that is opposed to the People of God.

"And it continues into the next chapter. Where chapter 17 is like an apocalyptic political cartoon, chapter 18 is more like Old Testament prophecy in that it contains a lament concerning Rome's fall. In fact, there is a good piece of evidence in this chapter as to why the Seven Bowls are not referring to the total destruction of the world. If the Seven

Bowls did refer to the total destruction of the world, how could there be kings of other nations watching from a distance, mourning? How could there be merchants lamenting at how the markets for their produce have dried up? Instead, we see that the destruction is *localised*. It is *focused* on Rome, the city responsible for implementing the religious policies that resulted in the persecution of Christians."

"OK," replied Andy, looking at the notes on his computer screen, "but Dima said earlier that destruction would be 'soon'. What did you mean?"

Dima looked thoughtful for a moment. "Well, there are quite a few references to something happening 'soon'. And it sort of depends on where you think 'now' is in John's presentation of events."

"Hang on a minute," said Dr. Williams. He turned to his own computer screen, started up his Bible software, and entered in a search for the word 'soon' restricted to the book of Revelation.

"Look, the first verse in the book says, 'The revelation of Jesus Christ, which God gave him to show his servants what must soon take place.'[1] Verse 3 of that first chapter says, 'Blessed is the one who reads the words of this prophecy, and blessed are those who hear it and take to heart what is written in it, because the time is near.' In 2:16 Jesus says he will come in judgment against the Nicolaitans soon. In 3:11 Jesus says he is coming soon. And then right near the end, we find this passage: 'The angel said to me, "These words are trustworthy and true. The Lord, the God of the spirits of the

1 Rev. 1:1.

prophets, sent his angel to show his servants the things that must soon take place." "Behold, I am coming soon! Blessed is he who keeps the words of the prophecy in this book." I, John, am the one who heard and saw these things. And when I had heard and seen them, I fell down to worship at the feet of the angel who had been showing them to me. But he said to me, "Do not do it! I am a fellow servant with you and with your brothers the prophets and of all who keep the words of this book. Worship God!" Then he told me, "Do not seal up the words of the prophecy of this book, because the time is near." [1]

"The question we have to ask is, What are the events he is talking about? What precisely is near? It really seems that John believed himself to be in the time leading up to the end of the Roman Empire, but *not* the end of the entire world, and *certainly* not the end of the material universe. He is like those Old Testament prophets who prophesied over the enemies of Israel for their role in the exile of the People of God. Isaiah, for example, spoke about the fall of Babylon, often using 'end of the world' language to describe it, too."

He pressed a few more keys.

"Here, for example, in an oracle spoken against Babylon, Isaiah says, 'See, the day of the Lord is coming – a cruel day, with wrath and fierce anger – to make the land desolate and destroy the sinners within it. The stars of heaven and their constellations will not show their light. The rising sun will be darkened and the moon will not give its light. I will punish the world for its evil, the wicked for their sins. I will put an end to the arrogance of the haughty and will humble

1 Rev. 22:6-10.

the pride of the ruthless. I will make man scarcer than pure gold, more rare than the gold of Ophir. Therefore I will make the heavens tremble; and the earth will shake from its place at the wrath of the Lord Almighty, in the day of his burning anger.'[1] You see? Lots of end-of-the-world language, talking about the imminent end of a political empire."

He stopped.

"Ah, I seem to have taken over the discussion somewhat. Please excuse me."

"No, that's alright," said Andy. "What you say is interesting. But getting back to Dima, if what you have said is true, then *did* John's prophecy come true? The fall of Rome did not happen until 410 A.D. when Alaric and his barbarian hordes sacked the city. If, as you say, the book of Revelation was written towards the end of the first century, then that's not exactly soon."

"True," replied Dima. "I have been struggling a little with that. I guess it depends on how literally you want to interpret the fulfilment. You could say that Rome 'fell' when Constantine became a Christian in about 312 A.D. Even Domitian's death could have been seen as a partial fulfilment. He was, after all, the emperor alive at the time of the writing of Revelation, and it was he who the Christians were being forced to worship."

Andy looked down again at his notebook.

"Well, I guess that covers the questions I had prepared. But I'm left wondering, if Revelation was written into that specific situation, what use is it to us today?"

1 Is. 13:9-13.

Natasha, who had not spoken for a long time, finally saw an opening.

"It is extremely useful," she exclaimed, passionately. "Wherever there is persecution, the book of Revelation can bring encouragement. And there is more persecution of Christians in the world now than at any previous time in history, so that means Revelation is even more relevant today. Granted, the specific details might be different, but the broad thrust of the book holds true: that Christians are to endure persecution and not give in to the temptation to compromise one's faith. But at the same time, the very act of being persecuted will bring about the destruction of those doing the persecuting."

Dima continued, "Yes, and the church here in Russia knows what that means, for they endured decades of persecution at the hands of an athieistic communist government. And yet that government was eventually overthrown. Even now, there are signs that the evangelical church here in Russia is about to experience a resurgence of persecution."

"What do you mean?" asked Andy.

"Well, there has been some legislation passed recently that only really applies to those evangelical Christian churches that started up in the wake of the fall of communism. Little things, like churches are required to document and report all financial gifts that come from foreigners. But how can you do that if you are passing around a collection plate? And there are restrictions about participating in social welfare programs, and holding outreach events, things like that. Oh, I don't think it will get anywhere as bad as it was before. But

I still find that the book of Revelation encourages me to hold firm to what I believe."

"Indeed," agreed Natasha.

"Well," said Andy, "thanks for your time. I have everything I need."

∽

Laodicea – August, AD 93

" 'To the angel of the church in Laodicea write: These are the words of the Amen, the faithful and true witness, the ruler of God's creation.'[1]"

Finally, after so many weeks – months, even – it had come to this: the reading of the scroll to the seventh church. He was in a hamlet not far from Laodicea, since it was too dangerous for him to try and enter the city itself. Loukas looked around at the assembled people, many of whom wore expensive black woollen clothing and fine gold jewellery, and sighed inwardly. He was exhausted from being on the road for such a long time, most recently entirely on his own, and he was about to read out rather a stinging rebuke. Well, it had to be done, and when it was over he would be free to return home to Ephesus and be with his family – and Iounia! – through the trials to come.

" 'I know your deeds, that you are neither cold nor hot. I wish you were either one or the other! So, because you are lukewarm – neither hot nor cold – I am about to spit you out of my mouth. You say, "I am rich; I have acquired wealth

1 Rev. 3:14.

and do not need a thing." But you do not realise that you are wretched, pitiful, poor, blind and naked.'[1]"

There was an immediate reaction. Ioanneis, of course, had worked in this city as part of his itinerant ministry to the churches of the whole Asian region. So he well knew the city's reputation for reliable banking, its manufacture of a famous eye ointment, and a booming textile industry built on the back of the special glossy-black wool grown in the region. And yet here he was deliberately negating those very things! Loukas could see the people, especially the wealthy ones, squirming in their places. And what was their problem? Iēsus knew: indifference. They were neither hot nor cold. They were not hot in their enthusiasm for following Iēsus, and they were not cold towards the depravity of the pagan religions so prevalent in their society. Loukas was sure that these people would be quick to compromise their faith in the face of increasing persecution. And yet, that very persecution could be the agent of their salvation...

" 'I counsel you to buy from me gold refined in the fire, so you can become rich; and white clothes to wear, so you can cover your shameful nakedness; and salve to put on your eyes, so you can see.'[2]"

Loukas knew that these words would be explained later in the scroll: that those who were able to withstand the fires of persecution would be refined in the process; and those who did not compromise their faith would be given white clothes

1 Rev. 3:15–17.
2 Rev. 3:18.

to wear, the white clothes of the faithful martyrs.[1] He continued reading, despite the angry murmurings.

" 'Those whom I love I rebuke and discipline. So be earnest, and repent. Here I am! I stand at the door and knock. If anyone hears my voice and opens the door, I will come in and eat with him, and he with me. To him who overcomes, I will give the right to sit with me on my throne, just as I overcame and sat down with my Father on his throne. He who has an ear, let him hear what the Spirit says to the churches.'[2]"

Now there was an invitation! Each time he read those words, Loukas mentally answered that call. Oh, to eat with the Lord! And to sit with him on his throne! It would be worth any amount of suffering. But thoughts of persecution again drew his mind back to Ephesus and what he might find when he returned.

The reading of the rest of the scroll passed without incident. The people had clearly been challenged by the earlier rebuke, but they had also accepted the exhortation not to compromise when it came to Emperor worship. Loukas could hear small groups of believers discussing what they would do to avoid participation in the various civic festivals and guild feasts.

An elder in the church approached Loukas.

"Thank-you, young man, for your willingness to come here and read Ioanneis' scroll."

"You are welcome, sir," replied Loukas. "I promised Ioanneis that I would do what I could."

1 See Rev. 6:11; 7:9, 13–14.
2 Rev. 3:19–22.

"It has clearly come at some personal cost."

Loukas nodded. "Yes, it has not been easy. I began the journey with two companions. One left me in Sardis, the other I left in Philadelphia. I must return there on my way home."

"You will be wanting to leave soon?"

"Yes," replied Loukas with a sigh. "Perhaps tomorrow. I am eager to see my family and friends again. We have heard that there have been arrests in Ephesus, and I am concerned for their welfare."

"But are they not in God's hands?" said the elder.

Again Loukas sighed. "I know that. But it is still hard to bear."

"Did you not find encouragement in what happens to the Beast in the end?"

Loukas knew the passage well. He quoted from memory: " 'Then I saw the beast and the kings of the earth and their armies gathered together to make war against the rider on the horse and his army. But the beast was captured, and with him the false prophet who had performed the miraculous signs on his behalf. With these signs he had deluded those who had received the mark of the beast and worshipped his image. The two of them were thrown alive into the fiery lake of burning sulphur.'[1] Yes, that is an encouragement: to know that the Roman empire will fall, along with all its representatives and followers."

"Then may God grant us strength to endure that we may see that come to pass!"

"Indeed," replied Loukas.

1 Rev. 19:19-20.

"Well," said the elder, suddenly all businesslike, "let's see what we can do for you to help you on your way. You will be needing some food for the journey, and... just look at your shoes! They are more hole than leather! Martha!" he called out to a woman standing to one side of the meeting room talking quietly with some other women. "Loukas here is in need of new shoes. Can you take care of him, please? I will see about that food."

"Certainly," the woman replied, coming over. "Let's see what we can find, shall we?"

Loukas smiled and went with her. Suddenly he felt an amazing sense of relief that the task had been completed, and it was now time to head for home. *Iounia*, he thought, *I'm coming...*

❧

St. Petersburg – March, AD 2006

The phone call from Nadezhda came late one night after Dima and Natasha had retired to their bed to read.

"Oh, who could that be?" asked Natasha with annoyance.

"I hope it is nothing serious," said Dima, as he got out of bed. He walked quickly into the other room and lifted the receiver. "Hello?"

"*Dima? It's* Babushka."

"*Babushka*! Is anything wrong?"

"*No, dear. But I thought you would want to know as soon as possible.*"

"Know what?"

"*Well, you know how you were looking for an extra piece of parchment? Something has come up. I think you will want to see for yourself.*"

Dima was suddenly very excited. "Did you find it?"

"*No,*" Nadezhda replied, "*I didn't. But I know where it is. How soon can you visit?*"

Dima turned to look at Natasha who had come in from the bedroom to listen in. "I think we could come this weekend. Will we be able to see the parchment when we arrive?"

"*Yes, dear. And you can take it with you. Perhaps it could be added to the display in the Hermitage.*"

"Of course," replied Dima. "That is, if it is related to the scroll Revelation. Is it? Can you tell?"

"*I think you will have to decide that for yourself. I look forward to seeing you soon, dear. Give my love to Natasha.*"

"I will. Goodbye, *Babushka.*"

He hung up the receiver.

"She found the parchment?" asked Natasha.

"No, she said she didn't find it. But it has appeared all the same."

"Well, it looks like we are off to Nizhny Novgorod *again...*"

They returned to the bedroom, but were too excited to pick up their respective reading books.

"I wonder what the parchment will say?" said Dima. "I keep hoping it will be an explanation from the original author. You know, giving some extra details to some of the more difficult passages."

"But haven't you been saying that the original readers of Revelation would have known what the book meant? That implies that none of the passages would have been considered 'difficult'."

"I guess so. Still, it would be nice. I mean, take chapter 20. This is the chapter that deals with the millennium: a one-thousand-year period when Satan is bound and Jesus reigns on Earth with the victorious saints. This is the passage about which all the major interpretations turn. You get pre-millennialism and post-millennialism, depending on whether you think Jesus will return before or after the millennium. Alternatively, there's a-millennialism if you think the millennium should be interpreted metaphorically. I just think it would have been nice for John to give us just a little bit of extra help. It might have narrowed down the interpretive options somewhat..."

"But what would the first readers have thought?" asked Natasha.

"I don't know!" replied Dima with some annoyance. "I wasn't there."

"Well, it seems to me that if someone was to read Revelation, and understand that most of it up to and including chapter 19 was about Rome persecuting the church and being punished as a result, then when you come to a passage that talks about 1000 years, then what comes *after* that must be events of the distant future."

Dima was thoughtful as he considered this.

"OK, that makes sense. The millennium is a significant temporal marker, clearly separating imminent events – imminent, that is, for those first century believers – from final events. The fall of Rome is an imminent event, but the last judgment which comes up in chapter 21 is a final event."

"Right," nodded Natasha, picking up her book again.

"But what *is* the millennium?"

Natasha put her book down again. Clearly the discussion was not over.

"I think we need to look at the text."

"OK," replied Dima. He got out his Bible. "Here it is."

"Well, what does it say?"

" 'And I saw an angel coming down out of heaven, having the key to the Abyss and holding in his hand a great chain. He seized the dragon, that ancient serpent, who is the devil, or Satan, and bound him for a thousand years. He threw him into the Abyss, and locked and sealed it over him, to keep him from deceiving the nations anymore until the thousand years were ended. After that, he must be set free for a short time. I saw thrones on which were seated those who had been given authority to judge. And I saw the souls of those who had been beheaded because of their testimony for Jesus and because of the word of God. They had not worshipped the beast or his image and had not received his mark on their foreheads or their hands. They came to life and reigned with Christ a thousand years.'[1]"

"Now draw out the clues John has left for us," said Natasha, patiently. "The first is clear: Satan is bound for the thousand years to keep him from deceiving the nations. So Satan's activity is restricted in some way."

"Right. I know that a-millennialists see this passage as referring to the age of the church, and that although Satan is

1 Rev. 20:1-4.

still active in the world, he is unable to prevent the spread of the Gospel."

"Sounds to me like you already know which way you are leaning," said Natasha, with a sly grin. "Well, the next clue is these thrones."

"Right, but the passage doesn't say where these thrones are. Are they in heaven or are they on earth? A-millennialists would say the former, pre-millennialists would argue the latter."

"Well, what does the text say? It says that the victorious martyrs come to life and reign with Christ. So wherever Jesus is, that is where you will find these Christians."

"OK, but that doesn't necessarily get you off the hook. Pre-millennialists would say that Jesus is now on the Earth having returned to bring judgment upon all nations."

"But that is not how we would interpret the previous chapters of Revelation. The judgment was only upon Rome. If that is right then there is no need to see Jesus as *physically* present on the Earth at this point in the book. In fact, listen to this earlier verse: 'To him who overcomes, I will give the right to sit with me on my throne, just as I overcame and sat down with my Father on his throne'[1] This is clearly happening in the heavenly realm."

"OK," said Dima, slowly. "So what you are saying is that these martyrs are brought to life to reign with Jesus in heaven."

"Yes, and that here on earth life goes on, and death too, since Death has not been dealt with yet. Those Christians who were not killed by Rome continue to spread the Gospel,

1 Rev. 3:21.

278

and people from all nations are given the chance to become Christians now that Satan is restricted from deceiving them completely. In other words, ordinary life as *we* know it now."

"So that would make you a-millennial, too," said Dima.

"Yes, and to be honest, I really think it fits with the broader sweep of Scripture far better than the alternatives. Pre-millennialism suffers from what I would argue was an un-biblical form of dualism nicely summarised by the phrase 'I am going to heaven and this world can go to hell.' It's too pessimistic. It doesn't do justice to the Biblical theme of redemption: that God's ultimate purpose is to to bring all things in heaven *and on earth* together under Christ. Yet post-millennialism is too optimistic. It plays down the sinfulness of humanity in thinking that good will gradually triumph over evil bringing in a golden age of Christian prosperity and dominance. Such a view might have been possible a hundred years ago, before the two World Wars. But now? If the twentieth century has taught us anything it is that things are *not* getting better. No, in my opinion a-millenialism best fits the tension between the 'now' and the 'not yet' that categorises Biblical eschatology."

"Wow, how did you work all that out?"

"Well, I can read, too, you know."

Natasha picked up the book she had been reading. It was G. B. Caird's commentary on the book of Revelation.

"Ah, I wondered where that had got to," said Dima, laughing.

Between Philadelphia and Ephesus – August, AD 93

The summer sun was hot on Loukas' and Artemas' heads as they walked along the Roman road. They were able to keep up a decent speed since Artemas' ankle had healed well during the time he had stayed in Philadelphia. But the pace was still not fast enough for Loukas. He wanted to be back in Ephesus, to be with his family, to see Iounia again. He knew that Artemas, too, was worried. But they had not spoken much about it.

Yet, even if the worst was to happen, he knew that God was still in control. There would be an ultimate judgment, Ioanneis' scroll made it clear, and all those whose names were written in the Book of Life would be restored to a better life on the new Earth. In his mind, he recited the words from near the end of the scroll:

Then I saw a new heaven and a new earth, for the first heaven and the first earth had passed away, and there was no longer any sea. I saw the Holy City, the new Jerusalem, coming down out of heaven from God, prepared as a bride beautifully dressed for her husband. And I heard a loud voice from the throne saying, "Now the dwelling of God is with men, and he will live with them. They will be his people, and God himself will be with them and be their God. He will wipe every tear from their eyes. There will be no more death or mourning or crying or pain, for the old order of things has passed away." He who was seated on the throne said, "I am making everything new!"[1]

It reminded him of the time when he had entered Ioanneis' home on Patmos, and had overheard him reading

1 Rev. 21:1–5a.

from the book of Isaiah. What had Ioanneis said then? Something along the lines of, 'This is how the story ends. Through all your pain and suffering remember this: it will be entirely forgotten when we are living in the joy of God's New Jerusalem.'

It was true: it was comforting to know that things would work out in the end. Wrongs would be made right. Justice would be done. Oppressors would be over thrown. Death itself would be destroyed. And the followers of Iēsus would be together, forever, with their King.

That thought brought new strength to Loukas' weary feet. The remaining miles to Ephesus would fly by...

❧

Between St. Petersburg and Nizhny Novgorod – March, AD 2006

There were four of them in the train compartment: Dima and Natasha, Yevgeny and Marina. When Yevgeny had heard that the parchment had apparently been found, he had wanted to come; and Marina had not wanted to be left behind.

There was plenty of time to talk. Initially the men had been discussing the recent ice-hockey season, while Natasha had been hearing from Marina how her pregnancy was progressing. But all their thoughts were centred on the parchment, and how it related to the scroll of Revelation.

Eventually, after a pause in the conversation, Yevgeny spoke.

"So, Dima, what have you learnt about the book of Revelation?"

"That's a broad question," replied Dima, smiling. "A broad answer is 'a lot'!"

"OK, let me refine the question. I know that you now view the book as primarily applying to the original recipients. But where does that leave us today? How does the book of Revelation relate to us?"

Dima nodded. "Now that's a better discussion starter. Hmmm, let me see. I think we should start by saying that we cannot simply assume that a particular passage of the Bible can be directly applied to us today. To do so is to ignore its original context and even purpose, and you can easily end up misapplying the passage. Instead, we have to try and look at the passage in its original context, being especially mindful of the culture and setting. Only then can we see how the writer has applied his teaching to the situation. Actually, if we do it right, we may find a more general principle at work than the one the passage more explicitly appears to teach."

Yevgeny nodded in agreement. "Right, and a good example of that is Titus 2:3-5: 'Likewise, teach the older women to be reverent in the way they live, not to be slanderers or addicted to much wine, but to teach what is good. Then they can train the younger women to love their husbands and children, to be self-controlled and pure, to be busy at home, to be kind, and to be subject to their husbands, so that no one will malign the word of God.' Some people would want to say, 'This is what the Bible teaches; therefore, this is what you must do.' In other words, they are saying that this teaching of Paul's is true for everyone, for all time, that it is universally applicable. Now, you probably wouldn't argue in this case..."

"Well," interjected Marina, with a laugh, "I'm not sure about that 'busy at home' part."

"The point is," continued Yevgeny, "those who advocate universal applicability will not want to see the passage as having been written in a particular cultural setting. For them, it doesn't matter, since it is true for all time. But if you deal with the passage in its culture and setting, you will realise that the external culture was impacting on Paul's teaching quite considerably. And you can see this when Paul says, 'so that no one will malign the word of God.' In fact, following what you were saying, Dima, you can argue that the general principle underlying Paul's teaching is cultural sensitivity. Paul is teaching the church to behave in such a way that outsiders looking in will find nothing to hold against them."

"And you can find the same teaching elsewhere in the New Testament," said Natasha. "I've just been reading First Peter, and he says in verse 11 of chapter 2: 'Live such good lives among the pagans that, though they accuse you of doing wrong, they may see your good deeds and glorify God on the day he visits us.' "

"Good," said Yevgeny. "But then what do we do with some of Paul's other teaching about women, such as not allowing them to teach men? After all, he's pretty clear: 'I do not permit a woman to teach or to have authority over a man; she must be silent.'[1]"

1 1 Tim. 2:12. See also 1 Cor. 14:34.

"Well," said Dima, cautiously, "if we were to apply *that* in our current cultural context, and plenty of churches do, then people outside the church will do precisely what Paul doesn't want: they will malign the word of God."

"In other words," said Natasha, "in this situation we might actually need to do the opposite of what Paul teaches in order to follow the underlying principle of cultural sensitivity: we have to allow women to teach and even have authority over men."

"Yes," said Yevgeny, nodding. "Of course, we cannot allow the external culture to dictate entirely. We can only overturn Paul's *surface* teaching when there are good grounds to do so. And in this case we can see that there is a fundamental equality between the sexes underlying Paul's theology, most clearly stated in Galatians 3:23: 'There is neither Jew nor Greek, slave nor free, male nor female, for you are all one in Christ Jesus.' In fact, many scholars argue that women in some of Paul's churches had taken this and were *really* applying it. In Corinth, for example, we hear of women praying and prophesying in church. But Paul is trying to hold them back: he doesn't want them to go *too far* and bring the Gospel into disrepute by their actions."

"So how does this help us with Revelation?" asked Marina.

"Simply this," replied Dima. "We cannot simply assume that the book of Revelation applies to us *directly*. We have to examine what the book meant for those who first received it, and hopefully find underlying principles that we can then apply to situations today. In the case of Revelation, we can see that it was written to people in the context of persecution. And it teaches them not to compromise their faith, for those who withstand will be rewarded in the end. And it promises them that those who persecute them will ultimately be judged. In fact, it promises something even stronger than that: it says that the very act of persecuting Christians will directly bring about the destruction of the persecutors."

"And does that apply to today?" asked Yevgeny.

"Yes," said Natasha, "wherever and whenever the church is persecuted. In the context of persecution the book of Revelation exhorts believers to resist the temptation to compromise, and to rest in the promise that the martyrdom of the saints will directly result in the fall of the persecutors."

"And since," added Dima, "there are more people today suffering persecution for their faith in Jesus Christ than at any other time in history, you could say that the book of Revelation is even more relevant now than when it was first written."

"Wow," exclaimed Yevgeny, "you guys have learned something!"

❧

Ephesus – August, AD 93

They came upon Ephesus late in the day. The city gates did not appear to be closely watched so Loukas and Artemas walked through unopposed. Once inside the city they paused in the shadow of a large building and rested for a few moments. Citizens were hurrying about trying to finish their business before nightfall. Artisans were closing their shops; market vendors were packing up their stalls.

"I'm not sure what to do," said Loukas, softly. "Do I go home? But what if the Romans are watching the house?"

"Well, I know what I want to do," said Artemas. "I want to go home."

Artemas' house was certainly closer, and sort of on the way to Loukas', so it made sense to stay together for a while longer.

Leaving the relative obscurity of the shade, they made their way up the crowded streets, dodging out of the way of the occasional cart, ever watchful for Roman soldiers.

Eventually, they came to Artemas' street. There did not appear to be anyone watching his house, so they walked up to the door and knocked.

"Who's there?" asked a gruff voice, after a few moments.

"Father? It's Artemas. I'm back."

They could hear bolts being drawn and the door was thrown open.

"Quick, come in. Before anyone sees."

Suddenly, they were in the gloom of the house. After a while his eyes adjusted and Loukas was able to see Artemas being given an enormous hug from this father.

"Artemas!" said his father, through tears, "I am so happy to see you. You were gone so long, and there have been terrible things happening."

"We heard that some people had been arrested," replied Artemas. "Hermas' family, for one."

"Yes, they were the first. But there have been many." He turned to Loukas. "I am sorry to say that your family have all been arrested."

Loukas knew this moment would come, but his heart was heavy all the same.

"And Iounia?" he whispered.

Artemas' father was silent for a moment. "She, too, I am sorry to say. They are in prison, to be tried soon. And the Romans have been asking for you, Loukas, by name. Is it because of the scroll? Do you still have it?"

Loukas clutched the travel-bag closely. "Yes, it is here. I need to put it somewhere safe."

He thought for a few minutes; and then it came to him. There would be just enough room in the secret place in the wall at the side of his house. As children, he and Iounia had left messages for each other there. At the moment he had a scroll of Petros' gospel[1] in a stone box. He could put Ioanneis' scroll in that, perhaps even leave a note for Iounia. Yes, she would be sure to look there, if she knew that he had returned. Assuming she was released.

"I have to go," said Loukas. "But first, do you have some parchment and a pen I can use?"

"I do." Artemas' father went over to a shelf and came back with what Loukas had requested. Then sitting cross-legged on the floor, Loukas wrote a letter to Iounia. When it was finished, he got up and went to leave.

"Be careful, Loukas," said Artemas.

"Yes, may God go with you," said Artemas' father. He unbolted the door again and let Loukas out onto the street.

Carefully, Loukas went back to the main street and headed for home. Once he crested the hill and could see down the

1 The Gospel of Mark, which according to tradition is based on Peter's eyewitness testimony.

Street of Curetes he became even more wary. Was anyone watching the house? As he got closer it did not appear so. He stopped and stood underneath one of the statues that lined the Street. But he felt even more visible just standing there, so he decided to risk it. He walked quickly up to the house and headed to the side wall. It only took a few moments to loosen the brick and place it on the ground. Then, he reached into the dark space, grabbed the stone box and lifted it out. Carefully, he lifted the lid, removed the other scroll, and put Ioanneis' scroll in its place. Then placing his letter to Iounia on top, he closed the lid and put the box back in the secret place.

He was just replacing the brick when he heard running feet coming up the Street. He stood up, placing the Petros scroll in his travel bag and went back to the front door of his house. It was then that he noticed that the door was ajar, looking as though it had been forced open. He went inside, and tried to shut the door again.

He could hear the footsteps getting closer, as he looked around at his house. It had been ransacked, as if someone had been looking for something. Did the Romans know about the scroll? It was a good thing he had hidden it when he had had the chance.

"Hello? Is there anyone there?" he called out softly. But there was no answer.

Then the door burst open, and a number of Roman soldiers pushed into the room. They grabbed Loukas, but he made no sign of resistance.

"Lucius! Or should I say Loukas. I have you at last!" It was Sergius Maximus. He had come in behind the soldiers, and now he came over to Loukas and looked him squarely in the eye. "My, but you have been causing trouble, unless I am very much mistaken. You and your scroll. You have it with you, I presume?"

Roughly, he grabbed the travel bag from Loukas' shoulder, ripping it open.

"Ah yes, the scroll. You received it from a traitor on Patmos, and you have been spreading its foul teachings across the province. But I have it now. I can put a stop to this treason at last."

Loukas remained silent. It seemed the best thing to do in the circumstances.

"Nothing to say?" asked Sergius Maximus. "Well, we'll see about that later. Bring him. He can join with the rest of the atheists, those that refuse to acknowledge the gods of Rome."

As he was led away, it took all of Loukas' will-power not to look at the side wall with its secret hiding place.

∽

Nizhny Novgorod – March, AD 2006

"Well, where is it?"

It was the question on everyone's mind, but Dima was the first to say anything. They had got off the train from St. Petersburg, straight onto the Metro, and had then walked the two blocks from the nearest Metro station to Nadezhda's apartment. It was cramped, what with Dima, Natasha, Yevgeny and Marina squeezed around Nadezhda's tiny kitchen table.

Dima's grandmother smiled. "It isn't here. Not yet. You'll need to be patient. Who would like some tea while we wait?"

Everyone was happy to have some tea.

"What are we waiting for?" asked Natasha.

"Not 'what' but 'who'," replied Nadezhda, mischievously. "I found someone. At least, a friend of a friend who turned out to be the granddaughter of a friend of Nikolai's."

There was a buzz of excitement from all those sitting at the table. Nadezhda poured the tea, and continued.

"Yes, it turns out Nikolai never did get that parchment translated while he was on his travels. So when he got back home, he sought out an expert in ancient languages. He found a man named Victor and they became firm friends. I only learned about Victor and his friendship with Nikolai when I was recently chatting with a mutual friend. She remembered *her* friend talking about her grandfather and how he had had a well-travelled friend who had been a spy in the late 1880s. We put two and two together, and she introduced me to the granddaughter, a lovely old lady named Olga. We are waiting for her to arrive."

They all turned to look in the direction of the front door. But there was no ring.

"That would have been perfect timing..." said Dima, sadly.

And then the doorbell rang.

"Oh, that was so close!"

Nadezhda went to open the front door. When Olga entered the room Dima and Natasha stood up to give her and Nadezhda a seat. Olga sat down, gratefully. She was in her seventies, and there was no lift in Nadezhda's building, and Nadezhda's apartment was on the fourth floor.

While she was recovering her breath, Nadezhda made the introductions. After they had exchanged pleasantries, and Olga had been poured a cup of tea, she spoke: "Well, I guess you are wanting to see this."

She reached into her carry-bag, and drew out a glass picture frame that held a large piece of cardboard. Onto the cardboard they could see that a piece of yellowish parchment had been stuck. Clearly, it had been falling apart, since there were gaps between sections of the parchment. The writing, too, was very faint.

"This is it. It was passed down from my grandfather. My father had it mounted and framed ages ago, but when I heard from your grandmother that it probably came from Nikolai, I got it down for you to see."

They all looked at it, careful not to spill any tea on it.

"But what does it say?" asked Marina. "Zhenya, can you read it?"

"Well, my Greek's not what it was. And it really is *very* faint. I'm not sure I could read it, even if my Koinē Greek was fluent."

"You don't have to," said Olga, happily. "You see my grandfather made a translation of it and we kept it in the picture frame all this time, too. It's here."

She pulled out a piece of old lined paper, with spidery Cyrillic letters on it. She passed it to Dima. He had a look, but struggled to read it.

"Here, Natasha, you have a go. You were always better at this than me."

She took it carefully and spent some time examining it. Finally, she started reading:

" 'From Loukas,

" 'To my beloved Iounia,

" 'May the Lord Jesus Christ protect you by his mercy and grace. My heart aches to think of you in prison, but I can only hope that the authorities will soon let you go, for you are so young. Perhaps I will even see you soon. But when you are released, I know you will look in this our secret place for a message from me. Iounia, take this scroll to the leaders of the church in Galatia – that should be far enough away from the terrible claws of this beast from the land. The scroll will be safe, and so will you, my beloved. When I am released, I will check for the scroll here and then come to you there.

" 'Grace and peace be with you.

" 'Come, Lord Jesus, come.' "

There was silence for a while. Eventually, Dima spoke: "Well, it's not from John."

"I wonder who Loukas is?" asked Natasha.

"Whoever it is, he had the scroll," replied Dima.

"And he wanted it kept safe from the authorities," added Yevgeny.

"So presumably this Loukas person had hidden the scroll, left a note for someone called Iounia, hoping that she – I assume it was a 'she' – would find both and take the scroll away."

"That sounds right."

There was a long silence.

"But the scroll was still there. I wonder what happened to them?" Dima asked, sadly.

Pergamum – October, AD 93

Sergius Maximus was sitting in his favourite spot in the Library. He was staring in the direction of Athena's statue, but he was not really focused on it. His mind was wandering, thinking over the last few months.

Where did I go wrong? he thought, frowning.

With a slight shake of his head, he tried to force himself to concentrate on the papers in front of him, notes for an upcoming law court appearance. But it was no use. His eyes just glazed over of their own accord and he found himself once again staring into the middle distance.

He had no idea how much time had passed when there came the sound of someone gently clearing their throat. He looked up to see Crispus standing in front of him.

"Greetings, O Sergius Maximus. Please excuse this interruption."

Sergius smiled briefly. "It is no bother," he replied. "What is it?"

"Well..." Crispus paused, uncertainly. "I'm afraid the proconsul is asking for you."

Sergius felt his heart lurch in his chest. Would this be the moment he had been dreading? The moment when his failure to stop the rebellion against the Emperors would receive its just penalty?

With a loud grunt, he ground his right fist into the open palm of his left hand.

"Oh, if only I had captured that scroll!" he exclaimed. "I thought I had it, that day when we arrested Lucius. But it wasn't the right one."

Crispus nodded. He had listened to Sergius raging about this before. He had also been present while Lucius had been illegally tortured, in an attempt to learn the whereabouts of the scroll. But to no avail. In the end, Lucius' Roman citizenship had saved him from an ignominious death at Sergius' hand.

"You did your best," he said, in an attempt to encourage Sergius.

"Do you really think so?" replied Sergius, wearily. "I am not sure the proconsul shares your view..."

"But if Lucius remains silent, what more can you do?"

Sergius frowned deeply. "Perhaps you are right. I comfort myself with the knowledge that Lucius' end is sealed, if he continues to refuse to offer worship to Domitianus."

"May he reign forever[1]," said Crispus, after he realised Sergius was not going to say the words. Then, more quietly, he added, "Also assuming that you can get the proconsul to Ephesus to sign the death warrant..."

There was a further silence for a couple of minutes; Sergius had gone back to staring at Athena again.

"Now, about the proconsul?" asked Crispus, eventually.

"Oh yes," said Sergius, getting to his feet. "The proconsul. Do you know what he wants?"

Crispus shook his head. "Not precisely, but there have been more reports of rebellion. The cities of Laodicea, Adramyttium, and Synnada have all sent in requests for the proconsul to visit so that they might execute those who have refused to participate in venerating the Exalted Ones."

1 He didn't. Domitian died in AD 96 when he was assassinated by some of his own court officials.

"But Lucius can't have travelled to those cities, could he?" replied Sergius, with a start. "Adramyttium is *north* of here, and as far as I know Lucius went south. He couldn't *possibly* have had the time to get there before his arrest in Ephesus."

Crispus shrugged. "Perhaps there is more than one scroll?"

Sergius groaned. "By Athena, I pray that you are wrong. I couldn't stop this rebellion when there was only one scroll! What hope if there are more than one?"

Slowly, he made his way to the doorway, with Crispus following. They left the Library complex and made their way up towards the top of the hill, where the proconsul's palace was located. He was not sure what fate awaited him once he got there, but he would face it with honour and dignity.

And as for that scroll, it seemed it would not be silenced so easily...

About The Author

Ben Chenoweth lived in St. Petersburg, Russia with his wife and two children for almost ten years. He currently lives in Melbourne, Australia where he works at the Melbourne School of Theology as their eLearning Coordinator. He enjoys reading, writing, music and playing computer games in equal measures. He has a particular interest in the intersection between theology and the arts.

His first novel, *Meeting of Minds*, dealt with exploring the galaxy through virtual reality (available as an ebook from Smashwords and Amazon and as a paperback from CreateSpace). He has also written a play based on the life of Saul (also available as an ebook from Smashwords and Amazon and as a paperback from CreateSpace) and a musical based on the Biblical book of Esther (a free download of the 1998 performance at Lilydale Baptist Church is available on NoiseTrade).

For more information, go to http://www.ephesusscroll.com.

Appendix 1: Names and Pronunciations

Most of the names used in the first century strand of this novel have been taken straight from the Greek New Testament and transliterated into English. Note that there is no character for a word-initial "Y" in New Testament Greek. Consequently, a "Y" sound is approximated by using the letter "I". Also note that in the following pronunciations 'oo' is pronounced as in the word 'book'.

Ioanneis [yoe-AH-nace]
Iēsus Christos [YAY-soos KRIS-toss]
Loukas [LOO-kuss] (2 Tim. 4:11)
Iounia [YOO-nee-ah] (Rom. 16:7)
Stephanos [stef-AH-noss] (Acts 6:5)
Tychicus [TAICH-i-kuss] (2 Tim 4:12)
Markos [MAR-koss] (Acts 15:37)
Tertios [TER-ti-oss] (Rom. 16:22)
Paulos [pa-OO-loss] (Acts 8:1)

The Russian names and places should be fairly self-explanatory. However, the letters "ZH" represent the sound in the middle of the word 'leisure'.

Appendix 2: St. Petersburg Metro (circa 2005 AD)

Made in the USA
Charleston, SC
30 October 2014